"That's the biggest rifle I've ever seen," Professor Anne McCaine said, making small talk as Will Casey gingerly unpacked his Barrett M107 sniper rifle.

"Oh, the elephant gun?" He laughed. "It's eighteen pounds heavier than a bolt-action M40 sniper rifle, but it's got twice the effective range, a bigger clip, and the .50-caliber rounds have more than twice the throw weight of a .308 Winchester slug. Another reason I'm partial to this puppy is that they make 'em in Murfreesboro, Tennessee, which is about twelve miles from where I grew up."

"I suppose that this thing could do some damage," she said, looking at the fearsome-looking weapon that was nearly five feet long now that Will had it fully assembled.

"Well ma'am, as I like to say, any of those jokers that I hit with this thing tend to stay dead for a very long time."

RAPTOR
FORCE

Bill Yenne

BERKLEY BOOKS, NEW YORK

THE BERKLEY PUBLISHING GROUP
Published by the Penguin Group
Penguin Group (USA) Inc.
375 Hudson Street, New York, New York 10014, USA
Penguin Group (Canada), 90 Eglinton Avenue East, Suite 700, Toronto, Ontario M4P 2Y3, Canada
(a division of Pearson Penguin Canada Inc.)
Penguin Books Ltd., 80 Strand, London WC2R 0RL, England
Penguin Group Ireland, 25 St. Stephen's Green, Dublin 2, Ireland (a division of Penguin Books Ltd.)
Penguin Group (Australia), 250 Camberwell Road, Camberwell, Victoria 3124, Australia
(a division of Pearson Australia Group Pty. Ltd.)
Penguin Books India Pvt. Ltd., 11 Community Centre, Panchsheel Park, New Delhi—110 017, India
Penguin Group (NZ), Cnr. Airborne and Rosedale Roads, Albany, Auckland 1310, New Zealand
(a division of Pearson New Zealand Ltd.)
Penguin Books (South Africa) (Pty.) Ltd., 24 Sturdee Avenue, Rosebank, Johannesburg 2196,
South Africa

Penguin Books Ltd., Registered Offices: 80 Strand, London WC2R 0RL, England

This is a work of fiction. Names, characters, places, and incidents either are the product of the author's imagination or are used fictitiously, and any resemblance to actual persons, living or dead, business establishments, events, or locales is entirely coincidental.

RAPTOR FORCE

A Berkley Book / published by arrangement with the author

PRINTING HISTORY
Berkley mass-market edition / August 2006

Copyright © 2006 by Bill Yenne.
Interior text design by Kristin del Rosario.

ISBN: 0-425-21105-3

BERKLEY®
Berkley Books are published by The Berkley Publishing Group,
a division of Penguin Group (USA) Inc.,
375 Hudson Street, New York, New York 10014.
BERKLEY is a registered trademark of Penguin Group (USA) Inc.
The "B" design is a trademark belonging to Penguin Group (USA) Inc.

PRINTED IN THE UNITED STATES OF AMERICA

10 9 8 7 6 5 4 3 2 1

PROLOGUE

November 25, 1997
10:45 P.M.
Shakaraband, Iran

A narrow band of darkening orange still defined the western horizon, but across the heavens, the darkness of night had thoroughly enshrouded the east in its impenetrable black velvet. Overhead, the stars were beginning to appear in uncountable numbers. The air was still, but the temperature was plummeting fast.

Colonel Dave Brannan looked around. His team, dressed in a shade that matched the hue of the eastern sky, were all but invisible. To even a trained observer scanning the rooftops of the compound, they could not be seen. It was as though they were not there. But there were no trained observers casting their practiced eyes across these rooftops. Hidden in the shadows of the parapets, those who might have observed Brannan's team slept. It was the deep and uninterruptable sleep of death.

Operation Raptor had proceeded with amazing precision, but that was the minimum that Dave Brannan expected of his team. They were fast and invisible. From that ICBM silo in Uzbekistan to the tarmac of the airport in Djakarta, where they'd thwarted three simultaneous hijackings, Brannan's team had silently and invisibly prevented unspeakable crimes against Americans and attacks against American soil.

Nobody knew what they had done, and it would have to stay that way. The enemy could not know, so nobody could know.

Through the window, Dave Brannan could see them. With a miniature microphone attached to the glass, he could hear them clearly as they laughed and congratulated one another. Three of the five French arms dealers he knew from having poured over their dossiers. The other two were familiar to him personally. He had met them and had shared affable banter with them.

If this were a cocktail party at a chalet at the Paris Air Show, Brannan might even walk over and strike up a conversation in their native tongue. If this were a cocktail party at the Paris Air Show, the five men would be selling weapons, very high-tech and very deadly weapons. This was not Paris, but they *were* selling weapons, very high-tech and very deadly weapons.

This was not Paris, and Dave Brannan was not a participant in the conversation, rather, he was an eavesdropping fly on the wall. Soon, he'd be a fly in their ointment.

He listened to them through the earphone in his left

ear, clearly hearing and understanding every word. The earphone in his right ear was silent, as it had been for two hours, and as it would be for at least another two. Two hours ago, he had reported that his team was in place, and he had received the final go-code. The next conversation with his control would come in two hours at the final extraction point.

Tonight as Dave Brannan watched and listened, the familiar Frenchmen were selling their wares to the man whom all Iranians feared, and whom all but a few Iranians dreaded. Lounging in a huge opulent chair in his long, black cloak was the Mullah of Mullahs, the supreme sovereign of the Islamic Republic of Iran. The forbidding visage, which stared from countless billboards everywhere, instilling fear into millions, was twisted almost into a smile tonight.

A dozen supplicants moved about the room attending to his needs, refilling his glass and offering tempting trays of caviar and sweetmeats. The five Frenchmen who were gathered about him sought only to please him. They had even brought his favorite cognac, but as the spiritual leader of a nation of sixty million muslims, he had graciously declined to drink with infidels in public.

Nevertheless, the Mullah of Mullahs was pleased with these men who sought to please him. They had brought him many wonderful things. They had bought him weapons, very high-tech and very deadly weapons. He had paid dearly for these toys, but that was of no consequence. He had the money to spend. Indeed, he had more money than he could spend, and still it continued to flow into his pockets. The Islamic Republic of

Iran fed Europe's voracious appetite for oil, and they paid very dearly in return.

Dave Brannan chuckled to himself as he watched the Frenchmen squirming happily on their silken cushions as a fire crackled in the enormous fireplace and robed attendants swirled about. Soon this scene would change abruptly.

He looked around. Night had fallen. He checked the AN/PEQ-2 infrared illuminator on his M4A1 carbine. Good to go. He snapped his night-vision goggles into place, and a monotone of green showed the compound's rooftops as if in daylight. He could see the dead Iranian guards, each rolled up and tucked into a corner of the roof parapets.

Brannan gave a thumbs-up to the nine members of his team, and saw nine thumbs gesture back. The Americans had also come with weapons, very high-tech and very deadly weapons.

The plan was in motion. The sound of a truck on the highway a kilometer away was louder than the sound of nine men moving across the roof. They moved with absolute precision that would be the envy of any ballet company. Two men with plastic explosives moved in on two opposing doorways that led into the room where the Frenchmen and their host were enjoying their delicate Caspian fish eggs.

What would come next would come fast, and it would be very, very deadly.

Suddenly, Dave Brannan's right ear burned. It was as though a 50,000-amp public-address system was thundering in his ear—yet the earpiece was so well shielded that the sound would have been inaudible to someone standing next to him. Given the circumstances, that was a very good thing.

"Delta, this is Alpha. Abort immediately."

Dave Brannan couldn't believe his ears. His team was less than twenty seconds from blowing the doors off the sanctum sanctorum deep inside a heavily guarded compound, deep inside heavily guarded Iran—and Control was aborting the mission!

He held up his hand and each member of the team froze, motionless in the starlight. He moved away from the window and whispered into his mouthpiece.

"Alpha, Delta here. Repeat."

"Delta, this is Alpha. Abort immediately."

"Under whose authority?"

"The top."

"The top?"

"You heard me. Get outta there now."

RAPTOR

FORCE

DAYS OF MARTYRDOM

Time has passed, and it is the third year of the administration of President Thomas J. Livingstone. The world enjoys relative peace. Order and balance in the world are insured because the member states of the United Nations have subscribed to the notion that only the world body can issue an International Validation certification to permit any nation to act militarily outside its borders.

Unfortunately, only *nations* have subscribed to this noble ideal.

ONE

November 4
7:07 A.M. Pacific Time

"I was sure hoping that I'd have gotten those two days off so that I could finish the quilt for Jeanine's baby," Summer Brophy told her sister as the two Western Star Air flight attendants made their way through the terminal at Portland International Airport.

"I thought you *were* finished," Summer's older sister, Morgan, admonished her.

"I'm so, like, not finished."

"It looked finished to me."

"I still want to make it just right before she has her baby. He'll be our first nephew, and I want it to be just right."

Summer had been working on the quilt since the day that she and Morgan had found out that their sister Jeanine was pregnant. Their grandmother had been a quilter of the old school. When the girls were young, they used to like to watch their grandmother at work, and they loved to listen to her stories. Every scrap of fabric seemed to have its own story.

As the girls had gotten older, their grandmother had wanted to teach them quilting, but there was never enough time, and there were other interests. Gradually, the scraps of colored fabric with their individual stories seemed less and less important.

When her grandmother passed away a dozen years before, Summer was still in middle school, but she had saved all of their grandmother's collection of fabric scraps, thinking that some day, she'd teach herself what her grandmother had wanted to teach her. Seven months ago, she'd gotten the reason. She would pass on something of her grandmother to the first little face of a new generation in their family.

"How much time do you need?" Morgan asked.

"Just a few days," Summer admitted. "I wish I hadn't got this call."

"You can't turn down a flight, even if it's a last-minute fill-in."

"I know . . . I'm like . . . I just wish I'd had these few days."

"You'll be back from Dallas tomorrow night."

"Then I have my regular schedule."

"There's always next week."

"But she's due in six weeks."

"Well, the baby won't know the difference for a month or two . . . and it looks finished to me."

"I guess you didn't inherit any of Grandma Margaret's persnickety genes!" Summer said in mock exasperation as she turned toward the gate to catch her flight. "So long sis, see you in a couple of days."

"See ya!"

As Summer neared her gate and showed her identification badge to the security man, she saw a squabble in the passenger section. Three dark-complected men were arguing with a short rotund woman in a Transportation Security Administration blazer. Nobody liked security checks, but some just complained louder than others.

"You're profiling! This is a violation of their civil rights!"

Summer watched as a dark-haired woman with heavily framed glasses and a large metal stud in her nostril interjected herself between the three men and the TAS agent.

"You know that it is a violation of the law to profile these men because of the color of their skin. I can file a complaint on their behalf . . . I'm an attorney . . ."

With that, Summer Brophy turned and headed down the jetway.

November 4
8:39 A.M. Pacific Time

MORGAN Brophy had seen the three men arguing with the TSA agent at her sister's gate, but had thought little of it. This sort of thing happened every day, and on nearly every flight. When she reached her own gate, she noticed another cluster of dark-complected men sitting together in the waiting area, glancing furtively at one another. She wondered whether the TSA had hassled them as well.

Morgan swiped her ID card and pushed her hand into the thumbprint scanner. The light at the top of the heavy steel door turned green and the door itself opened with a loud thud. Moments later she acknowledged Anita Carlstrand, the purser, and headed aft to stow her luggage and prepare for the flight. It was a five-hour run to Houston, a two-hour layover, and she'd be back home by early evening. Summer had a longer run to Atlanta, so it would be a day or so before she returned to Portland.

Morgan realized that she hadn't even bothered to get an itinerary from her sister. Since it was a fill-in, she didn't even know for sure what the schedule was. That didn't really matter. She'd be talking to Summer tonight. The two sisters were very close, and called each other nearly every night when they were on the road.

The boarding went smoothly, and when everyone was seated, Morgan demonstrated the oxygen masks and floatation cushions and took her place near the galley as Anita admonished the passengers to stow their tray tables and bring their seat backs to the full upright position.

November 4
11:57 A.M. Mountain Time

AS the 737-800 crossed the Wasatch Range of northern Utah, the thermals from the mountain peaks served up a sudden patch of turbulence, and the captain announced that he was turning on the Fasten Seat Belts indicator. Summer began moving up the aisle to make sure that everyone was complying. She paused briefly to aid a woman in the second-to-last row with a bawling two-year-old, and continued forward. The smile on the woman's face was one of the reasons that Summer enjoyed her job. There were people on every flight who helped make her career choice seem worth it.

"I'm sorry sir, you'll have to sit down."

It was one of the dark-complected men who'd been arguing with the TSA agent before the flight.

"The captain has turned on—"

"Bitch," the man hissed at Summer.

There were always people on every flight who helped make her career choice seem *not* worth it, but she tried to think about the others and not let this get her down.

"Sir, you have to take your seat *now*." Summer was trying to be firm, yet polite, and wished she could make herself be rude to this arrogant young man.

"Listen young lady, you had better be respectful to this man."

It was the dark-haired woman with the stud in her nostril. The woman was seated next to where Summer was confronting the standing man. The woman reached out and touched the man's leather jacket.

"Listen young man, you call me and I'll file a—"

She didn't have a chance to finish as the man slammed her face with his clinched fist.

"Shut up, infidel bitch."

Summer recoiled in horror. The man had struck the woman who'd come to his aid. He had struck her full force. Her glasses were gone, knocked off somewhere, and blood was pouring from the nostril with the stud.

A male passenger stood up to intervene as the man grabbed Summer and jerked her right arm behind her back.

"Sit down," the dark-complected man hissed.

Summer could feel something sharp being pressed against her neck, and she could see that the eyes of most of the passengers in the last few rows were staring at whatever was in his hand.

"Zahir Al-Akhbar!" he screamed so loud that the people nearest to him jumped. "The martyrs of Mujahidin Al-Akhbar are here to destroy the Great Satan in its own nest!"

There was a shudder of turbulence, and he almost tripped as he dragged Summer back toward the aft galley. Her mind raced. Was there anything that she could say to diffuse a situation that was rapidly getting out of control? She could hear shouts in the forward section of the plane, and she could imagine that a similar scene was playing itself out up there. Poor Anita.

The man jerked her into the galley and flung her against the back wall with all his might. She stumbled against the beverage cart and fell across it as it toppled over. She could see the object that he had been holding to her neck. It looked like a ballpoint pen. Could that be all it was?

"Unclean infidel bitch," the man snarled as he looked down at her. He grabbed the intercom phone and thumbed the public-address button. This was obviously well planned.

"Zahir Al-Akhbar!" he screamed again before starting

to rail on about how all of the passengers were miserable infidels.

Summer's thoughts turned to the young mother whose smile had lightened her day just a few moments earlier. She had to do something for the sake of the young mother—and for the sake of all the passengers out there.

Summer braced herself so that she could move quickly, then sprang upward, grabbing the coffeepot in the same motion.

The young flight attendant glimpsed the man's stunned expression as the steaming cloud of boiling liquid engulfed his face.

He screamed like an animal and lunged toward her. She tried to defend herself, but she was a small woman and he was a large man powered by hatred and adrenaline.

She felt a strong hand grab her wrist and saw his angry, twisted face. A moment ago it had been olive-complected, but now his scalded flesh was a strangely unnatural shade of red.

Summer felt powerless. She felt the excruciating pain of the sharp object piercing her neck. She felt the warmth of her own blood as the pain ebbed and faded.

She was able to sit up now. The man was gone and the galley was peacefully quiet. There was a brightness in the forward part of the aircraft as though someone had opened a door and let the sunshine flood in.

Summer noticed a shadow of someone coming back into the galley. It was one of the passengers. An older woman came into the galley from the brightness up front.

It was Grandma Margaret!

Over her arm, she carried one of her quilts. It was the same one that had been on her bed that night that she passed away.

Margaret smiled and held out her arms.

"Grandma! What are you doing here?"

"It's so good to see you Little Button," Margaret said as she hugged her granddaughter tightly. "It's been so lonely."

Summer felt nothing but peace coming over her as she embraced her grandmother.

November 4
11:57 A.M. Mountain Time

WITH a jolly little ping, the captain turned off the seat belt sign and Morgan unlocked the wheels of the lunch cart. The turbulence had finally subsided, and the customers would be anxious for their sandwiches and chips.

As she began pushing the cart forward from the aft galley, Morgan noticed a muscular, dark-complected man wearing a black sweatshirt in the aisle seat seven rows away as he stood up. He glanced around nervously, stared briefly at her, then grabbed a girl in a red nylon jacket, pulling her out of her seat. This girl, who Morgan estimated to be about twelve, had probably unfastened her seat belt after the turbulence. Morgan gasped as the man began dragging the girl in red back toward the rear of the aircraft.

"Zahir Al-Akhbar!" the man shouted as the girl screamed.

"Zahir Al-Akhbar!" The shout was repeated toward the front of the 737-800.

Morgan had the cart between them and herself, but what could she do to save herself and aid the girl?

Suddenly, a passenger, a man with a salt-and-pepper beard, who was wearing a pale yellow sport shirt, stood up. The man in the black sweatshirt apparently saw him out of the corner of his eye and began to turn.

In a movement that happened so quickly that Morgan could barely see it, the man in the yellow shirt grabbed the other man's neck, turned his head quickly, and immediately sat back down.

Morgan's jaw dropped as she watched the man in the black sweatshirt slump limply to the floor. His head remained turned and his eyes stared at her blankly.

The girl in red, still screaming, felt his grip on her loosen and she ran toward Morgan. She scrambled over the food cart, grabbed Morgan, and began to sob.

In the aisle, there was a great deal of commotion, another large, dark-complected man, this one in a leather jacket, was running down the aisle toward the crumpled form of the man in the black sweatshirt. He was shouting in a language that Morgan did not understand.

As the terrorist passed the aisle where the man in the yellow shirt was sitting, there was a swift flash of the man's hand, and the guy in the leather jacket suddenly doubled up in pain.

In the forward part of the aircraft, a third man was shouting. He had what looked like a gun.

Morgan watched the man in the pale yellow sport shirt lean into the aisle. In his hand, he had the thing that he had taken from the man in the leather jacket. It looked like a ballpoint pen. He tossed it hard and fast, like a baseball pitcher throwing a fastball.

The man in the front of the plane dropped the gun— or whatever it was—and grabbed his face. There was blood spilling through his fingers. His shouts turned to screams.

November 4
11:57 A.M. Mountain Time

"**M**ISS Laval is here to see you," the executive secretary said crisply.

"Send her up, won't you Madge," Dennis McCaine replied with a smile. Madge just didn't understand—or maybe she *did* understand, and she was just jealous.

Dennis reared back in his large executive office chair and looked around. He had a splendid view of the Rockies from up here on the sixty-first floor of the NothalCorp Tower, and the view was unobstructed. The recently completed skyscraper was the tallest building in Denver. In fact, it was the tallest building between Chicago and San Francisco. It was a monument to the power of men like Dennis McCaine, men who enjoyed the luxury of wood-paneled walls, the luxury of cranking up the air-conditioning so that he could enjoy the warmth of a crackling fire in his fireplace when it was twenty-six degrees—or ninety-six degrees—outside the big windows.

As the hardware clicked and the heavy rosewood door began to open, Dennis hurriedly grabbed the framed picture of his wife and turned it facedown on his desk. One last detail before his "meeting" with Miss Laval.

Anne wouldn't want to watch. Of course, she was thousands of miles away, and what she didn't know about her husband wouldn't hurt her. Dennis just didn't want to have her smiling face intrude on his "meeting" with Miss Kristee Laval.

Dennis had once loved his wife passionately. Maybe he still did. They met at the University of Colorado in Boulder. Dennis was in the business school, and Anne was studying archaeology, but when they met, they were both just undergraduates with the likes and lusts that define college kids as a species unto themselves.

Twenty years later, Dennis was still in business, and Anne was a world-famous archaeologist. While Dennis climbed the corporate ladder with a single vision of the view from the top, Anne scattered herself, teaching mostly, but going off for months at a time to, as Dennis put it, "dig up old bones."

"Hiya Denny," Kristee Laval said as she closed the door.

She insisted on calling him "Denny," but as far as he could tell, that was the only thing that Kristee did that was not absolutely perfect. He loved the way the young twenty-something moved across the room. That brought a smile to the face of the hardworking CEO of Nothal-Corp.

He loved the way she dressed. Her silk blouse had a deep V-neck that revealed just the right amount of cleavage. The cut of her rose pink suit flattered everything she had, and she had a lot to flatter. Her skirt was short, but not too short, and her heels were high, but not too high.

Anne would have been in khakis, with an old denim shirt and sandals. She had once had a body that men noticed, but years of digging bones had turned her hands rough, and her legs muscular. He remembered the last time he had looked at her hands, and at the broken nails cut short. By contrast, Kristee's were perfection, painted in a color that perfectly matched her suit. Kristee had done this for him, he thought. Such a thing would never have occurred to Anne.

"I booked a table at Raphaello's," Dennis told Kristee. "I know that you like their Caesar."

"I like *your* Caesar, Denny," she purred.

Kristee came around to his side of the enormous desk and sat on it, facing him and crossing her legs seductively. Nobody came around to his side of the enormous desk—except Kristee. Nobody sat on it—except Kristee.

"I was kind of in the mood for dessert." She smiled, slipping off her jacket and tossing it to a side chair. "It sure is warm in here with the fireplace burning."

She said what she meant. That was another in the long list of things that he liked about Kristee.

"I'm kind of in the mood for dessert myself," he said as she smoothly moved off the desk onto his lap.

He felt the strands of her long blonde hair caress his cheeks as she bent forward to kiss him. He drank in the sweet intoxication of her fragrance as she skillfully undid his necktie. Anne would have had her hair tied back, and her fragrance would simply have been Anne. There was a time when the fragrance of Anne was enough.

Dennis stroked the smooth skin of Kristee's bare arm, the back of his thumb feeling the contour of her breast beneath the silk. The silk was so luxurious. Kristee was so luxurious.

He basked in the luxury of her smile, and in the luxury of the way that she touched his face—the *adoring* way that she touched his face. It made him feel young, so much younger. These were more things in that long list of what he liked about Kristee.

He gazed up at Kristee's face as she adjusted her perch on his lap slightly. She was staring out the window, probably enjoying the view of the mountains. Slowly the smile faded from her perfectly painted lips. What was she looking at?

An expression of concern quickly changed to one of horror. Dennis squirmed to turn around to look just as the room went dark, as though the sun had just gone behind a very ominous thunderhead.

November 4
10:57 A.M. Pacific Time

"**WHAT'S** the holdup?"
The man in the silver Cadillac Escalade was third in line to exit the underground parking garage on Spring Street in downtown Seattle. He was irritable, impatient, and growing angrier by the moment.

"The card machine is jammed," shouted the attendant, a short, beefy man with dark hair and a receding hairline.

"Well, get it fixed!" demanded the man in the Escalade as he loosened his Salvatore Ferragamo necktie.

"People are in a hurry to get out of this damned garage."

"I'm working on it as fast as I can," the attendant said, wiping his sweating hands on his dark blue jumpsuit.

"I've got a client meeting in Ballard in fifteen minutes," the man in the Escalade said, continuing to badger the attendant. "You working-class heroes obviously don't care a whit about anything more important than your little world . . . and you can't even manage to keep that working properly."

"Asshole," the attendant muttered without looking up from the work that he was doing on the card machine.

"What did you say?" the man in the Escalade screamed, his voice cracking.

"I called you an asshole," the attendant said, pushing the jammed lever within the machine and watching it spring free. "You're a pompous, self-important *fucking* asshole!"

The man leapt out of the Escalade and squared off with the attendant. He quickly realized that the little man was built like a linebacker and was not going to back down. The standoff seemed to last minutes, but it was actually a matter of seconds. With the machine having been cleared, traffic was moving again, and the drivers stacked up behind the Cadillac were laying on their horns.

The driver climbed back into the huge SUV and scowled one last time at the attendant as he swiped his monthly parking card and accelerated out of the garage.

"Fuck you!" screamed the attendant. The vise grips that he hurled at the Escalade nicked the "No Blood for Oil" bumper sticker and bounced to the concrete floor as the SUV careened out of the garage in a blue cloud of exhaust.

"Boyinson, I saw that!"

The attendant saw his boss striding toward him through the blue haze of the garage, the veins on his neck throbbing.

"Bastard always takes everything too damn serious," muttered Boyinson to himself.

"Boyinson, that's the last straw. I've told you count-less times that temper of yours is going to get you and this garage in trouble. You might have hit that car. Next time maybe you will. We can't have that. Turn in your time card. You're through!"

"Whaddya mean, through? I got three hours left on my shift."

"No you don't. You're through, as in *fired*."

"You can't do that."

"I can, and I just did. I've documented enough of your outbursts to have gotten you fired a half dozen times. You just crossed the line, Boyinson, and you're outta here."

Greg Boyinson skulked up to the windowless busi-ness office on the third floor, drew his final check, and went across the street to the bank where a teller named Judy knew him. Now he was headed down Second Av-enue with $218 and some change in his pocket and a chip on his shoulder. Damn, he needed a drink.

He took a seat at the bar, ordered a pint of Redhook, took a long drink, and exhaled. The bar was nearly empty. It was the middle of the day. Only losers like him would be drinking in a seedy joint like this in the middle of the day. There was a couple in one of the booths, arguing in hissing whispers, and two old guys at the bar. Boyinson guessed from the way they were dressed that they were probably losers just like him.

The television was tuned to some kind of vapid day-time talk show. Some Oprah wannabe was talking to a well-dressed woman and a teenage girl with a sneer on her face. The sound was turned down low and nobody in the bar was paying attention.

Boyinson took another long drink and centered the pint glass on the cocktail napkin. For nearly an hour, his mind had been seething about the asshole in the Es-calade and the asshole boss. Now, his mind was starting to turn to what came next in his life, a life that had been one screwup after another, ever since he left the service. Maybe he would try to get back into flying. There were millions of acres of forest land in the Northwest, and people were always looking for helicopter pilots. Then he remembered that he had gotten fired from his last job doing that.

"Fuckin' loser!"

"What's that?" asked the bartender.

"I was talkin' to myself," Boyinson said, almost apologetically, not wanting to have the bartender or anyone else in the bar think that he had meant the epi-thet for them.

"You're being pretty hard on yourself, doncha think?" asked the bartender.

"No. I don't."

"Whatever you say. You wanna 'nother beer?"

"Sure. Why not?"

"Hey lookit that!" screamed one of the other men at the bar, pointing to the television.

The screen was filled with the image of a burning high-rise building. There were shaky telephoto shots of furiously burning flames interspersed with long shots of huge clouds of smoke billowing across a skyline. The tag at the top of the screen said "Live"; the one at the bottom identified it as Denver.

The bartender grabbed the remote and turned up the volume. The couple that had been arguing in the booth were on their feet now, staring at the screen.

Nobody said anything. They just watched in horror as the huge, steel-frame building began to buckle and collapse. Memories came surging back. Everyone remembered where they'd been the last time, and each person knew that those memories were just as sharp, and just as bitter, for everyone else in the room.

"Those bastards have done it again!" one of the men shouted, almost sobbing.

On the screen, the scene of the crumbling building was repeated, and the crawler at the bottom said something about an airplane hitting the NothalCorp Tower in Denver.

"Why can't somebody stop them!" the woman screamed, breaking into tears.

"I only wish I could," Greg Boyinson said angrily as he put his glass down on the bar.

TWO

"**M**ORE coffee sir?"

President Thomas Livingstone shook his head as he cradled the phone. He was exhausted, but running on a mix of adrenaline and the dozen or so cups of coffee that he had gulped down over the past twelve hours.

He put his face in his hands. He'd been up all night, sitting at his desk in the Oval Office making and receiving calls. He had been speaking to so many time zones that he had lost track of what time it was in Washington. The sun was up. It must be the day after.

When it had happened, he had been in a meeting with the secretary of agriculture. The Secret Service had bundled both of them into the bunker deep beneath the White House until the Air National Guard secured the airspace over the capital and the Secret Service established a perimeter around the White House. The secretary was still in the White House, waiting for transportation. The Secret Service and D.C. Police had closed off every street within a ten-block radius. Even cabinet secretaries had to wait for the Secret Service to decide that it was okay for their cars to come and go.

They had insisted that President Livingstone remain below through the night, but he said he'd be damned if he'd get on the phone to assure the world that all was well within the capital, if he was making those calls from a hole in the ground.

The reports that had come in reflected a terrible situation that could have been a lot worse. Two Western Star Air 737-800 jetliners out of Portland International had been hijacked. One had slammed into the sixty-first floor of a Denver skyscraper. The other had been retaken by the passengers and had made an emergency landing at McConnell AFB near Wichita, Kansas. The loss of the tallest building between Chicago and San Francisco was a horrible disaster, but the victory of the would-be victims over the hijackers on the other flight was a mitigating triumph of sorts.

"Sir, a briefing from the secretary of state in the Cabinet Room in five minutes."

The president looked up. It was Steve Faralaco, his chief of staff. Steve had been doing a magnificent job of running things through the night, of screening calls, of weeding out nonsense so that Tom Livingstone could get what he liked to call "Jack Webb" briefings—in other words, "Just the facts."

"How'd he manage to get through?" the president asked. "I thought they'd grounded every flight in North America."

Secretary of State John J. Edredin had been in New York City when it had happened, attending a foreign ministers' conference at the United Nations.

"Only the commercial flights." Steve Faralaco smiled. "I arranged for him to fly into Andrews in the backseat of an Air Guard F-16."

"I'll bet he liked that!" the president said, almost laughing.

"I don't know sir, I haven't spoken to him. You can ask him yourself, though. He's just arrived."

Livingstone stood up. Oh, he was stiff. He had no idea how long he'd been sitting there. What time was it? He watched Faralaco walk briskly out of the Oval Office, and found himself limping to catch up.

Secretary of State John Edredin sat in his usual place at the cabinet table. He was wearing an expensive suit that was unbelievably wrinkled, and no necktie. The stubble on his cheeks showed that he'd been twenty-four hours without a shave. Tom Livingstone wondered if he looked that bad, and guessed that he did.

"I'm afraid that the news is not good," Edredin said, obviously in a hurry to get down to business. "Secretary-General Mboma will make a public announcement condemning the attack in no uncertain terms in about an hour or so, but privately, the United Nations is not going to permit us to act."

"What? We were attacked."

"Yes, but under the International Validation rule, we are barred from taking unilateral action when there's no clear aggressor nation," Edredin cautioned. "We need to ask the United Nations to issue an International Validation in order for us to respond."

"What if we find out who did it?"

"On the record, he's sympathetic. Off the record, he's let it be known that he won't back the issuing of an International Validation to the United States for anything. We can submit a formal request, which might work, but it will take time."

"Damn him!" Livingstone said emphatically. "We'll take it to the Security Council."

"We don't have the votes," responded Edredin. "China will vote against us, and so will France. Russia and Britain are too scared of the Middle East governments to do any favors for us."

"That goddam International Validation," Livingstone said in disgust. "It won't let us use our own troops to go after these bastards."

"We all thought that it was a good idea at the time," Edredin replied.

"Dammit, even I supported it at the time," Livingstone said. "We all thought that it would be a good idea if only the United Nations could declare the validity of international conflict. The Senate voted fifty-nine to forty-one to allow the United Nations to have sovereignty over our armed forces. As you said, it seemed like a good idea at the time."

"There's not much we can do." Edredin shrugged.

"Most Europeans, and damned near everybody in the Third World, think it's *our* fault for making the rest of the world mad at us."

"So do a lot of people in *this* country," Livingstone said with disgust.

"It's the battered wife syndrome," Edredin mused.

"Whaddya mean?"

"In a lot of wife abuse cases, women allow themselves to get attacked over and over because they think they *deserve* to be punished. A lot of people in the United States are like that. They think we got attacked because we deserve to be punished."

"That's sick," the president said, shaking his head.

"So was what happened in Denver yesterday," Edredin added.

"I have to go there," the president said, leaning toward the intercom button to summon his chief of staff. "See and be seen."

"Steve," the president said when Faralaco appeared in the Cabinet Room, "make the necessary arrangements. I've got to make a trip to Denver in the next twenty-four hours, and I *don't* want to fly in the backseat of an F-16!"

"Don't worry." Steve Faralaco smiled. "*Your* plane has the necessary clearance."

November 5
5:56 A.M. Central Time

MORGAN Brophy moved numbly about the large cafeteria. Awake now for nearly twenty-four hours, she was still on duty, still doing her job. She was comforting the passengers as best she could, sitting by an eight-year-old unaccompanied minor with tears streaming down her face, or securing a blanket for an elderly man who was shaking uncontrollably.

Morgan guessed that she was in a state of shock herself. She knew that the other 737 had been lost with no survivors. Intellectually, she knew that the 112 people on that flight, including Summer, had perished, but it still had not registered. She felt as though she was in a trance, and that somehow it was all just a bad dream. At last, as she focused on her last conversation with Summer—about the quilt that would now never be finished—she sat down and began to cry.

When the 737 had landed at McConnell AFB, the Air Force Security Forces SWAT team that had come aboard the plane had stunned the passengers as much as the hijackers had, but as they began seeing the United States flags on the airmen's shoulders, there was spontaneous applause. The troops found themselves fighting off hugs and kisses.

Aside from two people who had suffered possible heart attacks, all of the passengers had been taken directly into the cafeteria. Here they remained. Nobody was allowed to leave, under the theory that the one hijacker who had been taken alive might not be the only one who had survived. Night had come, and soon it would be the dawn of a new and uncertain day.

Meals had been offered, and most people had eaten. Cots had been brought in, and some people were sleeping. Counselors were talking to some of the people, and a group of people in FBI Windbreakers were

interviewing people one by one. Everyone had shown
their IDs, and presumably there had been a background
check of some sort. Now the FBI was working the room
a second time.

"Miss Brophy. We need to speak with you."

Morgan looked up. Two FBI agents scarcely older
than she was had descended upon her with cool effi-
ciency.

"We understand that you were the flight attendant in
the back of the plane when the hijacking occurred."

"I was in the aft galley, yes," she said, wiping away
the tears and trying to appear more professional than
dishevelled. She went on to explain how the man had
grabbed the girl in the red nylon jacket, and how he had
screamed something and had threatened her with a
sharp object. Morgan then explained how the man in
the pale yellow sport shirt had apparently broken the
man's neck, and how he had proceeded to kill two other
hijackers.

"What man?" one FBI man asked incredulously.
"Nobody else said anything about a man in a yellow
shirt."

"That's probably because they were all distracted or
facing forward and keeping their heads down," the other
agent suggested.

"Yeah, I was standing behind," Morgan said. "I had a
clear view. And he also moved so quickly, and without
hardly getting out of his seat."

"We need to talk to this guy," the first FBI agent
said.

November 5
6:05 A.M. Central Time

JACK Rodgers sipped cold coffee from a paper cup and dabbed at the coffee stain on his pale yellow sport shirt. He was trying to keep a low profile and avoid being noticed while the hours clicked slowly past. He had just wrapped up a gig as a security consultant for a software zillionaire in Portland and was headed south to talk to a Louisiana retail magnate about a similar job.

Of all the bad luck to be caught up in this thing yesterday! It had been years since he'd been fighting these fundamentalist nutcases all over the world for Uncle Sam. It had been years since that night in Iran when Colonel Dave Brannan had been ordered to abort Operation Raptor. It had been years since the night that Greg Boyinson had managed to fly the team out in that single MH-6 chopper after the other one was destroyed.

Rodgers saw two FBI agents moving toward him and shifted his gaze. It was too late.

"Sir, I understand that you had a role in neutralizing the hijacking," the agent with the blonde crew cut announced.

"Well, I don't think *anybody* on our flight wanted to see those guys get control of the plane," Rodgers explained.

"Well, we hear that you did a bit more than *anybody*, Mr. uhh . . ."

"Rodgers, Jack Rodgers."

"Rodgers," the man in the blonde crew cut said as he scanned a twenty-page list that he was carrying. It was the results of the background check that the FBI had done on the passenger list and then e-mailed to the field agents at McConnell.

"Rodgers is it? Oh, I see, it's *Captain* Jack Rodgers. Retired Special Forces. Why didn't we spot you sooner?"

"I dunno, I guess I'm just an inconspicuous guy."

"Why didn't you come to us with this information six hours ago when we started interviewing people?" the man in the crew cut asked suspiciously.

"Because I really had nothing to tell," Rodgers explained. "The only ones of those clowns that I had any contact with will never have anything else to say. You should be talking to that one that got captured alive."

"We are," growled the other FBI agent, "but we want to find out what *you* know."

"As I said, there's nothing much to tell. I did as I was trained. I neutralized a situation. The other part of my training is to not stand up and crow about what I do."

November 5
2:45 P.M. Ankara Time

"**A**NNE, I'm going back down to the camp, can I bring you anything?"

Anne McCaine looked up at the young grad student silhouetted against the late afternoon sun.

"Yeah, thanks, Robert," she said, straightening up and shading her eyes. It was getting close to dinnertime and the volunteers would be yearning to knock things off for the day. "Get me some water. I don't want to stop now. I want to finish this section before it gets dark."

As Robert Pauwel headed off down the hill, Anne McCaine turned her attention back to the remarkable sandstone structure that her University of Colorado archaeological team had been excavating since July. Dating back to the thirteenth century B.C., in the far distant Bronze Age, the temple was built in celebration of Teshub, God of Tempests. It rivalled the famous sites at Alacahoyuk and Yazilikaya. In fact, this complex was the largest Hittite outpost yet discovered in this part of eastern Turkey.

At least on paper, it was Turkey. It was sometimes hard to tell out here in the high mountains north and east of Lake Van. The Iranian border was less than a day's ride to the east, and the Iraqi border not much farther to the south. Georgia lay to the north, and Armenia to the east. None of the borders was terribly well defined in these parts. To the Turks and Armenians, it was no-man's-land. To the Kurds, it was all Kurdistan. For the smugglers, whether their stock and trade was opium or ammunition, there were *no* borders.

It was a starkly beautiful landscape, this high plateau country surrounded by high, snowcapped mountains. To the distant north, you could barely make out Agri Dagi, the 5,165-meter mountain that the rest of the world knew as Mount Ararat, the final resting place of Noah's Ark. The terrain reminded Anne of Colorado.

For all its physical beauty and the familiarity of the terrain, this part of the world had taken some getting used to. Anne had come from an academic environment where the system bent over backward to avoid gender bias. Here, she entered a world where she couldn't be seen in the nearby town without her head wrapped in a black scarf. In Ankara or Istanbul, women had been allowed to bare their heads for more than a couple of generations, but out here, the old ways changed more slowly, or didn't change at all.

It was an exceptional opportunity to be given the grant to excavate the Teshub Temple, and she had jumped at it. Her work on that ancient site down in the Mogollon Mountains of New Mexico had certainly raised her profile in the archaeological community, and after that, she could write her own ticket. In her way, she was just as ambitious as Dennis. He had NothalCorp, and she had these holes in the ground. They were both seeing their professional ambitions realized, but he was the one getting manicures, while her fingers were tipped with chipped nails.

Today, she was chipping her nails on a bas-relief of Puduhepa, the consort of Hattusilis III, and the mother of the Hittite king Tudhaliyas IV. More than three thousand years ago, Puduhepa's face had been left to the centuries proudly uncovered, and now women had to wear sacks over their heads.

Working without gloves, Anne was carefully removing the last bits of dirt from the folds of Puduhepa's cloak when Robert returned. He was running—uphill. Running, especially running uphill, was certainly out of character for the lethargic Robert.

"Anne," he gasped breathlessly. "News. It's terrible. Denver."

"Sit down, Robert," Anne replied. "Sit down and catch your breath. What are you talking about? What's terrible in Denver?"

"There was a terrorist attack," Robert gasped. "The NothalCorp Tower was destroyed."

"When?"

"Yesterday. Middle of last night our time."

"What time was it in Denver?" Anne asked, frantically trying to do the math in her head.

"Just before noon."

"Dennis would have been at work," Anne said nervously. "Maybe he was . . ."

"I'm sorry, Anne," Robert said, lowering his eyes. "He was killed."

"How do you know that?" Anne demanded.

"The news reports. At the camp. Donald finally got his Internet connection restored, and he was downloading CNN on his laptop. Dennis is CEO of NothalCorp. He was in the news report. He never got out."

"There has to be a mistake!" Anne was distraught. She and Dennis lived in their separate worlds, but she still loved him, and she believed that he loved her. She had never looked at another man, and she believed that he remained true to her as well. Though they were spending a lot of time apart, she looked forward to the time they could spend together. When she was finished here, she was assured a senior professorship, maybe even head of the department. Then they could spend a lot more time together in their sprawling home near Boulder.

"This can't be true," Anne assured Robert. "There has to be a mistake."

Robert looked at her sadly. He could read her

expression, and he knew that she knew that it was *not* a mistake.

November 5
9:31 A.M. Central Time

FRESH air, at last. The cold wind pushed hard against the heavy door as FBI Special Agent Rod Llewellan exited the cafeteria. The bleak winter morning was a refreshing change. He had spent a sleepless night in a room full of shell-shocked hijacking victims. It had been like a nightmare. It *was* a nightmare. In the best of circumstances, it would have been unbearable for the passengers to have been cooped up like this, but these people were suffering with everything from posttraumatic shock to hypertension.

Llewellan's mandate was to debrief everyone. Don't let anyone go until they had been interviewed at length. He had done the best he could with seven agents and two bureau psychologists. If the news media could have a small army at the main gate of the air base within six hours, why the hell couldn't the Bureau get him more agents?

Finally they were being released in groups of fifteen. The next batch would make seventy-five, and that was more than half of the people who had been on the flight.

The worst part, Llewellan fumed, was that they had made no progress with the lone surviving hijacker. Under current law, he had more rights than the passengers. The U.S. Air Force security people could restrain him, and the FBI agents could talk to him—but they couldn't touch him. He hadn't told them a thing.

They had managed to ascertain that he spoke English, but about all that he had said was that he was proud of himself and he'd do it again.

They had gotten his name from his Arizona driver's license, which they guessed was probably an alias. The address on the license had been checked by agents from the Phoenix office. It was a vacant lot in Scottsdale.

Overlaying the whole situation was the frantic fear that another attack was imminent, and that this man could help the Bureau know when and where. Soon, if not already, FBI headquarters would be demanding answers. Llewellan felt the pressure. What could he do?

Maybe it was the fresh air flushing the stale atmosphere from his head, or maybe it was the umpteenth cup of coffee. Suddenly, Rod Llewellan had a brainstorm.

He chucked the Styrofoam cup into a barrel outside the door and pushed his way back inside. He looked around the room for that man in the yellow shirt and tan jacket, the ex-Special Forces guy, Jack Rodgers. Llewellan prayed that he hadn't been among those who had already been let go. He looked left, then right. He crossed the room and doubled back, realizing that part of this man's training was to make himself inconspicuous. If he had been Rodgers, he'd have done exactly the same. At last, Llewellan spotted his quarry, sitting next to a woman in a bright red down coat. He hadn't noticed the drab figure next to the eye-catching brightness of the red.

"Mr. Rodgers, I'd like to speak with you."

"Again?"

"Privately?"

"Do I have a choice?"

"Not really."

"Okay."

When Llewellan got the man off to the side he wasted no time in acknowledging Rodgers's Special Forces credentials and spilling his frustration with the rules of interrogation under which government agents operated.

"We need to know what's going to happen next," Llewellan continued. "He's not talking, and there are limits to what we can do."

"Even under an emergency like this?"

"Even under an emergency like this. An agent of the government is limited . . ."

"And you are thinking that a civilian with a background in getting people to talk about things they don't want to talk about might be able to . . ."

"I can't ask you to do that."

"But if a civilian were to convince this gentleman to share some secrets, that would please you?"

Both men understood the next step. Without any further conversation, Llewellan led Rodgers to the locked room where the surviving hijacker was being detained. Jack recognized the agent with the blonde crew cut who had interviewed him earlier. Llewellan nodded, and the younger man left the room. The hijacker was handcuffed to a steel table, but his defiant expression was that of a man who feared nothing and craved a glorious death.

"Mr. Mahmoud, this is Mr. Rodgers," Llewellan told him. "He would like to speak with you."

"I told you," Mahmoud said angrily, "I have nothing to say to agents of your infidel government."

"Mr. Rodgers is not an agent of any government."

Mahmoud simply sneered, eyeing Jack angrily.

"Let me get you a cup of coffee," Llewellan said to Jack, glancing at his watch. "I'll be back in ten minutes."

As Rod Llewellan closed the door behind him, leaving the retired captain alone in the room with the hijacker, he hoped that he had done the right thing. It was a desperate move, but he was out of options. He had to try something—anything. Time was running out.

When the ten minutes ran out, Llewellan opened the door to the room, unsure of what to expect. Jack calmly took the coffee as Llewellan handed it to him, and took a sip through the hole in the plastic lid.

Mahmoud, who had previously been the picture of arrogance, now looked like a man who'd been through an all-day IRS audit. His shoulders were slumped and he was trembling slightly. His eyes were wide and glassy. They were ringed in red as though he had been crying. His once sneering mouth hung open, a bead of saliva dangling from his lower lip.

"Kansas City," Rodgers said when Llewellan shut the door behind him. "A shopping center in Kansas City with the word 'gate' in the name. After that, medical facilities in Chicago. These things are in sequence, but Mr. Tough Guy here is not a Mr. Big. He hasn't been briefed on too much."

"Incredible," Llewellan said with amazement. "How did—"

"Don't ask," Jack replied. "You really don't want to know. The main thing is their staging base. It's in the Sierra Madre about 100 clicks south of Agua Prieta. A place called Rancho de los Bichos. Middle of nowhere."

"Mexico? How did they get into the United States?"

"They walked."

THREE

"**STEVE,** I've been thinking," President Thomas Livingstone said, turning to his chief of staff.

For most of the three hours since Air Force One took off from Andrews AFB in suburban Maryland, the president had been staring out the window of the big Boeing VC-25 executive jet, watching the fields and meadows of mid-America roll past. Beyond the wingtips of the big aircraft, at least a half dozen F-15Cs, armed to the teeth with AIM-120 AMRAAM air intercept missiles, kept the president safe, but he was nagged with his responsibility for the safety of all those people in those farmhouses and on country roads down there.

"I can imagine you've been thinking," Steve Faralaco said, sitting down across from his boss.

"Yeah. I've been thinking a lot about where we're

going today, but what I was thinking specifically was one thing I'd like to have you help me with in Denver."

"Anything. We have the schedule all laid out and the Secret Service has the route from the airport into town all buttoned up. The National Guard has—"

"I'm sure all that is in fine shape," the president interrupted. "What I want you to do is get hold of somebody for me."

"Sure," Faralaco replied, a tone of mystification in his voice. "Who?"

"Ever hear of General Buckley Peighton?"

"The name rings a bell."

"Buck and I went to school together at Penn a long, long time ago. We were great friends once. Had some wild times. I got into politics. He became a soldier. Went our separate ways. Haven't seen him in years. He retired with four stars. I hear that he lives in or around Denver."

"And you want to see him when you're in town."

"Right," Livingstone said hopefully. "I know it's very short notice . . ."

"No problem, I'll have Barb or Jo get right on it and we'll line him up."

"No," the president cautioned as Faralaco stood up. "I want *you* to handle it . . . personally. There is a lot going on. He values his privacy. I want as few people as possible to know about this."

"Just us," Faralaco replied. He could tell by the president's expression that he was serious. They had known one another since Livingstone was a freshman senator and Faralaco was a rookie staffer. Over the years, an absolute trust had evolved between them. It was one of the few things in the backstabbing world of Washington backrooms; it was one of the things upon which both could rely.

November 6
10:25 A.M. Eastern Time

SECRETARY-GENERAL Baudouin Abuja Mboma stared out the window of his spacious apartment on East Sixty-Sixth Street in New York City. It was raining hard, and the traffic down there on Madison Avenue was just a blur of headlights. The secretary-general swirled the scotch in his glass and looked across the cityscape. It was America's most powerful and most vulnerable city. He had lived here for the past eight years. He enjoyed the good life, and the good life was certainly good in New York City, especially if you had diplomatic immunity, and a virtually unlimited expense account.

Baudouin Abuja Mboma enjoyed New York City, but he longed to get back home. By home, he did not mean Djambala, the squalid back corner of the Congo where he was born and raised, but Paris, where he had gone to university and where he had reinvented himself as an urbane man of the world. He had left Djambala far behind and had climbed to the pinnacle of global power. He was, to turn a phrase, the king of the world. He had made a comfortable life for himself here in his well-appointed co-op in a very exclusive building, and had filled it with the finest things in life. His extensive collection of erotic etchings contained three Picassos.

It had been two days since the terrorists had struck

the United States, and the world was reacting. There were perfunctory condemnations, but mostly there was a global nervousness. If it could happen in Denver, it could happen nearly anywhere.

The bell rang and Mboma's personal secretary picked up the intercom. Mboma smiled. His personal secretary was young, but not too young. She was blonde, but not too blonde. And she was efficient, very efficient.

"The doorman said that Mr. Bin Qasim is here to see you, sir."

"Have him sent up."

Muhammad Bin Qasim was, like Mboma, a Third-World success story. The son of an Egyptian college professor, he had grown up in Cairo. The two crossed paths at the Sorbonne in Paris and had been friends ever since. With the International Validation Treaty, Bin Qasim had emerged as one of the most powerful men in the world. As head of the International Validation Organization, he could decide when and where nations could go to war, and over what issues.

"Greetings my friend," Mboma said, kissing Bin Qasim on both cheeks.

"Care for a drink?" Mboma asked.

"Merci, I'll have what you are having."

"Have you been following the news?" Mboma said, handing the International Validation Organization chief a tumbler of blended whisky.

"The Americans are certainly distressed." Bin Qasim smiled. "But the world, or most of it, cannot but rejoice when the Great Satan is struck."

"I have no more love for the Americans than the next person." Mboma shrugged. "But events such as this, and the bombings all across Europe, have got the Security Council worried. Even the French are worried."

"They know that they are safe from any major difficulties so long as they do nothing to anger the Mujahidin Al-Akhbar."

"And I suppose that they will avoid doing such a thing." Mboma smiled. "Let's get to work. What do you have for me today?"

Bin Qasim opened his attaché case and laid several large packets on the table. Each was brimming with American currency or British pounds sterling. The secretary-general had the ultimate authority to approve the contracts issued by the United Nations, whether it was a relief operation in East Africa or infrastructure construction projects in Southeast Asia. The firms and NGOs that received these contracts knew that they were not just receiving contracts, but getting their foot in the door of enterprises that would last for years, if not decades. Not just anyone received these prizes, and those who did were generous in expressing their gratitude to the man who had the ultimate authority to give and to take away.

For his part, Baudouin Abuja Mboma was glad to help these Third-World entrepreneurs, and he certainly appreciated their gratitude. He enjoyed the good life, and the good life was certainly good in New York City.

When Bin Qasim was finished going through this week's list of grateful NGOs with his boss, he took his leave, and the secretary-general sat down at his computer to scan his portfolio.

"Call my broker," Mboma said, stepping into his personal secretary's small office. "Issue a buy order.

The market's way down. This is a time of great opportunity."

"Buy what?"

"Anything. It's all down. Tell him to hold the oil stocks. Those will be going up, greatly."

November 6
3:55 P.M. Mountain Time

PRESIDENT Thomas Livingstone was visibly shaken. His visit to the massive field of wreckage that was once the NothalCorp Tower had taken an emotional toll that he had not expected. For the past forty-eight hours, he had seen it repeatedly on the small screen in the Oval Office, but he had not been prepared for seeing it live and in person. Nor had anyone traveling with him. Livingstone had even seen a tear running from Steve Faralaco's eye.

The sight was bad enough, but the thing that nagged Livingstone the worst was the *smell*. Even sealed into their heavy black limousine, with its bulletproof armor and airtight door seals, the stench lingered.

"He'll be meeting us at the airport," Faralaco said, breaking the silence.

Livingstone looked startled for a moment. The experience of the past three hours had seized him completely.

"Buck?" he said, remembering his having told Steve to get hold of Buckley Peighton. "That's wonderful. Will he be there when we arrive?"

"Then or soon after. I made a couple of calls and got

him. The Secret Service picked him up, and they'll meet us at the hangar where we staged all of the Secret Service vehicles when we arrived."

Ten minutes later, the presidential limousine and its long line of escort vehicles wheeled into the hangar, which was ringed by police cars, their lights flashing. Inside, Livingstone recognized Peighton. He was wearing a nondescript blue Windbreaker, and he was standing next to a Secret Service vehicle.

"Stop here," Livingstone ordered.

The two men greeted one another with a mix of joy and guilt, as old friends that have been too busy to stay in touch often do. Peighton had been to Livingstone's inauguration party, but they had not had a chance for more than a few minutes of conversation.

After exchanging lies about how neither had changed, Livingstone asked the old general to take a walk.

"Buck, I've got a problem."

"I'd say so," Peighton said, nodding toward the city from which Livingstone had just come.

"It's more than that. It's the damned International Validation. We can't do anything. Even if we could track down the assholes who planned this thing, we wouldn't be able to *do* anything."

"We're just players in the international community," Peighton said cynically. "If the French and the United Nations want us on a leash, that's what they do. If it doesn't pass the global test, our hands are tied. It's not like the old days."

"Let me cut to the chase," Livingstone said, pausing to look at his old friend face-to-face.

"Please do." Peighton smiled, noticing that their stroll

had taken them to a corner of the vast hangar that was well beyond earshot of anyone. "I hate beating around the bush, and you're on a tight schedule."

"Remember General Claire Chennault in World War II?" the president asked.

"Of course. He was the Army Air Corps general that went to China to set up the American Volunteer Group to fight the Japanese before the United States got into the war."

"Right. The Chinese Air Force was getting the shit kicked out of them by the Japanese. The Japanese had air supremacy over all of China. They were losing badly. China's first lady, Madame Chiang Kai-shek, went to Chennault. He was one of the best pilots and one of the best officers in the Air Corps, an aerobatic genius and a natural leader."

"Not to mention being a helluva tactician," Peighton interrupted. "Which is why Madame Chiang went to him. She wanted *him* running her air force. He quit the U.S. Army and went to work for her. Then he got Roosevelt to get him American pilots to fight the Japanese in China. They had to quit the Air Corps or the Navy or whatever, and do it on the sly as civilians."

"He organized the American Volunteer Group, the Flying Tigers," Livingstone said, retelling a story that Peighton already knew. He knew that Peighton knew it, but he was making a point. "They were all Americans, all ex-military fighter pilots who fought the Japanese in American fighter planes with Chinese markings. The United States military couldn't do anything because we weren't in the war yet. Our military had their hands tied behind their backs."

"I see where you're going with this!" Peighton said with a laugh.

"I figured you would," Livingstone said.

"Problem is that I'm about two decades too old to be your Chennault," Peighton admitted. "I'm closer to seventy than sixty, as you are. My ticker wouldn't take me chasing bad guys across the world for you . . . much as I'd like to."

"But you could *find* me a Chennault," Livingstone said, looking at him with what seemed like desperation. "You're plugged into the right circles. You're connected. You could make one phone call and be speaking to a twenty-first-century Chennault."

"You want as few links in the chain between you and him as possible," Peighton said thoughtfully. "I get it."

"Yeah, Buck. As few as possible, but there has to be at least one. It's like it was with Roosevelt and Chennault."

"Plausible deniability." Peighton smiled.

"Right. There has to be one link between me and whoever leads the new American Volunteer Group. I want it to be you. I don't want to *meet* the twenty-first-century Chennault or even know his name, but I want him two steps away from the Oval Office, and I want the step between to be someone that I can trust explicitly."

"This old general is honored to be called back into service, Mr. President," General Buckley Peighton said humbly.

"Don't call me that, Buck. You knew me when I wasn't president. That's my official title. This is about as far from being official as anything that I've done since I've had this title. But it's probably closer to the spirit of that promise to 'Protect and defend' that I made two years ago in January when I took this title."

"Okay Tom," Peighton said. "I'm still honored, and privileged to be part of this, as any old soldier would be. And I know your man. Problem is, it might take a bit more than a phone call to get to him."

FOUR

November 8
3:43 P.M. Mountain Time

IT was cold and windy in the high country of Montana's Bob Marshall Wilderness Area. There were a few patches of snow from last week's blizzard on the ground, and a few flakes in the air, but visibility was still generally good. Dave Brannan reined his horse to a stop and began to study the distant ridgeline through his binoculars. There was a bull elk out there somewhere, and the day after tomorrow, he would be steaks on Brannan's grill.

Brannan detected a flick of movement out of the corner of his eye and trained the binoculars on the spot. It was not an elk. It was a pair of hikers about a quarter of a mile away. They were walking on the main trail and were not carrying rifles, so they weren't hunters. Nor were they wearing high-visibility jackets or vests. They had dark jackets. Not exactly camouflage, but not exactly easy to see. What were hikers doing on this trail during hunting season?

As Brannan watched, they stopped. One man pointed to the ground and the other pointed down at the place on the trail where Brannan had been a half hour earlier. He realized that they were following him. They were following him by his horse's shit.

As the two men paused, he could see that at least one of them was carrying a holstered sidearm. Maybe they both were. Dave Brannan had made a lot of enemies in the world before he had retired from the U.S. Army Special Forces. He guessed that it had finally caught up to him. It seemed odd that it would come to this during hunting season in the middle of the wilderness, but maybe they thought hunting season was a good time to go hunting.

Dave Brannan stroked his auburn mustache thoughtfully and smiled. He had decided to make the hunters into the hunted. He pulled off his orange hunting vest and stuffed it in his saddlebag. Picking a course that screened him from the trail, he proceeded to outflank his pursuers. On horseback he could move more quickly than they could.

Keeping them in sight as they hiked across a bare hillside, Brannan quickly got behind the two men and followed them as the trail went into a thicket of jack pine. He was now as close as he wanted to get on horseback. Pulling his Winchester 30-06 rifle from the scabbard, he dismounted and turned his horse loose. He knew that Sandy wouldn't stray far, and he didn't want him tied up in bear country.

Brannan started down the trail after the two men, and within moments, he could see them just ahead. They both were, indeed, carrying sidearms. They walked without conversation as though they were making an effort to remain unheard. The taller of the two was obviously younger or in better shape than the other, but neither was a stranger to physical exercise.

At last, they reached a point where Brannan could bring this little cat and mouse game to a head. The trail dipped into a gully where there was no cover. Brannan could remain on high ground as they walked into the trough, and he would have a clear field of fire.

"Stop where you are and don't turn around," Brannan ordered.

Hearing the unmistakable sound of a round being chambered in Brannan's bolt-action Winchester, the two men complied.

"Hands clasped behind your heads and down on your knees."

Again, the two men complied, although the older man had obvious difficulty kneeling. They then complied with Brannan's order to pluck their pistols from their holsters with thumb and forefinger and to throw the weapons as far as they could.

"Colonel Brannan," the older man said without turning around. "I'm General Buckley Peighton and this is Rod Llewellan of the FBI. We're not here to harm you."

Buck Peighton. The name resonated with Brannan. He had known this man in Somalia long ago. He had never served under him directly, but he had briefed him a time or two and had seen him around. The name was certainly well-known.

"Stand up and turn around. Just you, not your friend."

As Buck Peighton turned, he could barely see Brannan crouched on the lip of the ravine, but there was no mistaking the fact that a rifle was pointed at him, and he knew that the crosshairs of the scope were trained on his head.

"We met in Mogadishu," Peighton said. "You were with the 334th Special Ops. Your commander was Smitty Smith. You took out that nest of skinnies up on what we called Crestline Drive. There was that French nurse. What was her name?"

"Lillienne."

"But everyone knew her as Nancy."

"Okay, General, I'm convinced that it's you," Dave Brannan said, standing. He lowered the rifle, but still kept it at the ready. He had left the U.S. Army with an honorable discharge, but in the world of special ops, there were always things that went unsaid, and there were enemies you never knew you had.

"Nice day for a walk," Dave said, not cracking a smile. "But you guys aren't out for a walk. You're following me, and you're armed. Why?"

"Colonel, it would be foolish of us to be walking around without protection out here where every man we are likely to meet will be armed. A few will be poachers trying for that third untagged elk, and then there are the bears. The grizzlies are in an edgy mood trying to top off their tanks before their long winter's nap."

"What do you want with me, General? I'm out of the Army now. Hadn't expected to see a general officer again on what I'm guessing is official business."

"I'm out of the Army, too, Colonel. But I've been called on by the president to undertake a special mission. It involves you."

"I'm not planning to reenlist."

"It wouldn't involve that. Not exactly," Buck Peighton said. "If you'd let us put our arms down, I'd like to explain."

Brannan whistled, and Sandy dutifully trotted to his master's side, knowing that a handful of oats from the saddlebag would be made available. As Brannan put his rifle back into the scabbard, the two men began to unfold a startling proposal.

"You want *me* to put together a mercenary team?" Brannan asked incredulously after the general had explained what the president had in mind.

"Except for the substantial sum that the president has authorized for you to be paid, there is no similarity with mercenary operations," Peighton responded. "You'd operate under the direct authority of the president with a very short chain of command in between. Obviously, it's going to be more secret than top secret, and we'll maintain the plausible deniability factor."

"Obviously," Brannan replied with a slight grin. "You're assuming that I'd have any interest whatsoever in getting involved in this thing," Brannan continued. "You know how and why I left the Army."

"Operation Raptor. Iran," Peighton recalled. "You were ordered to stand down by the highest command authority."

"After we'd risked lives and lost good men," Brannan said. "We were on the brink of success and we had the rug pulled out from under us. His job is to give the orders, but the highest command authority has a responsibility to let a soldier do his job once the orders are issued . . . not to cancel the orders at the eleventh hour because of cold feet. We lost two very good men egressing from that debacle. That's why I left."

"That was then, this is now," Peighton explained. "Back then, the Cold War was over and peace was breaking out everywhere. There were political considerations. There was a desire not to rock the boat. They thought everybody in the world was going to be friends."

"That's fine," Brannan said in disgust. "They can all be friends. Since my wife died eight years ago, I've sort of cut myself off from everybody out in the world. After those years, I've gotten to a place where I am quite content to wile away my time up here in the Rockies. As much as I miss some of the operational aspects of the old life, and as much as I miss some of the guys I worked with, I don't really want to come down off my mountain and go back into that world of backbiting and chain of command politics."

"You'll be given complete authority to form and train your team and to plan your actions. The president does not *want* to know any of the details. He doesn't even want to know your name."

"I can imagine."

"I'll get you whatever you need," the general continued. "Weapons. Explosives. Safe houses. Transportation. Whatever you need. The president has authorized me to get it for you."

"What's your role in all of this, Agent Llewellan?" Brannan asked, turning to the younger man.

"I'd be your liaison with National Intelligence," Llewellan replied, glad to have a chance to get into what had been a two-way conversation. "Through me, you'd get everything that National Intel knows about the target of your operations."

The snow flurries that had abated for a time were picking up now. Brannan knew that they had better hurry the conversation along.

"Which leads me to my last question," Dave Brannan said, glancing from Llewellan to Peighton. "What *is* the target of my operations? Would I be right to assume that it has to do with what happened in Denver last week?"

November 8
5:43 P.M. Eastern Time

"**I**T may surprise the infidel to hear me speaking in his own language," the bearded man said. "But that will not be the only surprise in store for the Zionist Crusaders of the Great Satan."

President Thomas Livingstone leaned forward in his chair, his eyes fixed on the television screen. Steve Faralaco had just dashed into the office with the word that the news channels would be broadcasting a message from the dreaded and enigmatic Fahrid Al-Zahir.

Al-Zahir was a cunning and charismatic rogue gangster in the mold of Osama Bin Laden, Ayman Al-Zawahiri, Khaleq Sheikh Mohammed, and Abu Musab Al-Zarqawi. Until now, his name, and that of his Mujahidin Al-Akhbar organization, was more commonly spoken at intelligence briefings behind closed doors than on international news channels—until now.

"Our martyrs know that it is God's will that they be slain in such a way as to kill Americans and all those who stand with them. With the gush of his blood, the martyr knows that he will be shown his seat in paradise. The Great Satan occupied the land of the two holiest of places, plundering its riches, dictating to its rulers, humiliating its people, and terrorizing its neighbors. But the brave martyrs of Al-Qaeda drove the infidels out of the country of the two holy places and took the jihad to the land of the Great Satan itself. The time has come to finish the task. The time has come in which the martyrs of the Mujahidin Al-Akhbar have come to destroy the Great Satan in its nest. The time has come for the Mujahidin Al-Akhbar to demonstrate to the infidels that they are not safe in their own beds. They will never be safe until we triumph."

The hairs on the back of Tom Livingstone's neck were on edge, but he tried to appear calm. Steve Faralaco and a growing number of White House staffers were standing around, watching the man in the turban chastise the United States. As Al-Zahir spoke, the gold fabric behind him rippled slightly. His tirade had obviously been recorded in a tent in a windy location.

"I have spoken to God, and God has spoken to me," Al-Zahir bragged smugly. "He has blessed this jihad. The fatwa to kill the Americans and their allies—civilians and military—is our individual duty. We will do it in any country in which it is possible to do it. We will do it in America! It is God's will that we slaughter them on their streets and in their homes and in all places where they feel safest. It is God's will that we give them no rest. There is no more important duty."

The screen faded to black and suddenly it was filled with a pair of ashen-faced, tongue-tied network commentators who stammered to fill the dead air with something intelligent.

Livingstone took the remote control from Faralaco and surfed to another channel, and then another. Finally, somebody on one of the cable channels was giving some background on Al-Zahir. Like Osama Bin Laden, he came from a wealthy family. His father had been an old bedouin arms dealer who had made millions smuggling ordnance in and out of the world's trouble spots since at least the 1980s. He'd been indicted in France for a money laundering scam, but the charges had been mysteriously dropped.

Fahrid Al-Zahir had been educated at the London School of Economics and had been involved in his father's business until the elder Al-Zahir was blown up in a bomb blast at his seaside villa in Lebanon. The Israeli Mossad was widely condemned for the attack, but the evidence pointed to a rival gunrunner. After that, Fahrid donned a turban and wrapped himself in fundamentalism. The onetime economics student turned into a killer who was widely feared throughout Europe and the Middle East.

The commentator reminded his jittery viewers that in his early years, Al-Zahir's signature hit had been a brazen attack in which he always lingered to mutilate the dead. He killed an Israeli cabinet minister on a quiet residential street in Haifa and sent his right hand—

neatly packed in dry ice—to his grieving widow a week later. A Dutch journalist known to be critical of Al-Zahir's brand of fundamentalism spreading into Europe was on holiday in Norway when he died violently. His eyes turned up in a package delivered to his editor the following day. Now, Al-Zahir's signature seemed to have changed. As the commentator pointed out, he was trying to match Bin Laden at *his* game.

"What else do we know about this character?" President Livingstone asked without looking up. "What the hell is this Mujahidin Al-Akhbar?"

"The Mujahidin Al-Akhbar is another one of these organizations like Al-Qaeda or Hezbollah or Islamic Jihad or the this-or-that Martyrs Brigade," Faralaco recalled from the White House CIA briefings to which he had been a party. "They're one of a dozen or so Middle East gangs turned anarchist armies that are in the service of a silver-tongued demagogue. He is as the talking head was saying. We don't know too much about him. He's a lot like Osama Bin Laden and some of those. He holes up in the mountains, but unlike Bin Laden, he's been seen outside the Middle East, like in Europe."

"He thinks he's on a mission from God," Livingstone's secretary interjected, paraphrasing Dan Akroyd's line from the *Blues Brothers* movie. "Those guys are always the worst kind."

"He's a real firebrand, but in and of himself, Al-Zahir isn't necessarily the worst kind," the president said. "The worst kind are the unknown lemmings who are willing to kill themselves to slaughter innocent people because they *believe* that he's talking to God."

November 8
5:55 P.M. Eastern Time

SECRETARY of State Edredin had heard Al-Zahir's harangue on the radio as his limousine crawled slowly through the midtown Manhattan traffic. The drizzle outside underscored the gloom that he felt as he made his way to the twenty-eighth floor of the United Nations building and the office of International Validation Organization head Muhammad Bin Qasim.

The well-dressed and urbane Bin Qasim smiled warmly as he greeted Edredin in his office, with its spectacular view of the East River. After a polite exchange of niceties, Edredin got right to the point. Without getting into technical details, he explained that the interrogation of the surviving hijacker had revealed the existence of a Mujahidin Al-Akhbar training camp in the Sierra Madre of the northern Mexican state of Sonora, just 100 kilometers from the United States' border. Satellite imaging had confirmed both the existence and the location of the facility.

Because of International Validation requirements, the United States could not take action against this base without the United Nations' authorization. Edredin felt a certain sense of humiliation at having to make the case to a United Nations bureaucrat for what the United States ought to be able to do, but treaties were treaties, and the United States had signed the International Validation accords.

"I want to express my deepest personal sadness for what happened in Denver," Bin Qasim said. "Certainly the world community feels your pain and frustration."

"However," Bin Qasim continued—Edredin had gritted his teeth and waited for the inevitable other shoe to drop, and here it was—"a military invasion of a sovereign country that is not a party to the conflict is a serious matter. You know that Mexico is very sensitive to American intervention. Your country invaded sovereign Mexican territory in 1846 and 1916 and numerous other times. I'm not sure that an intervention in this case would meet the global test necessary for an International Validation."

"In 1916, it was to chase terrorists who had attacked and killed people within the United States," Edredin said in clarification.

"Yes, but it was an invasion nevertheless, and your General Pershing never succeeded in capturing Pancho Villa. Furthermore, the negative impact on Mexico far outweighed the tactical results of your invasion. As for the present situation, I will take the matter up with the full International Validation Organization Board when we meet again in three weeks."

"What do you expect us to do in the meantime?" Edredin replied. "We were attacked, and we know where the perpetrators are."

"To clarify the situation, most of the perpetrators of the Denver tragedy are dead, and you have the lone survivor in custody. Aren't the people supposedly living at this place in Sonora, as you say in your own legal code, innocent until proven guilty?"

John Edredin was fuming as he left the United Nations building. The damned International Validation Organization bureaucrats would debate this thing for weeks. The hands of the United States were tied, and everyone knew it.

As he walked toward his waiting car, one of his aides was running, literally running, toward him. There were tears running down her face.

"They did it again!" She gasped. "In Kansas City. Two truck bombs at a shopping mall. The roof collapsed. They are estimating at least 900 dead."

High above them on the twenty-eighth floor, Muhammad Bin Qasim was checking his stock portfolio online. He looked at his oil stocks, imagining what the numbers would be tomorrow. A smile came over his face as he leaned back in his large, comfortable leather chair.

November 9
7:41 A.M. Central Time

JACK Rodgers tossed his duffel bag into the trunk of the rental car and took a sip of hot coffee. He had just checked out of his Baton Rouge motel room and was headed for his 8:30 meeting with the huge midsouth retail chain that wanted him to consult on their security. He was four days late, but they understood why.

Jack's deal with Llewellan was that after he had done his civic duty, he was free to walk out of the cafeteria and board one of the shuttle buses that were taking passengers from the Western Star flight across town to the Wichita Mid-Continent Airport. When he had finally gotten away, airline flights were still grounded and everything was in absolute chaos, so Jack had decided to rent a car and drive to Baton Rouge instead. Renting a car had also been easier said than done, so he made his way over to the Greyhound bus station and paid cash for a one-way ticket. When he got to Baton Rouge, he picked up a car at a seedy place downtown. All of the major car rental companies were sold out.

He was four days late, but they were more anxious than ever to see him. After what had happened in Denver, they were scared. The whole damned country was scared.

Rodgers put his Styrofoam cup in the improvised cup holder and was about to jam the key in the ignition when his cell phone began to chirp.

"Jack?"

"Yep."

"This is Dave Brannan."

Wow. He hadn't talked to Dave Brannan in years—not since the wake of the Operation Raptor debacle, and not since Brannan's leaving the service had sent shock waves throughout the entire special ops community.

"How've you been, Colonel?" Rodgers asked.

"Fine. Couldn't be better. Listen, it's hunting season. I'd like to have you go hunting with me."

"That would be great, but I'm down here in Baton Rouge. I'm getting ready to talk to a guy about a job."

"Jack, I'd really like to have you go hunting with me."

"It love to, Colonel, but I'm about to take a job, and I need the dough—"

"Jack, I *really* want you to go hunting with me," Brannan interrupted with an insistent tone.

Reading the tone of the former colonel's voice, Jack Rodgers knew immediately that he was not talking about hunting elk. His mind quickly grasped exactly what it was that Brannan had in mind. Jack knew that he didn't really have a choice.

"Yeah, it would be good to go hunting with you again, Colonel."

"Can you meet me in forty-eight hours at that place where we bought drinks for that gal with the eyepatch?"

Jack grinned when he remembered that night. She had been a piece of work. A former East Coast debutante turned Montana logger, she had lost her eye in a freak accident, but she still had the looks to turn heads and the sense of humor to keep them turned.

"I'll be on the road as soon as I give these folks down here the bad news that something has come up and I can't take their job offer."

FIVE

ANNE McCaine stared at the bas-relief of Puduhepa, the consort of Hattusilis III, but all she could think about was Dennis, her own husband. Her *late* husband. It was hard to get her mind around the fact that she was no longer a wife, but a *widow*. In this remote corner of Turkey, the outside world seemed distant, but they had gotten the news about Kansas City. Somewhere beyond where the sun was starting to go down in the west, the angry demons that made her a widow had struck again.

"The guys have been saying that we had better be thinking about getting out of here," Robert Pauwel said nervously.

Anne brushed a long strand of hair out of her eyes and looked up at the jittery young grad student. He was right and she knew it. They had agreed to stay put after the Denver attack, but with the Kansas City calamity, the tension was growing. The excitement of a semester abroad in an exotic land had turned into anxiety and fear. The dig that had seemed to be of such great importance to everyone a week ago was now just a hole in the ground.

"You're right," Anne said, standing up and brushing the dust off her knees. "Let's get the gear packed up. We can leave first thing in the morning. We might be able to make it to Erzincan tomorrow. After that we'll be on pretty good roads and we'll be able to get to Ankara pretty easily the next day."

As Anne walked down off the mound, she glanced back at the Bronze Age temple of Teshub, God of Tempests, and thought about the tempests that now swirled throughout the world. She wondered when, or even whether, she'd see this place again. She surprised herself when she realized that she didn't even care.

November 10
7:11 A.M. Central Time

"**W**E have to stop meeting like this," General Buckley Peighton told his old friend. There was not a trace of humor in his expression.

"The day when we don't *have to* cannot come soon enough for me," President Thomas Livingstone told him. "Denver was bad enough, but a second one in four days is a horror."

The president was in Kansas City to tour the carnage.

It was his second trip to a scene of man-made devasta-
tion in less than a week. The death toll had already ex-
ceeded a thousand. He had felt terrible in Denver, but he
felt worse now. Four days ago, he could kid himself that
it might have been an isolated incident. Now it was a
pattern. This was now clear to everyone, and panic was
brewing.

"What can you tell me?" Peighton asked Rod
Llewellan, who was standing with the two men in the corner of the hangar where the well-guarded Air Force One
was parked.

"We have the dossier on Mujahidin Al-Akhbar, and
it's essentially what you've seen before. These are guys
who have been convinced that they have a free pass to
heaven if they kill Americans. Al-Zahir is your classic
fundamentalist. He has the colorful tongue to turn a
gaggle of street punks into a band of zealots ready to
martyr themselves. They get their cash flow like mob-
sters anywhere, through shakedowns and pushing dope,
and we've spent a lot of man-hours following their
money."

"Where does it come from?" the president asked.

"Al-Zahir has a background in money laundering
and under-the-table deals. He knows his business. He is
certainly a lot more of a gangster than a would-be martyr, although the Arab street seems to love a man in
flowing robes who can talk hatred about the evil Americans. If we cut off the head of this serpent . . ."

"If we can *find* the bastard!" Peighton snarled.
"Where the hell is he?"

"His base of operations is up in the Caucasus in eastern Turkey, where Iraq runs into Iran and Georgia into

Armenia, and the only borders are the ones that are drawn by the guys with the guns," Rod Llewellan explained. "Although he moves in and out of there pretty frequently."

"Can you get to him?" the president asked Peighton. "Do you have your team in place yet?"

"I've found your Chennault, Tom," Peighton said, looking Livingstone in the eye. "It's in his hands now."

November 10
9:11 A.M. Pacific Time

THE Seattle Division of the King County Jail is a deceptively cheerful-looking concrete building located at the northwest corner of the intersection of Fifth Avenue and the steep hill of James Street. Nearly 1,700 inmates can be housed here, and until about fifteen minutes ago, one of them was Greg Boyinson.

"Get your ass off that bunk, Boyinson," the guard demanded. "Your pals are here to get you out."

Boyinson's head was spinning. He had no idea that there was anyone who would *want* to come up with the cash to pay his fine and spring him.

The whole thing started innocently enough as a discussion of the Denver debacle. It was on everybody's mind. Greg had been pounding the pavement in the days afterward, trying to find a job, but nobody was hiring. They certainly weren't going to hire a guy who had just been fired from a job in a parking garage.

Dispirited, he'd stopped into a bar to cool his heels and try to figure out what to do. Some guy was in there shooting off his mouth about how it was all America's fault. The United States invited disaster by not being deferential to the rest of the world. Greg took exception, and there was a "spirited" discussion. The guy escalated the thing by tossing half a glass of chardonnay on an American flag that was hanging above the bar. Boyinson saw red. The guy threw a punch, but that was not his last mistake. When he left the bar with the paramedics, he had a broken jaw.

As the heavy doors swung open and the guard walked away, Greg couldn't believe his eyes.

He hadn't seen Colonel Brannan and Jack Rodgers in years. The sight of the two of them took Boyinson back to that night in 1997 when he had flown the MH-6 Little Bird out of Iran. A dozen men had gone in with a pair of MH-6s. They'd been ordered to egress without taking down the target, and the bad guys had got lucky. They managed to put an RPG into one of the Little Birds, killing the pilot and another man before Jack Rodgers had turned the bad guys into *dead* bad guys with a 40-mm grenade from his M203.

The ten remaining soldiers had gotten aboard Boyinson's MH-6, with half of them hanging onto the outside. He had flown them all more than 350 miles to the safety of an aircraft carrier in the Persian Gulf, often travelling as low as ten feet above the ground. They'd had to stop once to shoot up an Iraqi military post and steal gas, but they'd made it, and those ten men were still alive. Two of them had just bailed him out of jail.

Colonel Brannan had thought that Boyinson deserved a Medal of Honor, but he was told that nobody gets a medal for an operation that officially never happened.

That was part of the reason that Brannan had turned in his eagles over the Operation Raptor mess.

"How'd you do it?" Greg asked incredulously.

"The guy decided not to press charges." Jack smiled. Greg could imagine how that change of mind came about.

"Great, but what are you guys doing here?" Greg asked, breathing a sigh of relief.

"We'll tell you all about it in the car," Brannan said. "Let's go."

They hopped on Interstate 90, and as Brannan's big Buick dashed eastward across the Lake Washington Bridge toward Mercer Island, the whole story started to unfold. There was a job to be done. The job would depend on people travelling by helicopter, and the other two men in the car had agreed that there was no better man to be flying that helicopter than Greg Boyinson.

November 11
8:23 A.M. Ankara Time

THE dusty sport-utility vehicle carrying the University of Colorado archaeological team lumbered into the little Turkish village at the base of the canyon in which the Americans had been working for the past four months. The Americans planned to fuel the vehicle, fill their spare gas cans, and buy water before making their dash across Turkey. They had e-mailed the university, and plane tickets would be waiting for them when they reached Ankara in about forty-eight hours.

When they had arrived in July, the people around

here had been friendly and more than willing to be helpful. They had hired one of the English-speaking villagers as a translator, and he quickly became "part of the family." This usually jolly fellow, whom they nicknamed "Little Abdul," was anything but gregarious today. Since the news of the Kansas City attack had filtered across the wire, he had become cautious. Today, as they reached the village, he was especially nervous.

As they reached the edge of town, Anne McCaine pulled the SUV into the driveway of the little country store that had the town's only gas pump. She pulled a wad of Turkish banknotes from her purse and was about to climb out when two men with Kalashnikov rifles approached. As she opened the door, one of them began shouting angrily and pointing at her. Anne could understand enough Turkish to know that he was talking about the hijab that she wore on her head.

Little Abdul, who was riding in the passenger's seat of the Nissan Xterra, hopped out and began speaking to the men. They argued for a time, and finally Abdul turned to Anne.

"They say that you are in violation of Islamic law," he explained apologetically.

"What law?" she said angrily. As much as she tried to be accepting of cultures other than her own, she still couldn't embrace a culture that treated women like they weren't people. "I'm wearing the damned hijab."

"They don't think that you should be driving a car."

"This isn't Saudi Arabia," Anne replied angrily, looking at the two men with the guns. "It's legal in Turkey for women to drive!"

"Things have changed," Abdul said sheepishly. "In the last few days, some of the local jurisdictions are under pressure to start imposing Islamic law. They are afraid. Things are changing. Men with guns are enforcing new laws, which are actually old laws, but they are enforcing them now, and they said that you should not be driving."

"Okay, Abdul, you drive. Here are the keys. Let's get gas and get out of here."

"That's another problem."

"What's another problem?"

"Petrol."

"What about it?"

"There isn't any," Abdul said after a long pause. "They won't sell petrol to infidels."

"Infidel money is as good as non-infidel money," Anne snarled, holding up the wad of bills.

Suddenly, one of the men reached through the open window and grabbed the money out of her hand.

"You bastard!" Anne screamed, scratching the man on the wrist as he pulled the bills from her.

The man lifted his fist to punch her, but Little Abdul intervened, shouting at the man angrily in Turkish. Apparently, having the money made the two men forget about their little, self-righteous jihadi against the uppity Colorado woman, and they wandered off.

Anne could see that Abdul was shaking. He was obviously scared.

"What are we going to do now?" Robert said from the backseat. Abdul was scared, and poor Robert was in a panic. For Anne, losing a wad of money worth about twenty dollars was small compared to having just lost her husband, and compared to the threat of being stranded in this place without fuel.

"We don't have enough gas to make it to the main highway, much less to Erzincan," Anne admitted.

SIX

GENERAL Buck Peighton felt a sense of excitement that he had not sensed in years. His long retirement had turned him into a stale old man who got all of his excitement from an occasional paperback. All of his exercise consisted of knocking balls around the golf course with other old duffers like himself. Suddenly he was back in the saddle. Tom Livingstone had summoned him to active duty. He had answered out of patriotism, but it had changed his life. With the adrenaline in his bloodstream and the stale gasoline smell of the beat-up old Ford Bronco in his nostrils, he felt twenty years younger. The old general felt like he was a major again.

Dave Brannan had picked him up on a street corner in Las Cruces, New Mexico. It was cloak-and-dagger stuff and, *by golly*, it was exciting. They had stopped for gas at Exit 134, and a man with a faded blue ski jacket and a brown paper bag had gotten into the backseat. Rod Llewellan was trying his best to be inconspicuous, but after they pulled back onto Interstate 10, both Peighton and Brannan gave the FBI agent a hard time about his wingtips.

When they left the highway in the middle of nowhere, only Brannan knew where they were headed. In fact, by this time, the only man not present who knew that they had even come to New Mexico was in the Oval Office, and Thomas Livingstone did not *want* to know where Brannan would be taking them.

They had travelled about forty-five minutes on the old, rutted gravel road when they could at last make out a cluster of buildings in the distance. A few of them were well-worn relics of a World War II Air Corps training base, and there was a windowless shed made of corrugated galvanized steel that had been added in the 1970s, when the runway on this site had been used by crop dusters. Peighton and Llewellan had the distinct sensation of being watched from a distance as they approached the steel building. There were no other vehicles in sight.

"Welcome to our humble home." Dave Brannan grinned.

As they stepped out, they were struck by the empty silence of this lonely place. There was a trace of a breeze, but that was the only sound. Peighton and Llewellan looked around. The sun was sinking low in the west, tinting the patches of snow on the ground with its golden glow. Except for these few dilapidated buildings there was no sign of human habitation for as far as the eye could see. There was not even a sheepherder's shack out on a distant horizon.

As Brannan opened a side door on the corner of the steel building, the scene on the inside was anything but quiet and still. Parked in the center of the building that had once housed crop-dusting planes was a helicopter. A man with a paintbrush was putting the finishing touches on a tail number for the small chopper. Peighton recognized the "X" prefix of a Mexican civil registration, but the helicopter was obviously not a McDonnell Douglas civilian model 530. It was the military equivalent, the MH-6 Little Bird. It was equipped with a forward-looking infrared turret and a pair of launch tubes for AGM-114 Hellfire missiles. The small craft also boasted a pair of M134 7.62 mm, six-barrel, Gatling-type twin machine guns.

Neatly stacked along one wall were nylon backpacks of varying color, and other gear that was military issue. There were night-vision goggles, Heckler & Koch MP5 submachine guns, and other weapons. The night-vision equipment included PVS-15 binocular goggles that were especially suited for operations where depth perception would be critical for mission performance. As with all Litton night-vision systems, they featured instant "flash response recovery" to bright light sources so they recovered quickly from flares or weapons firing. This would give the user a great advantage over an enemy using older night-vision gear.

In contrast to the spotlessly maintained Little Bird and the thoughtfully placed gear, the men in the room looked like they might have been scraped off the floor of a skid row bar. They were dressed in faded jeans and

well-worn workshirts. All had mustaches, and three had
beards. They each wore a sidearm and four of them had
large hunting knives strapped conspicuously to one of
their legs.

"Gentlemen, this is your team," the man with the
auburn mustache said proudly as the six men gathered
around. Brannan introduced Peighton and Llewellan to
the men, and then identified the members of the motley
lot, one by one.

"Agent Llewellan, you've already met Captain Jack
Rodgers," Brannan said as the two men shook hands.
"The rest of this gang of thugs are Brad Townsend, Jason Houn, Ray Couper, and Will Casey. This guy working on the chopper is Greg Boyinson, the best damned
helicopter ever to fly with SOCOM. That is, when he
isn't beating unpatriotic SOBs within an inch of their
lives. General, I would have to admit that when you
asked me to put together a team, I didn't look too far. I
just tracked down guys who were with me on that last
mission in Iran."

Peighton beamed. He wouldn't be in combat himself, but for the first time since long before his career
ended behind a Pentagon desk, he was standing with
the men who would be fighting on the front lines. They
would be fighting for the flag that Peighton loved more
than he had realized the day before that 737 had hit the
NothalCorp Tower.

"What do you call your team, Colonel?" Peighton
asked.

"I guess we've been too busy getting our ducks in a
row to do our job to really think about that," Brannan

admitted. "We don't have much of a chain of command, so I guess we're *your* private army."

"I don't plan on telling you men how to do jobs you know a helluva lot better than me, but one thing I will order you *not* to do is call this outfit Peighton's Private Army. What do you men think?"

"Our last mission was Operation Raptor," Townsend spoke up. "It ended with unfinished business. I guess we're here to finish that business, so I guess this team oughta be called the Raptor Team."

November 13
4:15 A.M. Ankara Time

ANNE McCaine awoke so suddenly that she barely had time to grasp the last fading wisps of her dream.

Dennis had been in it. He had been in all her dreams since the day she had learned of his violent death. She loved him and missed him, and she longed to be able to tell him so. He had been murdered by Islamic terrorists just a few miles from their home, yet here she was, in the heart of the Islamic world, and still alive.

After the University of Colorado group had been denied gasoline, Anne had decided to take her young charges back to their former campsite near the Hittite excavation. She figured that pitching their tents back at a place they knew was a better bet than taking the risk that they'd run out of gas in a place they did *not* know.

As she watched the kids—they were young adults but they seemed like kids—the weight of the responsibility of caring for them really began to sink in. A week earlier, there had been nearly twenty people on the site, but most had returned home. Another contingent was due out after the Thanksgiving break, but for the time being, and with Little Abdul having offered to hike down to the next town to look for gas, Anne was alone with her three young charges.

There was poor Robert, reliable but ponderous and overweight. There was Donald, a brilliant geek who was inept beyond belief when it came to common sense or any mechanical device that could not be controlled with a mouse. Finally, there was Tasha, the brat from Connecticut. She was the daughter of a divorced couple of unimaginable wealth who had enrolled at the University of Colorado because of its proximity to her father's twenty-four-room ski cabin at Vail.

Tasha had defied Anne's order that they should conserve their cell phone battery time for emergencies and had burned through her own battery complaining to friends at home about being stuck abroad, and had "borrowed" Robert's. Anne was furious. They were down to precious little gasoline, and it was needed to run the generator to charge the batteries as well as to run the vehicle.

With her own phone, Anne had contacted the university to explain their situation and was told to hang on. They would think of something.

Anne had awakened to the sound of falling rocks. Someone was coming up the steep slope on the far side of the hill.

She sat up and stared through the opening of her tent. Across the crest of the hill, there was the faint sound of men talking.

Outside the warmth of her sleeping bag, it was unbearably cold. It had to be well below freezing. The nights were cold in these mountains anytime, but this time of year, it could fall below zero Fahrenheit. At least it hadn't started to snow yet.

The professor looked around the campsite. There were a handful of embers where their campfire had been a few hours earlier. She could hear heavy snoring in the tent that was shared by Robert and Donald. There was no sound coming from Tasha's tent.

What should she do? Were the men coming toward them or just passing by? What were they doing at this time of night? Maybe they were just shepherds.

Instinctively, Anne began pulling on her clothes. As she was lacing her boots, the sound of the voices grew louder and she could see the glimmer of a flashlight not far away.

At last the light fell on their Nissan, and the voices became more excited. They were speaking Turkish, and Anne could make out enough to know that whatever their various occupations, "car thief " was about to be added to the list.

There were two men. At least two. They opened the driver's side door and began looking for the keys. They ripped out the mats and pawed through the glove compartment. It was all for naught. The keys were in Anne's purse.

What should she do? What would *they* do? Should she just hand them the keys and let them take the vehicle?

She wished that Little Abdul had been there to talk with them, and perhaps to reason with them.

"What the hell is going on?" shouted Tasha. She had evidently been awaked by the clatter of the men rummaging through the Xterra. "Would you all, like *shut up*, so I can sleep!"

Anne wanted to tell Tasha that it was she who should shut up, but it was too late. Robert and Donald were awake and they were now looking out of their tent. Tasha had gotten up and stormed out of her tent ready to scold her timid male colleagues in her usual brash way.

It is hard to imagine who was more surprised—Tasha, who beheld a pair of men with long black beards and Kalashnikovs, or the two men themselves. They were two of the ones they had met the day before. Now, the man who insisted that all women should be shrouded head to toe was standing face-to-face with a well formed, twenty-three-year-old with long, blonde hair and a lacy lavender camisole that left little to the imagination.

They all stood dumbfounded for a moment, and finally Tasha screamed.

"Anne, *do* something!"

Slowly Anne emerged from her tent. She took the car keys and tossed them on the ground in front of the men.

"Take them. Take the keys," Anne said as firmly as possible. She was too frightened to remember any Turkish, but she hoped that the tone of her voice would convey the message. "Take the car. Just go away and leave us alone."

The man with the flashlight played the beam on the

ground, saw the Nissan logo, and understood immediately.

For a moment, they probably entertained thoughts of hopping into the Nissan and driving away, but suddenly Donald began sputtering and wheezing uncontrollably. He was having an asthma attack. Instinctively, he grabbed his coat and reached into the pocket for his inhaler. Equally instinctively, one of the armed men saw a man reaching into his pocket and imagined that he was going for a gun.

The Kalashnikov was on single shot and it spoke just once. The 7.62-mm round caught Donald in the chest, propelling him backward into the tent and ventilating his poor, constricted lungs for the last time. As Donald fell, the ponderous Robert leaned to get out of the way, lost his balance, and toppled onto the ground with a thud.

Tasha shrieked, and suddenly the weapons were trained on her. As the two men stared at her, shivering in the cold night air, their imaginations began to whirl. The taller man approached Tasha. He circled her as a coyote would approach its prey, slowly at first and then more assertively. She froze in terror as he set his AK-47 down and came toward her.

He grabbed her by the waistband of her University of Colorado sweatpants and threw her to the ground. He knelt beside her and jerked the sweatpants to her ankles in one swift yank. Next, the man pulled at the lacy camisole, which virtually disintegrated in his powerful hands. The sight of her breasts, so pale and so perfect, made his head spin.

Tasha lay shivering in the bitter cold, looking up into the face of the man who loomed above her. The faint light of a distant dawn revealed small details about his face. His dark teeth were crooked, and arranged in a gruesome grin. A small trickle of saliva dripped into his course, matted beard. He smelled horrible. Was that his breath, or his body? She now realized some of the dread that Anne had tried to convey about their being stranded in this alien land at a very unsettled time in history.

Tasha longed for her room at her mother's sprawling home in Greenwich. She longed for the softness of the pillows and the sweet smells of the perfumes, and of the body wash, and of the potpourri in the bathroom that the maid was always so diligent about replenishing.

The terrible pain jarred Tasha back to the reality of the moment. She tried to cross her legs, but she could not seem to move. The pain was unimaginable. She screamed, but the sound was muffled by the huge bearded face being pushed into hers. Was he trying to *kiss* her?

Anne felt the bile rise in her throat as though she was about to throw up. Her mind raced. What could she do to stop this? One man, the same one who she had scratched the day before as he grabbed the money, was on Tasha. The other man was convulsed in laughter. Tasha's wild screams had turned to loud, gasping sobs.

In the gathering light of the dawn, Anne saw a scabbard among the gear that the man had been carrying. It contained a very large knife, larger than the hunting knives that she had known as a kid growing up in the Rockies. The man's Kalashnikov was out of reach, but not this knife. Anne knew what she had to do, and she knew that she had to do it *now*.

In an instant, she had the knife out of the scabbard and had leaped onto the back of the man who was on Tasha.

She grabbed the man's beard with her left hand and jerked his head backward. With one swift motion, she drew the blade across his throat. The blade was very sharp. Anne could sense that it had cut a swath across his throat an inch deep.

As she toppled backward, still holding the head of the lifeless rapist, she saw the bigger man crawling quickly toward the rifle that he had set aside when he sat down to watch his friend rape Tasha. She was helpless. There was no way that she could untangle herself from this corpse in time to stop him.

November 13
6:33 A.M. Mountain Time

THE large and solid adobe main house at Rancho de los Bichos echoed with the shouts of angry and disciplined men. At first glance, the dark-complected men with their coarse, black beards might have been taken for the Mexican vaqueros who once worked here, herding cattle on the sprawling land grant. Had it not been for the huge banners with slogans scrawled in Arabic, or the large portraits of Fahrid Al-Zahir that were everywhere, one might have thought for a moment that these young men were, indeed, vaqueros.

In many ways, Rancho de los Bichos was just like the remote landing strip 150 miles to the north where

Peighton and Llewellan had first met the Raptor Team just twelve hours before. It was far from the prying eyes of anyone, and the men who worked here were at war.

The men at the rancho were part of a global war that had as its goal the destruction of Western civilization.

Meanwhile, the men at the steel building in New Mexico were like the brave citizen soldiers at Lexington and Concord more than two centuries before. They were a small band that were the tip of the spear of a people who had finally been pushed too far—and who were ready to push back.

There were nearly a hundred men in the old ballroom of the huge mansion at Rancho de los Bichos, doing their morning calisthenics and shouting slogans. Seething with hatred, a small man with a long beard with a distinctive grey patch, dressed in a black kaftan with embroidery near the collar and a grey skullcap, exhorted them to demand the death of the Great Satan that lay to the north. Khaleq Badr screamed, "Death to the Great Satan!" they screamed, "Death to the Great Satan!"

His nostrils flaring, the man with the long beard exhorted them to prepare to trade their lives for those of hundreds of infidels on their own infidel soil. They screamed, "Death to the Great Satan!"

Clutching a book filled with angry slogans, Khaleq Badr asked if they were ready to dress as migrant workers and slip across the Arizona border to carry out the sacred will of the holy Fahrid Al-Zahir. They screamed, "Death to the Great Satan!"

He was more than satisfied. He was ecstatic. Denver. Kansas City. Chicago. Phoenix. No place would be safe as he took the jihadi to the infidel heartland.

His mind wandered, but he was jarred back to reality by the popping sound of small arms fire. For a split second, he thought that someone outside was firing some practice rounds, but this wasn't the case. He stared in disbelief as the young jihadis in the room began screaming and crumpling to the floor. Blood was spattering everywhere. They were under attack!

Badr's instinct was to save himself. He ran toward the hallway that led to presumed safety, but felt a sharp sting in his abdomen. As he lay writhing in pain, the room was engulfed in a bright light that came from the direction of the huge barn that contained a million rounds of ammunition and hundreds of pounds of explosives. The eruption that came a half second later shook the big house, shattering windows and causing plaster to fall from the ceiling.

He tried to crawl, but it was too painful. The dust made him cough, and when he coughed, he spit up huge dollops of blood.

He saw a tall man with a stocking cap and a fiery auburn mustache. An infidel. It was the infidels. How could this have happened?

"He's not going to make it. We're not going to get anything out of him." Dave Brannan saw Brad Townsend eying the man with the long beard as he twitched on the floor drooling blood. The plan was to take prisoners who might provide useful intelligence, but to give the rest of the jihadis the same treatment that their brethren had given the Denver office workers. "Go ahead and make him a martyr."

Townsend fired one round into Badr's forehead, turned his head sideways with the toe of his boot, and put another into the side of his head.

The room was a scene of bloody carnage, but it was now quiet except for the moaning of the wounded jihadis who were systematically being put out of their misery. They had all come to the Western Hemisphere knowing that it was a one-way suicide mission. They had all come knowing that they would die violently and that they'd be rewarded with an endless supply of virgins. They just hadn't expected to die without taking any infidels with them.

Outside, the roar of the inferno that had been the barn was punctuated with a continuous snap, crackle, and pop as the ammunition that had been stored there cooked off. Greg Boyinson had fired just a single Hellfire into the structure. The ordnance inside had done the rest. Boyinson now circled the compound, prepared to send a stream of 7.62-mm slugs into anything that moved.

Farther out, the jihadis who had been tasked with guarding the perimeter lay quietly on the cold ground where they had fallen in the predawn darkness. The blood from their slit throats had already begun to congeal.

The Raptors moved methodically through the main building looking for documents and survivors. Brannan could read enough Arabic to know that their search for documents in the main building had turned up a wonderland of treasures. As for survivors, several jihadis had been discovered cowering in closets, entertaining second thoughts about martyrdom. One by one, they were turned over to Jack Rodgers, who was operating under more expansive rules of interrogation than at McConnell AFB a week earlier.

By 6:55 A.M., the compound had been declared secure and plastic charges had been placed at all of the
outbuildings. Jack was making one last pass through the
main building when he saw Colonel Brannan standing
over the body of Khaleq Badr. He was staring intently at
Badr and at what looked like a passport.

"I was just thinking," Brannan said without looking
up. "I was just thinking that Mr. Badr here might not
have outlived his usefulness. Let's bag him and take
him home."

As the small helicopter dashed toward the United
States border, skimming the ground just a few feet
above the sagebrush, a tall column of black smoke rose
high into the cold winter sky over the Sierra Madre. It
marked a resounding success for the jihadis of Mujahidin Al-Akhbar. Every one of them, every last man,
had achieved what he had come to North America to
realize. They had all become martyrs.

November 13
4:25 A.M. Ankara Time

DESPITE his solid middle-class upbringing, pretty
good health, and better than average academic career, Robert Pauwel had lived a difficult life. His hard-
ship awoke with him each day and dogged his every
step. Since his first day in the first grade, Robert had
been the "fat kid." He was not grossly obese, but neither
was he anything approaching average. Always the "fat
kid," he was a failure at sports. He could barely run as
far as first base, and was perpetually the last one picked

when sides were chosen. He was a caricature behind whose back the boys shook their heads and the girls giggled. Hard work kept him in the top quarter of his class academically, but he was never in the top ten. At the University of Colorado, he majored in archaeology in order to escape the present and live in the past.

Robert came to Turkey as part of the excavation team, and worked as hard as he could. Physical exertion came hard. He was still the "fat kid." Most people were kind and considerate, but girls like Tasha, with their perfect bodies, found it easy to make snide off-hand comments about the "fat kid." Still, Robert tried his best to be a reliable and conscientious worker, even though he found himself dripping with sweat before anyone else.

This morning, there were far more serious hazards in motion than sweat and catcalls, but Robert was still the "fat kid." His friend Donald, with whom he'd played video games in the off hours, had taken a bullet, a real bullet, that splattered him all over a tent. As for Robert—the "fat kid" had simply toppled over onto the ground like an unbalanced bowling pin.

Things could not have been more grim. Donald lay still, his eyes wide open. This meant that he was probably dead. The bitch Tasha had been raped, and Mrs. McCaine was about to be killed—or worse. Robert had to do something. He had to show that he was a man, not just a caricature.

With great effort, Robert rolled over and reached out, grasping the Kalashnikov that lay near him on the ground. The bearded man reaching for the other Kalashnikov saw him. Robert imagined that the man giggled.

Like all the others, he did not take Robert seriously. His eyes were on Mrs. McCaine. He saw her as the biggest threat. He would kill her and finish Robert off at his leisure.

Robert now had the gun. He had never fired a gun, but he had seen it in the movies. He pulled the trigger, felt the kick of the recoil and heard the round plink uselessly in the distance.

The man with the beard was turning his own gun toward Robert. With all the strength that he could muster, he lunged at the bearded man, jabbing the muzzle of the rifle into his gut. He pulled the trigger. The sound was muffled by the man's flesh.

Robert looked at the stunned expression on his face and pulled the trigger again, and again, and again.

Robert felt a hand on his arm. It was Mrs. McCaine. She gently pulled the rifle away from him.

"It's okay Robert, he's dead."

Anne sat back and took stock of the situation. The predawn light now illuminated a scene that had begun to unfold in nearly complete darkness. Donald was dead, as were the two bearded men. Blood was spattered everywhere. Both of the bad guys were literally in pools of their own blood. Anne had slashed open the carotid artery on one, and Robert had put four rounds into the other man's gut at point-blank range. In the center of the camp, Tasha was sprawled naked. Her blue white arms and legs extended from her torso, which was covered in blood. Some of it was her own, and some of it was from the man whom Anne had killed while he lay on top of her.

Anne's first order of business was Tasha. She had to

stop the bleeding and get her warm to try to offset the symptoms of severe shock. She had lost a great deal of blood, and her breathing was shallow and labored. Her eyes were fixed into a stare and she was shivering.

Robert too, was in a state of shock at the sight of the blood, and the trauma of all the violent death that had just occurred around him, including one of his own making. Anne ordered him to rebuild the fire, and he threw himself single-mindedly into that task.

Anne zipped Tasha into her sleeping back and hugged her, trying to warm her up. Tasha looked up and made eye contact, but there was no hint of an expression on her face.

SEVEN

November 13
2:43 P.M. Eastern Time

"**A MERICAN** forces were not involved," the Pentagon briefer adamantly told the clambering sea of reporters.

It had taken several hours for news of the conflagration at Rancho de los Bichos to reach the outside world. Indeed, the rancho was so remote that the incident would probably have been overlooked entirely had it not been that the world was so skittish. Also, the smoke plume was visible from north of the border, and it was too big to ignore. Initial speculation was that it might have been a terrorist attack against a target in Mexico. The rumor spread that Mujahidin Al-Akhbar was expanding the war into neighboring countries.

The Mexican *federales* had finally helicoptered out to the scene in an aging Huey, arriving just after a Bell Jet

Ranger news chopper from an enterprising television station in Tucson had touched down at the rancho. Had they not been so completely overwhelmed by the scene, the *federales* probably would have arrested the gringos. Instead, they just threatened them and demanded that they leave immediately. The Americans complied, taking with them videotaped images that would be on television screens around the world within two hours.

When it became evident from the pictures that the site had been a terrorist training camp, speculation obviously turned to the theory that this had been an American Special Forces action.

Nobody was more surprised than the crisis team that had been formed at the Pentagon in the wake of the Denver attack.

The chairman, a U.S. Navy admiral, angrily denounced his U.S. Army counterpart for sending in a Delta team without telling him. The general shouted back that it was not an Army operation, and that it must have been the Navy Seals. At last, they came to realize, just as the poor briefer had insisted to the reporters:

"American forces were not involved."

November 13
9:49 P.M. Ankara Time

FAHRID Al-Zahir was in good spirits. He had just finished videotaping his sermon taking responsibility for the Kansas City bombings, and had removed his kaftan and turban. One aide had just turned off the fan that was placed behind the fabric backdrop to subtly simulate wind, while another had gone upstairs in the palatial Black Sea villa to prepare to e-mail the recording to Indonesia for retransmission to Al-Jazeera.

He had watched as the pathetic Americans wanted to strike back, but could not. He had relished the irony of the constraints put upon it by the United Nations—a creation of Western infidels!

Al-Zahir was in front of a mirror carefully dabbing at his eye makeup when the aide who had gone upstairs began shouting for him to come quickly.

The big plasma screen television in the living room was tuned to the Dubai-based Al-Arabiya network, but regular programming had just been dropped to bring the viewers some breaking news concerning the death of apparent members of Mujahidin Al-Akhbar. Al-Zahir recognized Rancho de los Bichos. He had never been there, but he had approved the site selection from a number of photographs that had been e-mailed by his contacts in Mexico.

"How could the Americans find it?" Al-Zahir asked rhetorically. "And so soon."

"It wasn't an air strike," one of the aides pointed out. "Look at the bodies."

He was right. The video showed numerous men who had been shot from ground level. It was a massacre. Al-Zahir suggested that at least a hundred infidels had been involved. Perhaps more. There had to have been that many in order to kill his most zealous fighters.

"It wasn't the Americans," the other aide observed. "Look at the bodies. They were executed. The Americans would never execute prisoners. They are too weak. The fools have too much 'honor' to kill in cold blood."

"Who was it then?" Fahrid Al-Zahir demanded.

He was beginning to have a strange and queasy feeling. An hour ago, he was on top of the world. He was in control of the world's destiny. Now, he wasn't so sure.

November 13
3:02 P.M. Eastern Time

A S he watched the cable news report with his staff at the top of the hour, President Thomas Livingstone could feel the gooseflesh rippling beneath his Brooks Brothers suit. He was the only person in the room who knew what must have happened, yet it had happened with no warning to him.

"American forces were not involved."

Livingstone felt a bit guilty when he saw the press beating up on the Pentagon briefer. The poor guy was telling the truth, and they didn't believe him.

"Who could have done this?" Faralaco asked rhetorically. "It had to have been our guys from Delta."

"It could have been the Mexicans," someone suggested.

Suddenly the screen changed to a commentator with a furrowed brow speaking over a bright red banner that read "Breaking News."

"A tape has just been broadcast on the Al-Arabiya network. A spokesman for a group calling itself Ikhwan Al-Jihad has claimed responsibility for the attack in the Sierra Madre."

A dropping pin could have been heard as the spokesman came on the screen. The small man in a beard with a grey patch, dressed in a black kaftan with embroidery near the collar and a grey skullcap, spoke in Arabic, demanding the death of the Great Satan. The tape quality was horrible, as though it had been recorded in black and white on the worst possible equipment.

The president and his staff read along as the creeper on the bottom of the screen attempted to keep pace with an English translation. The exhortations about death to Americans were painfully familiar, but when the man turned his rage on Mujahidin Al-Akhbar, Thomas Livingstone felt his jaw drop as a murmur went around the room. He said that Fahrid Al-Zahir and Mujahidin Al-Akhbar were cowards who were as bad as the infidels. The man identified himself as Khaleq Badr.

The Americans followed the translation creeper on the bottom of the screen as it unfolded a tale of how Badr and hand-picked agents had infiltrated Mujahidin Al-Akhbar, and how they had killed nearly 100 members of this brotherhood at Rancho de los Bichos. He boasted that Ikhwan Al-Jihad had infiltrated Mujahidin Al-Akhbar and planned to slowly and methodically destroy them from within.

As the commentator came back on the screen to attempt an analysis of the Al-Arabiya clip, Livingstone turned to Faralaco.

"I've never been briefed on this Ikhwan Al-Jihad. Have you?"

"No, I've never heard of it."

"Then get me the CIA. I want a briefing."

Five minutes ago, Livingstone had felt the excitement of believing that Peighton's secret commandos had struck a blow against the Mujahidin Al-Akhbar. Now, it

turned out to have been a rival gang. The impossibly
complex world had just gotten way more complicated.

November 13
10:02 P.M. Ankara Time

IN few places in the world were people more stunned
at the viewing of the Badr tape than the White House.
One of these few places was a beautiful seaside villa
perched in the rugged coastal hills overlooking the
Black Sea on Turkey's northern coast.

"Can it really be him?" Fahrid Al-Zahir asked in disbelief.

"How can it not be?" asked one of the aides. "That's
his black kaftan. I've seen him wear it. The embroidery
near the collar. It's hard to see because this cursed tape
is such crap, but that's his kaftan, that's his beard. It *is*
him."

"That pig!" Al-Zahir screamed at the huge Panasonic
fifty-inch plasma screen as the tape was being repeated.

The terrorist leader was enraged. He beat his fist
against the silken arm of his lavish, overstuffed sofa and
cursed. Defections to the infidel were always a fear. No
matter how much the true and pure beliefs were
drummed into their heads, there was always a danger
that the young jihadis would fall victim to the tempta-
tions of the material pleasures of the West. Even in the
bazaars, the wretched pop music blared and the infidel
DVDs were sold. He had always dreaded that they
would succumb to that temptation, but how could he

have imagined that the young jihadis would come to believe that Mujahidin Al-Akhbar was *too compassionate* toward the infidels?

November 13
2:38 P.M. Mountain Time

IN the middle of nowhere, somewhere far north of Interstate 10, Jason Houn took off the black kaftan with embroidery near the collar and hung it on a hook on the wall. He stepped to the sink and washed the distinctive grey patch from his black beard. It took a bit of work with a comb to get the latex house paint cleaned out, but he finally had it.

An hour ago, the Arabic-speaking, third-generation Lebanese American former Special Forces man had taped a message that was e-mailed to Al-Arabiya by way of an old friend in the British SAS who was now living quietly in Manchester, England.

When Dave Brannan had found Badr's documents at Rancho de los Bichos, he realized that the man was of some importance within the Mujahidin Al-Akhbar organization. He was not a kingpin, but apparently the rough equivalent of a battalion commander. He was obviously a capable leader who had been given the responsibility to lead forces in a key operation. It was evident that if Badr had decided to defect, it would be a serious distraction for Mujahidin Al-Akhbar.

Brannan wanted to give Badr a life after his martyrdom. He had considered a posthumous defection to the

Americans, but he quickly rejected that as a bit too far-fetched. What if Badr left Mujahidin Al-Akhbar and moved even *farther* to the dark side?

With his mortal body unceremoniously interred in the New Mexico desert, the reborn Khaleq Badr had now become an extremist more extreme than Fahrid Al-Zahir.

November 13
5:49 P.M. Eastern Time

"**I**S there any way that it *could have* been the Americans?" Secretary-General Baudouin Abuja Mboma asked the head of the United Nations International Validation Organization.

"I told the secretary of state that I would refer the American request for an International Validation to the Security Council," Muhammad Bin Qasim replied. "He was angry, but I did not have a sense that his government would defy the authority of the United Nations. We saw the television pictures from the Sierra Madre. That sort of attack was definitely *not* characteristic of an American operation."

"Then who *is* this Khaleq Badr person?"

"He is apparently a former associate of Fahrid Al-Zahir who has turned against him."

"This is very troubling," Mboma replied. "If Badr is at war with the Mujahidin Al-Akhbar, there is no telling what he might do. The European Community is very concerned. They have deliberately distanced themselves from the Americans in order to keep the Mujahidin Al-

Akhbar jihadi isolated to the United States. Now they are worried."

"I'll make some discrete inquiries."

"I wish you would. Have you seen what has happened to the oil stocks since Badr has surfaced?"

EIGHT

November 14
6:38 A.M. Central Time

FEW people took notice of the tall man with the briefcase as he pushed his way through the heavy double doors at the Metropolitan Community Hospital, which was located just off Interstate 88 in Downers Grove, Illinois, and about twenty-two miles west of downtown Chicago. He was well groomed and well dressed in a dark overcoat, blue sweater, and grey slacks. He might have been a doctor, or an insurance man on his way to a meeting. It was the middle of a shift change, so numerous people were coming and going. Passes were required to enter certain wards on the upper floors, but the only security at the main entrance was an elderly guard from a private service who was tasked with watching out for "anyone suspicious." The man in the dark overcoat did not meet this criteria.

He was in. He entered the elevator with a large group of nurses coming on duty and a young couple with a bouquet of flowers. He exited on the fifth floor and made his way to a restroom on a hallway that led to storage rooms. Quickly opening the briefcase, he took out a set of scrubs. Moments later, the overcoat and sweater were in a large trash can beneath a pile of day-old newspapers, and the tall man was moving through the hospital dressed as an attending physician.

He took the stairway to the sixth floor and made his way to the maternity ward. Security here required an encoded badge to be swiped, but the guard at the desk was watching for "anyone suspicious," not matching faces on ID cards to faces of people who looked as though they belonged.

The bogus attending physician walked to the door of the neonatal intensive care unit, glanced both ways, and walked in. The atmosphere was quiet and serene. The murmur of the machinery was a soothing sound. He heard the faint cry of a tiny patient. He knew that at this time of day, only two nurses would be on duty. In a few hours, the place would be swarming with distraught infidels.

Fahrid Al-Zahir, bless his holy name, was brilliant. Just as the Denver attack had reminded the infidels of their defeat in September 2001, today's attack in Downers Grove would remind them of August 1990, when the brave soldiers of Saddam Hussein had destroyed the premature infants of the Kuwaitis who had collaborated with the Crusader Zionists and the Great Satan. Fear would be instilled by the deaths of the most helpless of the infidels, and it would happen in their own heartland.

"Can I help you, Doctor?" the young Filipino nurse asked.

"No," he answered simply, as he grabbed her small neck.

From her hiding place behind a partition, Amelia Gonzales watched in horror as her friend's neck was quickly and efficiently broken, and as she fell lifeless to the floor.

Amelia stifled the urge to cry out and hid herself. The man looked around, but did not see her. She had to summon help, but this man in the pale green scrubs was between her and the door, and between her and the panic button.

Amelia was overwhelmed with terror as the man thrust his hand into an incubator. Was he going to kill the babies too?

He had trouble with the small opening, and began to pry at the lucite cover with his large and powerful hand. Amelia listened helplessly to the tiny squeal as the man ripped off the lid and jerked the baby's air tube from his throat.

Suddenly the door to the nursery opened and there was another man in the room, a man with a salt-and-pepper beard. The tall man who was tearing into the incubator turned. There was a flurry of movement, and the tall man crumpled to the floor.

The second man knelt briefly at the side of the lifeless body of the man in the scrubs then looked directly at Amelia.

"You have a very small patient who needs your help, ma'am," he said softly, his voice barely more than a whisper.

Standing up, he punched the emergency call button and left the intensive care nursery.

It seemed like an hour, but he had been in the room for fewer than twenty seconds. Amelia's friend was dead, but a small baby—perhaps a dozen small babies—would live because of this man.

November 14
7:55 A.M. Central Time

A light snow was falling, but it wasn't sticking to the pavement yet. It was cold, but not unbearable, even for men who had grown up in the warmth of Saudi Arabia. The men in the florist van were nervous, but excited. In the distance, they could see the sign on the top of the nine-story Metropolitan Community Hospital. In a matter of minutes, they would be there. There were four ten-minute parking slots less than twenty meters from the emergency entrance. At least two were always empty at this hour.

As they paused at the traffic light, an old Chevrolet Monte Carlo with a noisy muffler pulled up on their left. Moving forward, the Chevy turned sharply in front of them. There was a slight jolt and the sound of breaking plastic as the car clipped the front fender of the florist van.

What could be done? Should they make a run for it? The hospital was just two blocks away.

No. Their orders were to avoid attracting attention until the final moment. They had to remain disciplined.

The big, noisy American car had pulled over to the

side of the street next to a sprawling city park, so the driver followed suit with the van.

"What the hell were you doing?" the man from the Chevrolet said as he walked back to the van. "Couldn't you see that I had my blinkers on? I was trying to make a turn when you speeded up."

"I did not," the Saudi man said. "I was driving with caution."

The driver of the van *had* been driving with caution. His orders were to avoid attracting attention until the final moment.

Another man had gotten out of the passenger side of the Monte Carlo and was surveying the damage. He was screaming and shouting. All four of the men in the van were watching him, and they did not see a third man approaching from their rear.

There were several popping sounds mixed with the sound of breaking safety glass. A few flakes of snow drifted into the van from the broken windows.

With the snow coming down harder now, the drivers on the heavily travelled street paid little attention to the Chevrolet with the broken taillight as it signaled for a left turn and merged smoothly into the morning traffic.

It would be nearly an hour before the florist van was surrounded by police cars and traffic on this section of the street was diverted.

November 14
3:55 P.M. Ankara Time

THE afternoon sun fell across the temple of Teshub, God of Tempests. Anne paused and leaned on her shovel, gazing up at the structure that grew ever more golden by the moment. It was so beautiful and serene, but it had been a tempestuous day and a half.

She had hoped that she would have been able to stabilize Tasha, bundle her into the Nissan, and get her to the nearest medical facility, but when the girl began coughing up large quantities of blood, Anne realized that she would not survive a two-hour drive over mountain roads with internal injuries this severe. Toward the end, she thought that she had seen Tasha smile, but the young child of privilege who once talked nonstop had not spoken a word after the rape.

Anne and Robert had buried the two bearded men under rocks as far away from the camp as they were able to drag the corpses. They buried Tasha and Donald in one of the trenches that they had excavated near the temple. This way, no matter what happened next, the bodies would eventually be found by whomever resumed the excavation, whether that was next month, next year, or a decade from now.

November 14
11:49 A.M. Eastern Time

"**T**HERE were enough explosives in the van to bring down a ten-story building," the National Intel briefer explained to President Thomas Livingstone. "The only building that size within a mile radius of the place where the van was found is the Metropolitan Community Hospital, so that is assumed to have been the likely target."

"I understand that it was an anonymous tip?" the president asked. "Any idea who might have called in the tip, or who might have killed those people?"

"Not yet," the briefer replied. "The FBI supposes that it may have been the Mujahidin Al-Akhbar organization because Chicago was mentioned by the terrorist that was interrogated, but that cannot be confirmed. Witnesses claim to have seen a late-model American car that may have been involved in the fender bender that damaged the van. Downers Grove police are investigating, but they don't have much to go on."

The president wanted to believe that it had been his own twenty-first-century American Volunteer Group that had made it possible for him *not* to have to travel to the Chicago suburb and stand with the grieving on the threshold of *another* smoldering pit where Americans had once gone about their everyday lives. He wanted to be able to celebrate this fact, but his own rules of engagement prevented him from knowing anything for sure. He had to be satisfied simply with knowing that he had something more to celebrate than just an undetonated truckload of high explosives.

"Are the deaths in the hospital related?" Steve Faralaco asked. "Were these a coincidence, or is there a connection?"

"We are assuming a connection, but there is no hard evidence," the briefer explained. "The greatest possible damage that could have been done by a car bomb was in the vicinity of the emergency entrance. The intensive care nursery is on the opposite side of the building, where it would have survived the bomb blast. Had both succeeded, it would have shown that the Mujahidin Al-Akhbar could attack simultaneously from two directions. The panic would have been far-reaching. As it is, we are keeping the info about the explosives quiet, and the nursery incident is being spun as a jealous husband incident."

"And you are sure that it was not?" Faralaco asked.

"There were two deaths. A nurse and her assailant. We ran his prints. He's on the terrorist watch list, associated with as many as three Mideast terror groups. We put out the cover story that he was related to one of the kids in the nursery."

"Do you have anything on the man who killed him?" Livingstone asked.

"There was a witness who said that he came in, killed the guy, and left. All in the space of less than a minute. We suspect that he had followed the guy into the hospital. We have no idea who he was. We have him from behind on two surveillance tapes, but that's it. It was lucky. The bad guy had it in mind to kill babies. It would have been just like Kuwait back in 1990."

"I thought that the stories of the Iraqi troops dumping newborns out of incubators turned out to be a fabrication," the president said hesitantly.

"Thanks to rumors spread all over the Internet by leftist and pro-Saddam groups," Faralaco said, shaking his head. "They put out such a blizzard of postings claiming that the Bush administration faked the story that a lot of people actually believe that it really *is* an urban legend. Not surprising. There are still people who believe the websites that claim that the Nazis never gassed any Jews."

"What do you have on Al-Zahir?" the president asked. "Has there been any progress on finding him?"

"The NSA has been trying to track cell phone traffic all over the Middle East, but it comes down to the fact that there's a shortage of analysts to sift through it all."

NINE

"**YOU,** of all people should know that any initiative that puts more authority in the hands of the Americans would be detrimental to the goal of limiting their already disproportionate power in the world," Muhammad Bin Qasim lectured the French ambassador to the United Nations.

"This was true when their enemy was Al-Qaeda or Mujahidin Al-Akhbar," François Lumiere replied. "We were content to sit by and let the Americans fight their wars. The world wanted not to be involved, but in the last forty-eight hours things have changed. Things have escalated. Ikhwan Al-Jihad has changed this. I wish to show you something in strict confidence."

Bin Qasim took the folder with the green cover that

the ambassador passed across his huge rosewood desk. The heading was that of the Direction Générale de la Sécurité Extérieure, the DGSE, France's external intelligence agency. Inside was a series of e-mails and analyses. Finally, there was a brief section marked as *sommaire*, the summary. This paragraph explained that the DGSE had deduced that a state of jihadi now existed *between* the Mujahidin Al-Akhbar and the Ikhwan Al-Jihad—*and* that Ikhwan Al-Jihad would began striking in Europe to prove that they were more daring than Mujahidin Al-Akhbar.

"We cannot have this," Lumiere explained. "American cities. Who cares? But what would happen if the great monuments of Europe were threatened?"

"But I don't see how you could possibly think that giving the Americans an International Validation would prevent bloodshed in Europe. As we have seen in the past, reacting aggressively only emboldens the terrorists. It is better for them to know that Europe continues to mistrust the United States as the greatest threat to world stability."

"With Badr's organization now in play, the balance has changed and stability is threatened." Lumiere shrugged.

"The United States will be asking formally for an International Validation at the next Security Council meeting. Edredin as much as stated that," Bin Qasim told the Frenchman. "I hope that I can count on you to vote to curb that request . . . to act in the best interests of the world community to keep the United States contained."

"France will act in her own best interest," Lumiere insisted. "We always have. We do not wish to have the world see us as being directly allied with the United States, but something must be done to diffuse the situation before this jihadi civil war spreads to the outside world."

November 15
9:51 A.M. Eastern Time

AS he swiped his ID card and pushed the button for the elevator, Rod Llewellan thought about the aftermath of his trial. The trial itself warranted no thought. He would be convicted for sure. No question. The president would, of course, disavow any knowledge of his actions. That's why they called it plausible deniability.

No, it was not the trial, but the aftermath that played out in his mind as he waited for the elevator. He could be executed. A death sentence in the case of espionage was not out of the question. The United States hadn't executed a spy in years, but there was no reason to believe that he would get off easily with life imprisonment. He hoped he could. In a few years, maybe ten, everything would be revealed and he would be pardoned. He'd be free again.

On the other hand, secrets often stayed secret. Especially deep, dark secrets. What would happen if everyone on the outside died with their lips sealed and there was no one left to tell the truth and save him?

Llewellan had done little to hide the four CDs that he had burned on the fourth floor of Bureau headquarters. He had thought of taping them to his body, or hiding them in his socks like Clinton aide Sandy Berger did when he purloined documents from the National Archives back in 2004. Finally, he decided that he'd just put them in the pocket of his suit jacket. If he was searched, they would not appear to have been consciously hidden.

He had labeled them with a marker as "Classic Country," but the CDs did not contain Johnny Cash singing "Folsom Prison Blues." If someone put them in a CD player, they'd know the truth. They contained data that could land Rod Llewellan himself in prison.

As he rode down to the lobby of the J. Edgar Hoover Office Building on Pennsylvania Avenue near E Street in Washington, D.C., Llewellan wondered what it would be like to spend the rest of his life in federal lockup. Convicts tended to treat child molesters very unkindly on the inside. What would they do to a traitor?

Each time someone got on the elevator, he imagined that they were there to search him. They'd find the contraband. He knew he was taking a chance, and he knew why. He knew why he was risking his own life and he was glad to do it.

He thought of the lives that would be saved, about the lives that would be lived by people who would live them because of what he was doing here—even though they would live those lives never knowing that Rod Llewellan stole government secrets on this cold winter day.

November 15
9:51 A.M. Eastern Time

"**I**T'S a sign." Ray Couper laughed as he pointed to the sign identifying the town as the birthplace of Patsy Cline.

"Yeah, it's definitely a sign." Jack Rodgers nodded as he slowed down for the first stoplight in Winchester, Virginia.

"No, I mean it's a *sign*."

"You mean that it's a sign that we're 'crazy' to have driven straight through from Chicago in the middle of the night and the middle of the winter?" Jack chuckled, picking up on his reference to the title of Patsy's signature ballad.

"Don't mind me," Ray said. "I'm just rummy from being awake all night."

"We'll have some time before Llewellan gets here. We can catnap for a couple hours."

November 15
10:51 A.M. Central Time

"**S**HE said it wasn't finished, but it looks fine to me." Morgan Brophy held up the colorful quilt for Jeanine to see, and the two sisters began to sob.

"We'd better stop bawling," Jeanine said as the tiny bundle that she was holding began to squeal. "We're perturbing little Charlie."

The quilt had finally been delivered. Summer Brophy's handiwork had finally reached the little nephew whom she would never know. Little Charlie had been born premature the day after Summer had died a violent death in Denver. The shock of the disaster had sent Jeanine into premature labor, but after some touch and go moments, the little guy was doing better.

It had taken Morgan until now to get here to see him, but she had finally made it. The security at Metropolitan Community Hospital in Downers Grove was more strict than it was at the airports these days. Morgan had showed her ID at three checkpoints before she reached the right floor and twice between there and the intensive care nursery. But that was understandable. There had been two killings—in the nursery.

"It was terrible, everybody was screaming," Jeanine said, telling her sister about the horrible events that had occurred here only one day earlier. "I had no idea what was going on. I was in my room. They started talking about somebody that was killing babies. All I could think of was that something had happened to Charlie. They wouldn't let me go in. The police were everywhere."

"I heard it was a nurse and some other guy," Morgan said.

"Yeah. He killed the nurse, but another man came into the room and stopped him."

At that point, Jeanine began to cry uncontrollably. Morgan already knew that the man had been stopped only seconds from ripping his way into the incubator where little Charlie lay helpless.

"That man saved little Charlie's life," Jeanine sobbed.

"Do they have any idea who it was?" Morgan asked. The news reports had spoken of a mysterious stranger who arrived in the nick of time and then vanished into thin air.

"The other nurse saw the whole thing," Jeanine reported, clutching little Charlie tightly to her body. "She said he was a man with a beard who was wearing a black overcoat and a pale yellow sport shirt. There must be millions of men who look like that."

There may be millions, Morgan thought to herself, but this made two that she could think of.

November 15
7:21 P.M. Eastern Time

"**I** don't like what I'm seeing," Secretary-General Baudouin Abuja Mboma said, taking off his glasses and disgustedly thrusting the papers onto the coffee table. He usually felt like he was king of the world, and he didn't like feeling out of control. "My portfolio is off 12 percent since Badr surprised the world. *Twelve percent.*"

"Those are the chances one takes in the market." Muhammad Bin Qasim shrugged. "I'm sure that the hedge funds will turn things around in a day or two. In the meantime, it might be a good time to buy."

As usual, the two men were meeting at Mboma's apartment on East Sixty-Sixth Street in New York City rather than at the United Nations. One could not speak frankly at the United Nations, where even the walls had "ears."

"At least the Americans haven't upset things by acting unilaterally. That would cause the rest of the market to rally and drive oil down," Mboma said, pacing toward the window to look out at the skyline of America's largest city. As much as he generally despised the United States and its people, he never ceased to marvel at the wonders they had built for themselves.

"Lumiere was in my office," Bin Qasim said. "It's not the fact that Edredin asked for an International Validation, it's that the French may be ready to support them in the Security Council."

"Lumiere said that?"

"Not in so many words, but he's clearly keeping that option open. The French don't want a global gang war spilling into their backyard."

"The Americans must remain isolated," Mboma said angrily. "We cannot return to a world where the United States can send its Marines willy-nilly into any corner of the world," Mboma insisted. He could tell that the International Validation Organization boss was nervous. He hadn't touched his tumbler of Seagrams.

"It's Badr who has upset the symmetry of the situation," Bin Qasim lamented. "For once the Americans are behaving themselves. If only we could get them to chase Badr instead of Mujahidin Al-Akhbar."

"That gives me an idea," Mboma said with a smile. "What if it were the French who undertook the pursuit of Badr?"

November 15
7:21 P.M. Eastern Time

"**THIS** is the best information we have. This is the briefing that was given to the boss this morning."

Rod Llewellan was walking the two Raptors through the data on two large plasma screen monitors in the little house on Dunlap Street in Winchester, Virginia. "It's a compendium of NSA, CIA, National Reconnaissance Office, and third-party data, sifted and sorted for his majesty, the director of National Intelligence."

"What does he say?" Jack Rodgers asked.

"I wasn't in the meeting, but I heard that he is livid that we can't do anything without an International Validation, and we haven't been able to get one."

"Has the president seen this?" Jack asked.

"Yes."

"Does anyone know that you're giving this to us?"

"Not outside of this room."

"You could be shot for this."

"Yes. I know," Llewellan admitted. "That thought *has* crossed my mind."

A week of processing mountains of intercepted digital data transmissions had narrowed the probable location of Fahrid Al-Zahir's headquarters to a small sliver of northeastern Turkey near the Black Sea. Jack Rodgers carefully compared the data to an extremely detailed 1:12,500-scale map of the region.

"This spot on the Black Sea is it," Llewellan explained, pointing to a place on the Black Sea coastline that had been highlighted for the director's briefing. "This is where Fahrid Al-Zahir spends most of his time and where he probably is now. The NSA figured it out by looking at areas where certain categories of cell phone traffic originated, and where they did not."

It was an old trick that signals intelligence analysts used. It was like identifying a hidden object by its shadow or its conspicuous absence. They had identified the place, triangulating on its location by the cell phone "chatter" that *didn't* originate there.

"Why don't they just notify the Turks and have them go in there?" Ray Couper asked rhetorically, already knowing the answer.

"They're scared to death that Al-Zahir and Mujahidin Al-Akhbar will declare war on *them*," Llewellan replied, even though he knew that it was a rhetorical question. "And Al-Zahir probably has people on the inside at Turkish intel, just like Bin Laden did with the Pakistanis."

"Do you have any Keyhole pictures of this place?" Jack asked, pointing to another location farther inland.

Rod clattered a moment on his own keyboard and brought up a digital photo that had been downloaded from one of the KH-12 "Keyhole" digital surveillance satellites that the National Reconnaissance Office and the Air Force kept on station over the Middle East.

Jack studied the two screens, murmuring to himself and moving images with the mice attached to the two computers. Llewellan and Couper watched him intently, curious about what he was seeing, but not wanting to break his train of thought. He pulled the map onto his lap and traced his finger along several small innocuous country roads that trickled across the plateau and mountain country south of the Black Sea.

"They missed something," Jack said at last.

"Who missed something?" Llewellan asked. He knew that the best minds in the United States national intelligence community had analyzed and prepared this data.

"Whoever prepared this briefing didn't have enough time in the field psyching out bad guys. They're focussing on this one site on the coast, but they missed another site."

"Where? What?" Llewellan asked.

"I'll let you know after we *go* there," Jack said cryptically.

Rod knew better than to ask again. It was a "need to know" world, and he didn't need to know *where* the Raptors were going, only that they *were* going.

November 16
10:33 A.M. Ankara Time

AS Fahrid Al-Zahir paced the floor in his beautiful seaside villa overlooking the Black Sea, his soft Gucci loafers made no sound on the thick Persian carpets.

The failure of the hospital attack troubled Al-Zahir deeply. He had postponed sending the message that he had taped after Kansas City. It had been overtaken by events. He had to change his plans, but first, he had to figure out what was going on. The infidel news reports had mentioned a lone assailant in the nursery, but that was all. Where were the others? There was no mention of the explosives. Had Badr stolen them? Was he planning an attack of his own?

Khaleq Badr had to be stopped. He had issued his fatwa against Mujahidin Al-Akhbar, but Al-Zahir would show him that he had crossed the wrong man.

"If Badr wants a jihadi with Mujahidin Al-Akhbar," Al-Zahir had screamed at his terrified aides, "if Badr wants a jihadi with *me*! Then a jihadi he shall have!"

Al-Zahir smiled when he saw the gate to the compound swing open and the dark SUV drive in. He would show Badr. He would show the world. It was like one of those infidel movies where the villain opens the gates of hell itself to call upon the very embodiment of the power of the underworld.

The massive front door opened, and in the foyer stood a balding man in a black cloak, a huge man with an aquiline nose, black beard, and fierce, piercing eyes.

The mercurial Muhammad Al-Abir had been one of the most feared men in the world since he had led the gang of hijackers who commandeered that Olympic Airways 767 and flew it all over the Mediterranean, daring someone to stop him. The U.S. Navy's Sixth Fleet had scrambled four F/A-18Es, but they had been ordered not to shoot. The world still remembered the sight of him pushing all those women out the back door of the jetliner as it sat on the runway in Algiers. He had screamed in English that he was killing the infidel women for not wearing veils. Only one of the thirty-three women had survived, and she had gone back to Yorkshire as a quadriplegic with a broken neck.

In the end, the Greek government had paid him a rumored $100 million to stop. Over the ensuing years, he had killed more than 300 people, mainly unveiled women, in a half dozen brazen and ruthless attacks.

He had dropped out of sight for several years, but now Al-Zahir had lured him out of retirement to hunt and kill the infidels, and that heinous traitor, Khaleq Badr.

TEN

November 16
9:02 A.M. Eastern Time

THE presidential limousine and its accompanying bevy of Secret Service vehicles streamed into the underground parking garage at the Hilton Hotel in Washington, D.C. Thomas Livingstone would be making some remarks at the annual convention of one of the youth groups that he had always championed, and he'd be back at the White House in plenty of time for a scheduled luncheon with some congressmen. It was a typical day on the presidential schedule, but one meeting was not on the official agenda.

At literally the last minute before leaving the executive mansion, Livingstone had requested a minor change in his route from the underground garage to the ballroom. Doing it off-the-cuff like this meant that nobody knew about it other than the president, a small number of Secret Service men, and an older gentleman from Colorado.

"How was your flight out, Buck?" the president asked General Peighton as they met in a narrow hallway. The Secret Service men, who recognized Peighton, stood at a discrete distance. "I was pleased to hear about the Downers Grove situation. That could have been very bad."

"Very bad indeed, Tom."

"Do you have any more information for me?"

"No."

"No?"

"When we started down this road, you said you didn't want to know any details. Remember? Plausible deniability?"

"Yeah. Right. But things are going okay?"

"Let's just say that plans are in motion," Buck Peighton said with a smile.

November 16
11:02 A.M. Mountain Time

DAVE Brannan studied the horizon with his N-Vision binoculars. The temperature was well below freezing, but the air was perfectly clear. Visibility could be measured in hundreds of miles, but the small speck on the horizon was much closer.

"I have it in sight," he said calmly. "We should have wheels on the ground in about seven minutes."

"Great," Ray Couper quipped. "I was about to freeze my delicate ass off."

They called it Granite Field, after the 7.068-foot peak that was about thirty miles away, but this remote landing strip in the distant corner of Tooele County, Utah, didn't have an official name. During World War II, the U.S. Army Air Forces had built hundreds of these airfields across the West to support their crash program to train pilots by the thousands. After the war, many of the ones that were close to towns became municipal airports. Others were simply abandoned. This one fell within the restricted and heavily guarded boundaries of the Dugway Proving Ground. Except for being lengthened to nearly 9,000 feet for use as an emergency strip during the Cold War, Granite Field was almost never used. This, and the long runway, made it ideal for what would happen here this morning.

Though it had been decades since it had become an airfield, the site had remained as quiet and isolated from human action as it had been for all the centuries before. Only brief moments of commotion had broken the solitude, and that would be the case today. The half dozen men who arrived an hour ago in their two vehicles might have been campers, arriving for a relaxing weekend of beer and tall tales—but they weren't staying that long. By noon, they would all be gone, and Granite Field would be as quiet as it had been for most of the past millennium.

"Where the hell is Boyinson?" Jack Rodgers said, straining his eyes to the south. He was starting to worry. They had driven up from New Mexico overnight after fitting their two Broncos with out-of-state plates, but Greg Boyinson had diagnosed a fuel line problem in the Little Bird, and had remained behind to fix it. Now they were within an hour of liftoff and he was long overdue.

"He should have been here ahead of us," Dave Brannan observed. Even he was starting to worry.

Gradually the faraway hiss became a rumble, and the speck on the distant horizon became an Apex Air 747-200F freighter on final approach. Boeing had delivered the big aircraft to Lufthansa decades earlier, but the carrier had sold the big ship when it took delivery of newer 747-400F cargo planes. After bouncing around on the used airplane market for several years, the aircraft was acquired by Apex Air, the "quiet company" of the air cargo business. Apex had long ago earned a reputation for being a reliable contractor that met schedules and asked few questions. They had numerous clients around the world, and among these was the United States special operations community. Today's clients were alumni of that community.

The big freighter touched down, taxied to the end of the runway, and turned 180 degrees. With the complete absence of wind, the pilot would simply take off the way he had come in.

The men climbed into their vehicles and dashed across the runway as the nose of the freighter tipped up, revealing 5,000 cubic feet of cargo space, more than enough for the Raptors. This would permit the aircraft to carry the extra fuel necessary for today's long flight.

Buck Peighton had known the owner of Apex Air since they had served in the army together long ago. When the general had called to say that he needed transport and payment would be deposited in a certain account in a certain bank, the big 747-200F had been earmarked with a flight plan. The crew on the flight deck knew that they would be carrying flowers. The loadmaster who was carefully guiding the two Broncos as they backed up the ramp and into the big airplanes, knew that he would be loading freshly cut flowers.

Dave Brannan was watching from the outside as the loadmaster moved backward into the cargo hold, motioning the two drivers forward. Everything was being done with hand signals. The flight crew were keeping the four big JT9D turbofans running so that they could throttle up for an immediate takeoff.

At last, the loadmaster signaled to the drivers to stop and cut their engines. As the Raptors piled out to assist in the tie-down, the loadmaster suddenly pointed to Brannan and gestured for him to turn around.

As he did, he saw Greg Boyinson's grinning face inside the Little Bird, which was hovering barely a foot above the tarmac just twenty yards from the 747-200F. With the big jet engines idling, he hadn't even heard him arrive.

November 16
1:02 P.M. Eastern Time

"**THE** saumon poëlé au fenouil et coriandre is excellent," the French ambassador assured the International Validation Organization chief. When Muhammad Bin Qasim had suggested that they get together away from the United Nations, where the walls have "ears," Lumiere had suggested La Grenouille on East Fifty-Second Street in Manhattan. It was one of his favorites, and a short, twenty-minute stroll from the United Nations

Building. It was one of the few places in New York that they could go without the nagging sight of American flags everywhere.

"I think the Château Figeac, St. Emilion 1999, would be good," Lumiere said, scrutinizing the wine list. "I enjoy a Bordeaux red with salmon, don't you?"

Muhammad Bin Qasim had the balance of world power on his mind. The Americans had to remain isolated. The Mujahidin Al-Akhbar jihadi had been directed against the United States alone. The world, and the United Nations, had stood back. As long as they did nothing to anger Mujahidin Al-Akhbar, the rest of the world would be safe. As long as the United States remained isolated, the rest of the world would be safe. Until Khaleq Badr came on the scene, the rest of the world had stood back safely. Now, even the French were threatening to support the American bid for an International Validation.

"I would like to suggest a hypothetical scenario," Bin Qasim began as they finished their appetizers. "What would happen if the French were to secretly seek to locate Badr and neutralize him? Hypothetically, of course. Certainly the Direction Générale de la Sécurité Extérieure has this capability?"

"Mais oui!" François Lumiere replied indignantly. To suggest that the DGSE was capable of any less was preposterous. "Theoretically speaking, of course, the DGSE could certainly locate this man. This is certainly possible. If the French government chose to do this, it would be done."

"Of course," Bin Qasim said with a smile. "And if they were to do so, the status quo would be maintained and the United States would remain isolated within its war with Mujahidin Al-Akhbar."

"But operations outside the European Community require special authorization." Lumiere shrugged. Nobody knew better than Bin Qasim that the need for an International Validation hamstrung not only the Americans, but that it would also be necessary for another country.

"I think that this might be less of a problem, hypothetically speaking, than you might think," Bin Qasim said with a wink. "France has an open International Validation, a carte blanche if you will, to operate unilaterally on the African continent. One might consider that authority to be, shall we say, flexible."

"*D'accord*," Lumiere said with a nod. "Introductions could be made."

"I'm actually travelling to France tomorrow," Bin Qasim told the ambassador. "The gallery that I deal with there has some things that they wish to suggest for my collection. Perhaps while I'm in Paris I would have time for lunch if there would be someone to meet?"

ELEVEN

GRUMBLING and swearing, the men most closely resembled a cave full of grizzly bears being aroused early from hibernation. Jack Rodgers was walking through the passenger cabin of the 747-200F cargo aircraft, nudging his fellow Raptors and cajoling them to wake up.

Dave Brannan was already in the jumpseat on the flight deck nursing his second cup of coffee. Below, broken clouds at about 10,000 feet covered the khaki-colored landscape. The big freighter had made landfall over the Gulf of Alexandretta a half hour ago, and would be entering the pattern for a landing at Erhac Airport momentarily. Brannan could see the dark waters of the Euphrates River snaking its way across the ground below as the pilot descended. He and the other men had passed through Turkey before, but always by way of the United States base at Incirlik. They picked Erhac for the current operation because it was located in the eastern half of the country, and it was just large enough so that air freight flights were common enough not to attract much notice.

Incirlik AB would not be available today, even if the Raptors had needed it. In the wake of Fahrid Al-Zahir's declaration of a jihadi, the nervous Turkish government had asked the U.S. Air Force to suspend flight operations at the base, and the Turkish ambassador had demanded that Secretary Edredin promise him that the United States armed forces would undertake no offensive operations from Incirlik. Edredin had agreed. He was telling the truth about United States military operations, and the ambassador had been very specific about Incirlik. The ambassador didn't mention Erhac, but then neither he nor Edredin had any idea that President Livingstone had an American Volunteer Group—and that the *last* place from which they would stage an operation was a military base.

With the minarets and cement plants of the city of Malatya visible in the distance, the 747-200F touched down on Erhac's 10,990-foot Runway Twenty-One and taxied away from the terminal to an air freight hangar on the opposite side of the airport. Inside, the customs inspector glanced at the stack of cardboard boxes shrink-wrapped onto pallets at the front of the cargo hold, accepted his personal "fee," signed the paperwork, smiled, and left the freezing cold hangar.

The empty boxes and their pallet were moved out of the way and Greg Boyinson's Little Bird was rolled off, already prepainted with a "TC" prefix tail number that identified it as having Turkish civil registry. Jack Rodgers and Jason Houn then drove the two Broncos off the aircraft and out of the building. As with the Little Bird, the two vehicles had "gone native." Each had been fitted with Turkish license plates and registration papers. Both had been gassed up at a truck stop as they turned off Interstate 15 in Utah the day before, so they would be good for a few hours.

"The clock is ticking and there's no time to waste, so we're going to hit the road," Jack called out to Dave Brannan as he put the Bronco into gear and waved.

"We'll see you at Dodge City tonight," Dave said as they drove away. Dave and Will Casey would remain with Greg Boyinson to prepare the helicopter for flight. They would then take off after dark and rendezvous with the others at the prearranged location high in the Caucasus foothills that they had nicknamed after the famous Kansas cowtown.

November 17
9:22 A.M. Central European Time

HIGH over the Atlantic, Muhammad Bin Qasim leaned back in his comfortable first-class seat, set down his snifter of Rémy Martin, and reached for the folder in his briefcase that detailed the life of Khaleq Badr.

A zealous jihadi since his teens, the Mujahidin Al-Akhbar capo was born in Waziristan, that ambiguous border country between Pakistan and Afghanistan that remains autonomous from each, and a veritable petri dish of fanatic sects. Badr attended a madrassa in Islamabad, where he acquired an obsessive hatred for all things Western. As with many of his contemporaries, he and his madrassa class were easy pickings for the Pied Pipers of Al-Qaeda, Hezbollah, or Mujahidin Al-Akhbar.

Bin Qasim could easily see how Badr was recruited into Mujahidin Al-Akhbar. However, he read and reread the thin dossier, longing for more information that would help him figure out what had caused Badr to rebel *against* what was arguably the most radically fundamentalist organization in the world.

November 17
8:31 P.M. Ankara Time

GREG Boyinson smoothly lifted the Little Bird from the asphalt pad behind the air freight hangar. The Apex Air crew was already loading a consignment of packaged hazelnuts that actually contained hazelnuts. Within an hour, they would be winging their way westward to Frankfurt.

Dave Brannan watched the lights of the traffic beneath him streak by, marveling that the Little Bird was so quiet that he could actually make out bits of traffic noise from the highway below.

Within moments, they were flying over open country where there was no more traffic, and no more lights. At the altitude of roughly 2,000 feet where Boyinson was flying, the helicopter was virtually inaudible from the ground, and in the darkness, it was almost invisible—almost.

An hour after take-off Brannan glanced at the radar. They were not alone. There was another aircraft within two miles.

"Looks like we've got a bogie," he said, looking at Greg.

"Yeah, I've been watching him," Boyinson replied without looking down. "He's far enough away that I don't think he'll see us."

"What is he?"

"Helicopter of some kind. Might be smugglers. Might be a Turkish Air Force copter chasing smugglers. Not much commercial traffic out here."

Suddenly, the blip on the radar turned. It was a mile away and heading directly for them.

Greg Boyinson jinked to the starboard to change his flight path.

"I can see him visually now," Greg said. With his AN/AVS-9, Series F4949 aviator's night-vision goggles, night was day. "It's a Huey. Must be the air force. A smuggler would be trying to get away from us, not come *toward* us."

Manufactured by Bell Helicopter back in the Vietnam era, the UH-1 Huey was still one of the most ubiquitous military choppers in the world. It had been standard in the United States armed forces until the Black Hawk came along in the 1980s, but the American Military Assistance Program had provided them to dozens of air forces around the world during the Cold War. Turkey, being a NATO ally, had gotten its share of UH-1s and many were still in service.

"Do you suppose he sees us?" Dave asked.

"Not visually, but he'll be painting us on his radar."

There was a flicker as the Turkish helicopter turned on its powerful searchlight. It flashed around the sky, trying to lock onto the Little Bird. It was a pretty low-tech system, but probably pretty effective against smugglers. The Raptors could see a burst of tracers just as Greg went into evasive action.

The second burst of tracers came even closer. Armed Hueys typically carried a side-mounted 7.62-mm mini-gun that could put out a devastating rate of fire. For the unarmored Little Bird, even a single round, if well placed, could be fatal.

The thought crossed Dave Brannan's mind that it could all end right here. They could augur into the gravel of eastern Turkey and that would be that. He knew that Jack Rodgers would assume command, and he had every confidence that he would succeed in completing the mission. Dave just regretted that he wouldn't be there to see it through.

The next round of tracers came so close that Brannan couldn't see why they *weren't* hit. His stomach was in his throat as Greg Boyinson whipped the chopper through turns of evasive action.

"You could go ahead and return fire," he calmly said to Boyinson.

"I've got another idea." Boyinson grinned. "He's mad. He's gonna chase me."

"As plans go, that's a really good one," Brannan said sarcastically, wishing that Boyinson would cut loose with a Hellfire.

Greg Boyinson was right; the Huey pilot was getting into the spirit of the chase. Boyinson also knew that with the Huey hot on his tail, the side-mounted minigun would be pointed *away* from the Little Bird.

Gradually, but not too gradually, he was pulling the Huey lower. He increased his lead over the Huey, and then throttled back to let his adversary catch up. He was practically on Greg's tail. The pilot was enjoying this kind of hot-rodding, and he wasn't paying attention to how low they were getting. The Huey pilot was just watching the Little Bird and clinging to its tail. This was fine with Boyinson. It was exactly what he wanted.

They had been flying low over the dark waters of a river, a tributary of the Euphrates. There were a few bridges on the river, but Greg was looking for the right one. At last, he saw it. It was a double arched bridge over a section of the river with higher terrain on either side. This meant that the bridge itself was relatively high, while the spans between the arches were narrow.

The Huey followed him down to near wavetop level as Greg lined up on the left-hand arch. He prayed that the span was at least eight meters wide as he eased the throttle forward.

The Little Bird sailed under the bridge at 150 mph.

The Huey did not. Its rotor blades clipped the structure of the bridge, throwing the helicopter widely out of control.

Helicopters out of control at zero altitude and 150 mph don't last long. The wreckage cartwheeled through the arch, crashing violently into the river. Had it been the movies, there would have been a glamorous, blinding explosion, but the fuel tanks sank almost instantly and moments later the loudest sound beneath the bridge was the roaring of the river.

"How wide do you suppose that was?" Dave Brannan asked calmly.

"Well, I knew it was nowhere near forty feet and I knew that all models of Huey have a rotor diameter more than forty feet," Greg Boyinson replied, breathing for the first time in thirty seconds. "I was just hoping it was more than twenty-six feet."

November 17
1:45 P.M. Eastern Time

J UST as the mystery of Khaleq Badr perplexed the head of the United Nations International Validation Organization, so too was it a conundrum for the director of National Intelligence and the entire national intelligence apparatus of the United States—that is, except for one man.

Rod Llewellan was literally the man who knew too much. He always felt a little uneasy sitting in on the meetings of the special joint task force that the Director of National Intelligence had set up to investigate and oppose the Mujahidin Al-Akhbar threat. He alone within the National Intelligence apparatus knew of the existence of the Raptor Team, and the fact that they, not Khaleq Badr, had engineered the Rancho de los Bichos raid. Or at least he thought he knew that it wasn't Badr, but he really wasn't sure. Who was Khaleq Badr, and how *did* he fit into the picture?

Rod Llewellan may have been the man who knew too much, but he was coming to realize how *little* he actually knew.

Llewellan listened patiently as the Director of National Intelligence blustered at a young agent who had researched Badr's background, and who could find no details that shed any light on his becoming the nemesis of Fahrid Al-Zahir. Llewellan was nervous about the resources being devoted to Badr rather than Al-Zahir.

His mind had wandered during the Badr portion of the briefing, but he was suddenly jolted back to the here and now when the slide on the PowerPoint presentation suddenly changed. Up on the screen and standing three feet tall was the face of a man with a scraggly salt-and-pepper beard. It was Jack Rodgers!

Rod Llewellan was glad that it was a darkened room, because he felt his jaw drop and all the color instantly drain from his face. He had not seen a ghost. He had seen a Raptor. What in the hell? How did a Raptor show up in this briefing?

"This man is retired Special Forces Captain Jack Rodgers," the briefer explained. "He was present on the second Western Star Air flight that was hijacked. He played a role in defeating the hijackers and saving the flight."

Llewellan knew this. He had interviewed Rodgers. That was how he got involved in this whole thing.

"He has possibly reemerged as a figure in the Mujahidin Al-Akhbar matter," the briefer continued. "By profound coincidence, the baby who was saved is the nephew of a Western Star flight attendant, a Miss Brophy, who was aboard the flight where the captain *also* killed terrorists. She has spoken to the only witness to the Downers Grove killings. The description is of a man generally matching Captain Rodgers. Miss Brophy thinks he might be the one who killed the terrorist and saved the baby. It was she who contacted an FBI field office when she heard the description."

"This is very interesting," the director of National Intelligence told the group. "Ordinarily, we wouldn't follow up on a lead as tenuous and improbable as this, but we are not working an ordinary case, and the improbable coincidences are just too intriguing. Llewellan, you were present at McConnell. You met both Rodgers and this flight attendant. I want you to head out there and talk to the hospital witness and the Brophy woman. Then track down Rodgers and find out where he was on the day of the hospital incident."

November 17
10:54 P.M. Ankara Time

JACK Rodgers, Ray Couper, Will Casey, and Jason Houn had bypassed the city of Malatya on the ring road, crossing the Euphrates and heading northeast through the apricot groves into the Taurus Mountains. Three thousand years ago, this city of over a quarter million had been Milidia, the capital of a small Hittite kingdom. Later, the Romans passed through. They called it Melitene and made it a military headquarters for the Cappadocia region. The Ottoman Turks arrived in 1516 and never left.

The Raptors reached Dodge City after nightfall,

where they were met by Jahar "Johnny" Ertegun, a retired Turkish Special Forces man with whom they had worked years ago. As with the quiet men who had set up the transfer at Erhac Airport, Ertegun was one of a myriad of names in Dave Brannan's Rolodex of old friends who were only too happy to help out.

Dodge City was little more than a collection of shacks on an apricot plantation. For half the year, it was a beehive of activity. For the rest of the year, it was deserted. The metal buildings that had been piled high with crates of fruit a few months earlier allowed plenty of space for the Raptors to park their vehicles and begin unpacking their equipment and ammo.

Just as they had finished the hardest part of organizing all of the Raptor Team gear, the Little Bird quietly touched down.

"It's about time you got here," Jack Rodgers told Greg Boyinson as he nonchalantly strolled over to where the men had stacked the equipment. "What kept you?"

"Oh, we just had to make a short detour."

It wasn't the most comfortable place to spend the night, but Ertegun and his son had a pile of lamb on the grill, so they wouldn't be going to bed hungry.

TWELVE

"**WELL,** at least this morning I'm glad that we didn't break into that beer last night," Greg Boyinson admitted. The night before, as they were enjoying their kabobs at Dodge City, he had discovered a couple of cases of Efes Pilsen stashed in the barn where they spent the night. After surviving the chase under the bridge with the Huey, a cold one would have gone down nicely, but he had resisted temptation. Today was a workday.

Ertegun and his son had gone out before dawn to wrangle some horses while Jack Rodgers briefed the rest of the team on what he had learned from the data that Rod Llewellan had plucked from under the nose of the director of National Intelligence. Jack had brought copies of his 1:12,500 map of Turkey for each of them. He had kept the huge maps whole until now, just in case the mission had been compromised and the maps picked up by the wrong hands. He had gotten up early to trim out the relevant parts, and he had used the excess to start the fire that was reheating the morsels of lamb that would be their high-protein breakfast.

"We have two targets," he explained, having told them how the analysts in Washington had missed one. "There's one target that the spooks in Washington know about, and another that they missed. One is on the Black Sea, and it will be heavily guarded—this almost certainly is where Al-Zahir is hiding. It probably has been his little Tora Bora all along. The Turks may or may not know that, but if they do, they're afraid to do anything. The other place is on the plateau to the south. As you know, when you're running an operation like this, it's ideal to have two locations in completely different areas. Nobody except us and the bad guys know about the second one."

"The plan is to recon the plateau place first and then take down the Black Sea one as soon as possible afterward," Dave Brannan said. "We'll leave the Broncos here and travel overland on horseback. It will be faster because we can cut straight across terrain that's too rough for any wheeled vehicle, and nobody will be suspicious of guys on horseback around here. After that, we'll continue north to the Black Sea and take that place down tomorrow night. Greg will fly in for an air strike and to extract us back to Dodge after we're done."

November 18
8:34 A.M. Ankara Time

FISHING boats could be seen in the distance, and one was left to wonder whether they were trolling for mackerel and sea bass—or whether they were shuttling toward Trabzon or Istanbul with a hold full of the drippings of the poppy.

The houseboy shuffled silently into the luxurious living room with the commanding view of the Black Sea carrying a silver tray with tiny cups of very black coffee.

The men had spent the previous day planning their next move. The Mujahidin Al-Akhbar operation in the United States had been compromised. It had been stalled. The Downers Grove attack had been stopped in its tracks. The date for the Phoenix attack had come and gone. Al-Zahir had heard nothing from the jihadis who were supposed to cross the border and execute the attack. They had probabaly died in the Sierra Madre.

When asked, Al-Abir said he was eager to help restart the Mujahidin Al-Akhbar jihadi in the United States. He would even consent to shave his beard, which was as dark as the Black Sea on a moonless night. He was eager to travel to America to kill the infidels in their heartland.

Al-Zahir's immediate concern though, was Khaleq Badr. The rogue had to be stopped, and he needed Al-Abir's help. He handed the man a folder with a green cover. The heading was that of the Direction Générale de la Sécurité Extérieure. Al-Abir, who did not read French, asked for an explanation, so Al-Zahir turned to the section marked as *sommaire* and began to read. France's external intelligence agency had concluded that in the state of jihadi that now existed between the Mujahidin Al-Akhbar and the Ikhwan Al-Jihad, the latter would soon threaten Europe.

"If he means to challenge you in Europe, you must respond in Europe," Al-Abir said at last. "You must strike before he does, and you must strike savagely. You must take the initiative away."

November 18
8:47 A.M. Central Time

"I'M Agent Llewellan, we've met before," Rod told the young flight attendant as he greeted her at the door to her sister's modest little home on a quiet street in Downers Grove, Illinois.

"Yes, please come in. Thank you for coming," Morgan Brophy said, with the faint trace of a smile. "I hope that this won't be a wild-goose chase. It's been a roller coaster these past weeks. I wasn't really sure, but I knew that if I didn't say something, I would always wish that I had."

Llewellan was glad that she wasn't really sure. She had heard a general description, and she had heard something about a yellow shirt. She had connected the two. Llewellan would carefully reassure her that there were lots of men in the world with grey in their beards who also wore yellow shirts.

"You connected these facts with the man on the plane because you connected the two acts of terrorism in your mind," he told her. He was no shrink, but he had learned interview techniques at Quantico. Of course, he had never imagined that he would one day use his training to steer people *away from* identifying someone who was probably the man in question.

They had already spoken to the nurse at the hospital. She couldn't identify Rodgers. That was understandable. She had been in a state of shock. A friend had just been murdered. Rod had also gently coaxed the nurse. He hated having to finesse a witness like this, to convince her that she was wrong when she probably wasn't. He hated being the man who knew too much, even if he wasn't certain how much he really knew.

However, as much as Rod disliked his role as the man who knew too much, he was delighted that the director had teamed him with Erik Vasquez. This young agent was the man who *talked* too much. He loved to talk. Yesterday on the flight out, Vasquez had talked Llewellan's ears off. Today, Llewellan would let him take the lead in the interview of Morgan Brophy. The man who talked too much, knew too little, so there was less chance of him *saying* too much no matter how much he said.

November 18
3:47 P.M. Ankara Time

ANNE and Robert had hiked nearly ten miles since they left the cryptic note at the campsite that they hoped Little Abdul would find and be able to understand. She was in very good shape for being forty-something, but poor Robert found the going difficult. He had not, however, complained a single time since they had left.

Anne had decided that remaining at the camp would invite trouble. They could have driven toward town, but they didn't have the gas to get any farther, and being stuck in that town also seemed like a prescription for trouble.

She had managed to reach the university just before her cell phone died. The head of the department was at lunch, and the receptionist could not comprehend what Anne was trying to say. Luckily she put Anne through to voice mail. At least there was a recording of her explaining the situation. Hopefully *someone* who heard it could figure out what to do.

She decided that heading across the ridge and trying to get to a larger town on the main highway was the best of their unappealing choices. It was easier said than done. It was rough terrain, and the thin air of the 6,000-foot plateau made each step a chore, even for people used to the mile-high country around Boulder. At least the weather was perfect for hiking. The daytime temperature was in the forties, but with the body heat generated by the exertion, that was perfect. The air was still clear and dry, but if it started to snow, that would be more than an inconvenience.

They also struggled under the load of gear that they had taken with them—food, water, and sleeping bags for the freezing nights. They had finally abandoned one of the two Kalashnikovs, but Anne decided to continue to carry the other no matter how heavy it was getting. She had also kept the large knife that she had used to kill the bearded man.

As they walked, they had been crossing what seemed to be an endless series of ridges. Anne wanted to find a valley between ridges that was wide enough to contain a road or a trail. Following this would be more likely to lead them to a main highway and less likely to get them even more lost. As they reached the crest of each ridge, they found only a downhill slope into a gully, across which there was another ridge to climb. Finally, they crested a ridgeline, expecting yet another narrow, empty canyon, but instead, they saw a dirt road and some buildings.

"It looks like a sheepherder's shack, like you'd see in the Southwest," Robert observed.

"It looks deserted," Anne added, scanning the area surrounding the small cluster of tin-roofed mud huts. She shaded her eyes and squinted into the distance, following the deeply rutted dirt road that led away from the shack and down the narrow valley. The road followed and occasionally crisscrossed the dry rut of a seasonal stream. In the spring, there was probably a lot of water up here and the now-barren hills would be used for grazing livestock.

"Good news," Robert said. "I see a water pump."

They hiked down, refilled their water bottles, and began looking around the area. There was evidence that several vehicles had been at the site since the last major rain, but that had been nearly a month ago.

The door to one of the buildings was open a few inches, and Anne pushed her way in. She was not ready for what she saw. There was so much paperwork that she was reminded of being back at the university. It certainly seemed out of place in a remote location like this. There was paper everywhere. It was collated and stapled and placed in neat stacks. It was sorted and color coded and placed on shelves. There were comb-bound booklets and a few hardcover books. Most of it, however, seemed to be in Arabic, not Turkish.

"Oh, my God!"

It was Robert. He had followed her in and had moved ahead of her into an adjacent room.

"What is it?" Anne asked, as she headed toward the sound of his voice.

Anne found him staring slack-jawed at a huge map on the wall.

She too was speechless as she tried to comprehend what she was seeing. It was actually several maps tacked up next to one another. There was a large one of Europe that extended from the Catalonian part of Spain all the way to Armenia, and another of North America.

Pinned next to the North America map were a postcard and four large pictures clipped from a magazine that showed the NothalCorp Tower in Denver. The postcard showed it as Anne had last seen it. A small tree in the foreground and fluffy clouds above. The magazine pictures showed it engulfed in smoke and fire. She knew that Dennis was in those pictures. He was in his office on the sixty-first floor. The man she loved. With her picture on his desk. A picture of her was in those pictures. Was her picture the last thing that had been seen by the man she loved?

Robert watched helplessly as the tears began streaming uncontrollably down Mrs. McCaine's cheeks.

It was hard to grasp, but here, in the middle of nowhere, 6,500 miles from Denver, they had stumbled across a place that was frequented by someone with an intense interest in the destruction of the NothalCorp Tower. At the very least, these people were nuts. In the worst case, these people had been involved.

As Mrs. McCaine left the room sobbing, Robert reached out to comfort her, but she pushed him away.

"It's okay, Robert. I'm okay. Let me just get some air. It's too much."

As he followed her, he paused in the first room and thumbed through one of the booklets. He couldn't read any of it, but the pictures told a terrible tale. It was filled with crude drawings of people killing other people. These were terrorist manuals! This place was a terrorist base!

Outside, he found Mrs. McCaine rinsing her mouth out with water. He guessed that she had been throwing up. Her face was as white as a sheet.

He walked around to the other side of the building to give her some space to pull herself together. Beneath a makeshift lean-to was a fuel tank like one often sees at remote farms and ranches in the western United States. There was also a large shipping container like he had seen on container ships. He could imagine what might be in there. Guns? Explosives? Terrorists?

He didn't want to look.

As he started back to the side of the building where he had left Mrs. McCaine, Robert could hear the sound of a motor in the distance.

"Somebody's coming," she shouted. "Up the road. Coming here. We've got to get out of here."

They grabbed their packs and gear and looked around. They were surrounded by high ground. They had to get up there, but how? It would take five to ten minutes to climb the ridgeline in any direction. If the vehicle that was coming arrived sooner than that, they would be seen struggling up a hillside in full view.

"Hide," Anne instructed. "We have to hide and hope they don't stay long."

She pointed toward a small shed about twenty yards past the cargo container. From the main building, it was partially hidden from view. It was not perfect, but it was better than any other option.

They ran. The sound of the vehicle was getting louder. Anne knew that they were right not to have climbed the hill. Not enough time.

Anne looked sideways. Robert had been panting at her side, and now he wasn't.

She looked back. He was on the ground near the container. His face was twisted in agony and he was clutching his ankle. He tried to stand but he toppled over. He did not scream, nor cry out. He was trying hard to be as brave as his ponderous body would allow.

Only when Anne started back for him did he speak.

"No," he said emphatically through clenched teeth. "Go. Hide yourself. I'll let them think I'm alone."

"Okay," Anne said hesitantly. "Get behind that pile of cinder blocks if you can. Try to hide."

Anne reached the small shed just as the vehicle arrived. It was a late-model SUV with four men in it. They were younger than the men who had invaded the camp the other night. She guessed that they were about the same age as her grad students.

What a difference there was between people of the same generation. The same was true of her own generation. People had such a different take on the world. Usually that made things interesting. Sometimes it made things complicated. In the university environment, everyone seemed to blame the United States for terrorism. Terrorists were people with whom reasonable people could reason. Beyond the ivy walls, Anne met more and more reasonable people who blamed the *terrorists* for terrorism.

Since she had watched her husband die in streaming video on a laptop, Anne had come to think of terrorists as being people with whom trying to reason was impossible. She saw these four young men, realized that they were involved in murdering Dennis, and found herself wanting to kill *them* before they killed again.

Each of the men had a black beard, but the beards were more neatly trimmed that those of the men from the camp. Except for the driver, each man carried a black assault rifle. These guns had curved clips that were similar to that in the rifle that Anne had been lugging. She guessed that it must be a similar model.

Anne fingered the trigger guard of the Kalashnikov, wanting to start shooting, wanting to kill *them* before they killed again.

She watched as they walked toward the building, laughing and shouting. Then they stopped. They were near the water pump. Now they were looking around, scanning the hillsides. They must have seen something.

The water!

Anne and Robert had spilled some as they were filling their water bottles and as Anne washed out her mouth. The men were seeing that. The men knew that someone had been here recently—very recently.

Anne watched as two of the men searched the house and the others stood guard.

Now all four were outside and moving away from the building, guns at the ready.

A pair of the men moved left and another pair to the right. They were not coming toward her yet, but she could picture them circling around and coming toward the shed where she was hiding. She thought that she had figured out how the gun worked. At least she hoped that she had. She had taken off her pack and her heavy down jacket so that she could move more easily, but it was very cold out of the sun in the shed. She started to shiver, and she wondered whether it was the temperature or her nerves.

She could see Robert. He was lying very still near the pile of cinder blocks. He had pulled a piece of canvas over himself. Unless they got within about a dozen feet of him, they might not see him.

Hours seemed to go by as the men circled this way and that.

Bang!

There was a gunshot, and Anne nearly jumped out of her skin. One of the men had fired into a pile of brush. There might have been a rabbit or a rodent of some kind. Maybe he was just nervous and shooting at ghosts.

The fact that he had his AK-47 on single shot rather than full auto indicated that these guys were a great deal more disciplined and methodical than would have been a gang of crazy young gangsters spraying things with bullets for the adrenaline rush—but Anne did not know this chilling fact.

One pair of men was out of sight beyond the building. The other was moving toward where she was hiding.

There was a shout, and the two men turned away from her. They had seen Robert!

The two thugs converged on the hapless grad student, screaming in what sounded like Arabic, not Turkish. Robert didn't know Arabic.

They tried to get him to stand, but his injured ankle crumpled and he toppled over again.

One man set his assault rifle aside and jerked Robert to a kneeling position. He crouched down and started yelling at Robert, who was trying to reply.

The man screamed at Robert and finally slapped him. Robert slipped sideways, but caught himself before he fell. He looked defiantly at the man, who continued to scream at him. This time, Robert made no attempt to reply—he just stared at the man.

Anne watched as the other man grew more and more fidgety. Finally, he raised his assault rifle. The first man shouted at him and they began to argue. They were fighting over whether to murder poor Robert in cold blood.

Anne decided to do something. She quietly crept from the shed and inched toward them. The man with the gun was standing with his back to her, and she moved so as to use him to screen herself from the other one. She noticed that Robert had seen her out of the corner of his eye, but he did not turn his head.

Anne moved forward quietly until she was about

twenty feet from them. She raised the rifle and trained it on the man's back. She thought of Dennis and how he died. She wondered if he had seen it coming. She wondered how much warning he had. Had he seen the airplane before it hit the NothalCorp Tower?

She squeezed the trigger and felt the recoil slam her shoulder.

The man seemed to leap slightly as the round hit him. The second man leaned sideways to get out of the way as the first one fell. Anne aimed at the second man's face and pulled the trigger. His head jerked and he fell.

All of her years growing up with a bolt-action .22 rifle in the house came back to her. She had never fired an automatic weapon before, but that was okay. She was so nervous that she would probably have forgotten to eject the spent shell.

"Get down!" Anne shouted to Robert, who was staring at the two men.

Anne crouched as Robert flattened himself to the ground.

She heard a shot and saw a puff of dust as a bullet struck the ground only two feet from where she was. She jumped toward the pile of cinder blocks just as another bullet hit where she had been lying.

The other two men had heard the shots and came running. She could see one moving toward her on the right side of the building. She didn't have a clear shot, so it didn't occur to her that she should fire anyway.

She saw a flash of movement to her left. They were trying to surround her. The one on the left was working his way behind her position, while the other man continued to fire round after round. She thought of counting the shots like they used to do in the movies, but she stopped. She had no idea how many bullets were in their clips.

She realized that the man on her right was just there to keep her pinned down. It was the second man who was going to kill her, and he didn't know that she had seen him. She crouched as low as she could, watching him out of the corner of her eye while the other man fired wildly. He was almost in line with the shed now and creeping toward her. It was the man who had been driving, who did not have an assault rifle. He had something in his hand but she couldn't tell whether it was a knife or a pistol. Anne decided not to wait to find out.

She turned, aimed, and fired.

The man was hit and went down screaming.

Anne fired again. She thought she might have hit him again, but he was still screaming.

Realizing that she was exposing herself to the man with the assault rifle, she ducked down. Again, luck was on her side as a bullet whizzed past her head so closely that she could hear it.

The man had used the distraction to work himself closer.

She could see him. Was this a clear shot?

She took it. The bullet ricocheted harmlessly off the wall of the building and the man ducked.

Anne leaned up and squeezed the trigger again, bracing herself against the recoil.

Instead of the sound of powder exploding and the kick of the gun butt, there was just a dull *click*.

She squeezed the trigger again. Again there was just a *click*.

Anne's heart sank. Was she out of ammunition? Was the clip loaded incorrectly?

The man had heard the first click and paused.

When he heard the second, he stood up and started moving in her direction with his gun pointed at her.

What could she do? If she raised her gun to try again, he would fire before she could aim. She wondered whether she could lure him close enough to hit him with the gun or attack him with the large knife that she had used on the rapist. It was absurd, but this might be her only chance.

As she watched the man in the beard moving ever closer, she thought about Dennis, and wondered if he'd had this much time to prepare to die.

November 18
3:55 P.M. Ankara Time

THE Raptors had been making good time on horseback. Dave Brannan wished that he was on Sandy, rather than on this old grey mare, but she was a pretty good horse. He also knew that the Little Bird, for all its remarkable capabilities, couldn't extract horses after an operation, and he would not have wanted to leave Sandy behind.

They had reached the canyon that led up to the Mujahidin Al-Akhbar's remote safe house and were following it toward their target when they heard the sound of a vehicle roaring up the road. They had been keeping to the top of the ridge so that they could easily duck out of the way if someone came along, and so they did.

"Looks like probably four of them in there," Dave said as he studied the SUV through his binoculars. "Two in front, two in the middle, and nobody in back."

The vehicle disappeared out of sight around a bend, and the Raptors urged their horses to a trot until at last they saw the SUV again. It was parked near a small cluster of sorry-looking shacks. Just as they were dismounting to make a more cautious approach on foot, they heard a shot.

Brannan quickly crept to the crest of the ridge with his binoculars, while the other men tethered the horses. As he looked down into the valley, he could see four men in heavy winter coats. Two of them appeared to be looking for something or someone. Some distance away, the other two were shouting at a fifth man who was sitting on the ground.

"Look over there," Jack Rodgers whispered.

They watched as another figure emerged from a small hovel and began creeping toward the men who were shouting at the sitting man.

Suddenly there were two more pops, and two men went down.

"Good shot, whoever it is," Jason Houn observed.

"Let's get down there," Brannan said as he rose to his feet.

They spread out and slipped quietly down the hillside. There were more shots. A real gun battle was now raging down there. The men in the SUV were almost certainly the Mujahidin Al-Akhbar, but who were the others—and how did they get here?

Dave Brannan reached the main building first and pressed himself to the side as he crept toward the rear. The shooting stopped. He peeked around and saw one of the men from the SUV advancing toward two people who were next to a pile of cinder blocks. The one who was standing looked like a woman!

Dave knew that the Mujahidin Al-Akhbar didn't recruit women, so he raised his Heckler & Koch MP5, put a short burst into the man and moved in closer.

The woman came slowly toward him, holding a rifle in one hand, its muzzle pointed toward the ground. She wore a pair of substantial, but heavily scuffed boots, dirty khaki trousers, and a close-fitting, long-sleeved T-shirt. It was evident from the enormous knife in the scabbard strapped to her thigh that she was not someone to be trifled with.

She was a small woman, about five-foot-five, with dark wavy hair and dark grey eyes that cast a riveting gaze. The streak of grey in her hair and the lines around the corners of her eyes told Dave that she was probably in her forties, but her lean, well-formed body was that of a woman of twenty-five. She was slender, but well toned. Her hands were perfectly proportioned, but her nails had the nicked and worn look of someone who worked with her hands.

"Merhaba," she said cautiously.

"Merhaba," he replied, repeating the Turkish word for "hello."

He was trying to place her accent. She wasn't

Turkish, but there were an infinite number of nationalities and dialects in these mountains and plateaus.

"Do you speak English?" she asked hopefully. "I really am not very conversant in Turkish."

"Yes ma'am," Brannan replied. "I do know a word or two of English."

"American?" she asked.

"Yes ma'am, American. It sounds like you are as well."

"What are you doing out here?" she asked pointedly.

"Well, we're just doing a little hunting here today," he replied, after a pause to decide exactly what to tell her. He couldn't tell her exactly what they *were* doing, but he was an old-fashioned gentleman to whom lying to a lady came hard. In fact, she looked like someone who could probably figure out what they were doing, and she probably already had.

"Hunting? With *that*?" she said skeptically, pointing to his submachine gun.

"What are *you* doing out here?" Brannan asked cautiously, observing how she handled weapons. "Are you with Special Forces?"

"You have *got* to be kidding me!" Anne said emphatically. "My name is Anne McCaine. I'm a professor of archaeology at the University of Colorado."

"You're studying archaeology with *those*?" Dave said, pointing to the AK-47 in her hand and the knife with the ten-inch blade that was strapped to her leg. "Who's kidding who?"

November 18
4:07 P.M. Ankara Time

"**I**T is heartening to know that these fools are so frightened by Badr." Fahrid Al-Zahir smiled as he and Muhammad Al-Abir watched the Al-Arabiya television rebroadcast of a press conference held earlier in Washington. The two men watching the fifty-inch plasma television screen in the villa overlooking the Black Sea were pleased to see that the Americans were completely baffled by the mercurial Badr.

"The infidels are frightened by everything," Al-Abir growled.

The spokesman from the office of the director of National Intelligence had flown into a thunderstorm of questions about the elusive Khaleq Badr. There was a growing groundswell of public concern in the United States about the possibility of anyone and everyone being caught up in a gang war between rival terrorist groups.

Al-Zahir was especially pleased that one of the jihadis who had arrived with Al-Abir knew the location of a safe house in Livonia, Michigan, that Badr had used in the days before he left Al-Qaeda to join Mujahidin Al-Akhbar. Badr had last been seen in Mexico, and because the whole world was watching for him, it was correct to surmise that he was not far from the borders of the Great Satan. If he was not in Livonia, there might at least be clues there.

With this knowledge, the plan had virtually developed itself. The day after tomorrow, Al-Abir would leave Turkey with eighteen men. They would split up to board international flights from Ankara and Istanbul; following various routes across Europe they would go on to Toronto and Montreal. From there, they would enter Michigan, crossing from Sarnia to Port Huron, or by way of the heavily travelled International Bridge from Windsor into Detroit.

He wished that he could watch Muhammad Al-Abir in action in America, but he knew that soon his exploits would be widely televised. His signature was a ruthless brutality that was visually riveting. Like the airliner in Algiers, it was tailor-made for television. Body after screaming body falling to the tarmac. Why was it that the infidel television networks were so eager to broadcast infidel pain?

Al-Zahir still weighed the possibility of taking the jihadi to Europe to outflank Badr, but he hadn't yet decided. The Europeans were no threat—yet. They had generally cooperated with terrorists out of fear—so far. Bin Laden had discovered this in 2004. When he had blown up a train in Madrid, the Spanish whelps had changed their government and run home whimpering from the Middle East with their tails between their legs.

On the other hand, maybe it *was* time to give Europe a taste of the Mujahidin Al-Akhbar whip!

Al-Abir had never before set foot in the heartland of the infidel and he looked forward to it. Al-Zahir wanted Badr dead, and so be it, but there would be plenty of opportunities to spill infidel blood as well. Al-Abir longed to kill the infidels, to take the jihadi into their homes. He could almost smell their blood.

The cable news commentator came on the screen. She had long, blonde hair that fell to her shoulders. She had glossy, red lipstick that accentuated her pouty lips. She wore a low-cut top that revealed the flesh of her neck.

Al-Abir clinched his teeth and closed his eyes. Oh! how he *hated* women. He despised all women, except of course his late and saintly mother. The sight of them made him ill, physically ill. In his world, they were properly covered so that they could not be seen. In his world, they did not speak. In the West, against which he had declared a personal jihadi, their flesh was visible everywhere, their faces visible anywhere that anyone turned. He wanted to kill them—kill them all.

As he tilted his head back, his eyes still tightly closed, Al-Abir imagined that the voice ringing in his ears was not that of a woman, an infidel woman. He imagined that the voice was that of a boy, a sweet and beautiful prepubescent boy, and he wished that such a boy could share his bed tonight.

November 18
4:07 P.M. Ankara Time

ANNE McCaine took a sip of water from the plastic bottle and looked across the dusty patch of ground in the middle of godforsaken nowhere on which she had just killed three men. The experience of killing four people in fewer than four days had been numbing. A few days ago, the very thought of such a thing would have torn her apart. She was surprised that the reality

had not. More numbing than the fact of having killed
was the experience of nearly being shot to death herself. Had it not been for the tall man with the auburn
mustache, that probably would have happened.

The men who had been with this man had descended on the small complex of buildings in a flurry
of activity. One of them had wrapped Robert's ankle,
given him a couple of painkillers, and pronounced him
"good to go." He wasn't, but he was limping around
the place as though to prove that he soon would be.
Others busily removed the bodies and picked up shell
casings that were strewn across the ground after the
shoot-out.

She hadn't asked any more questions, but it was
clear to her that these "hunters" were not hunting the
bezoar ibex that were so plentiful in these mountains.
They were American, and they were part of some sort
of military operation. She had seen the artifacts on the
wall, and she was left with little doubt that these
hunters were hunting the people who had murdered
her husband.

Inside the building, Brannan and Rodgers studied the
map and took pictures with their digital cameras, while
Jason Houn studied the Arabic text of the manuals.
What they found was information that confirmed the
supposition that the Black Sea site was where Al-Zahir
had his headquarters. More ominously, the maps told
the story that Mujahidin Al-Akhbar planned much more
far-reaching mischief than they had suspected from
what they had found at Rancho de los Bichos.

As they studied the ephemera in the small house,
Dave Brannan couldn't stop himself from thinking

.

about that woman. Maybe it was the brisk country air, or maybe it was the thought of an attractive woman close to his own age who walked around with a goddamn sword strapped to her leg, but he was feeling unnaturally happy. Maybe it was just the exhilaration—for the first time in many years—of being hot for a woman while he was in the middle of an operation.

Finally, he couldn't stand it any longer. He had to talk to her.

"How's your friend?" he asked, nodding at Robert as he approached the woman.

"It wasn't too serious," Anne replied, "but your man fixed him up."

She caught herself smiling as she spoke. The big man with the red mustache was what a girl might find ruggedly attractive. He wasn't smooth and well groomed like her husband, but in another lifetime, she might have been attracted to him. He had huge hands, but they had seemed gentle when he had shaken her hand when he introduced himself. She found herself wondering whether he had killed people with those bare hands, but then she realized that *she* had killed a man with her own hands.

"You guys look like you're planning to leave pretty soon," Anne said, nodding toward where the Raptors were tightening the cinches on their horses.

"You're very observant, Doctor," he replied.

"Full professor," she said. "Not a PhD. It's easier to get out into the field without those initials."

"How long were you at Teshub?" he asked. She had earlier told the story of what had happened there.

"Since the summer. The plan was to stay until late

December and come back in the spring if there was continued funding."

"You crossed to here on foot?" he asked.

"Yes we did, Colonel."

"Sounds like you can take care of yourself pretty well outdoors," he said nervously. He knew that they would have to leave these two Americans out here. He didn't like that idea, but he was trying to rationalize that in her hands, they would be all right until they could be picked up.

"You mean 'pretty well' for a woman," she said, stifling a smile.

"When we leave, we'll give you rations for four days. I'll see that someone picks you up as soon as possible."

"You're *not* going to leave us out here," she said angrily.

"I'm sorry," he argued. "We have things to do. We can't—"

"Well, I'm sorry. What you *can't* do is leave us here. What happens if more of those guys come up here? I know what you're doing in Turkey. Any fool could figure that out. I've been inside that shack over there. I've seen what's on that wall. I know what you're 'hunting' in Turkey. I want to go *with you*."

"We can't—"

"Of course you can," she demanded. "You have four packhorses. They're packed light. Obviously you did that so that you'd be able to double up the loads if you needed to. Well, now you need to. You can put us on two of the horses. Robert may be a full load, but I don't weigh very much."

"If you've figured that out, you've probably figured

out that where we're going, it's not going to be a classroom environment," Brannan cautioned.

"I've already been outside the classroom, Colonel," she said, pointing to where she had just shot three terrorists. "I know where you're going, and I want to be there. Those bastards murdered my husband!"

THIRTEEN

November 19
3:09 P.M. Central European Time

THE slender man with the thick glasses sat down in
a wicker chair at the sidewalk cafe on Boulevard
St-Germain and ordered a coffee. He lit a Gauloise and
watched passersby carefully out of the corner of his eye
as he pretended to read his copy of *Le Monde*. It was an
unusually clear day for Paris this time of year, and it
was pleasantly warm on the sunny side of the street. It
was sunny enough that it didn't seem unusual that the
heavyset, dark-complected man who sat at the adjoining
table was wearing dark glasses.

"*Il pleuvra demain,*" he said without looking at the
man with the thick glasses.

"*Pas a Paris,*" the man replied without looking up
from his newspaper.

"My sources tell me that your government has considered supporting the United States' request for an International Validation," Bin Qasim told the man, speaking in fluent French. "That would embolden them and undo all of our best efforts to curb their dispropor- tionate influence in the world."

"The terrorist war has escalated." The man shrugged. "France must act in its own best interest to prevent this war from reaching French soil."

"The reason that it has escalated is one man. Khaleq Badr," Bin Qasim reminded the Frenchman. "As I told Monsieur Lumiere when he arranged this meeting, Badr is the reason that the war has escalated. If he were to be removed, it would leave the confrontation solely between the Mujahidin Al-Akhbar and the United States. As in the Cold War, the two will be locked in a stalemate that is de- tached from Europe and the world. The Mujahidin Al- Akhbar has declared war on the United States, *not* against the rest of the world."

The man in the thick glasses nodded thoughtfully.

"If the DGSE removed Badr, the status quo, the stale- mate, would be restored," Bin Qasim said, pressing his case.

"What if the United States were to obtain an Interna- tional Validation?"

"I'm the head of the damned International Validation Organization!" Bin Qasim responded in a peeved tone. "I can prevent that."

"Will France need an International Validation?"

"You have an open International Validation for opera- tions throughout Africa and the European Community, but the DGSE has never relied on diplomatic niceties when French interests are at stake. You sank the Greenpeace *Rainbow Warrior* in Auckland Harbor in 1985."

"Our sovereign interests are paramount." The man sniffed. The 1985 incident was still a sore subject. "We believe that he is not in Africa nor the territory of the European Community."

"If you were to undertake to eliminate Badr, it could be done quietly. Nobody need know. Do you think that the DGSE would be able to locate him?"

"Of course."

"Do you know where he is?" Bin Qasim asked.

"I am not at liberty to say."

"Of course." Bin Qasim nodded. "I understand."

November 19
4:09 P.M. Ankara Time

"**T**HAT'S the biggest rifle I've ever seen," Anne said, making small talk as Will Casey gingerly unpacked his Barrett M107 sniper rifle. The Raptors were situated on a bluff high over the Black Sea that looked down on the villa that was the lair of Fahrid Al-Zahir. Anne watched as they all prepared their equipment for the night's work that lay ahead.

"Oh, the elephant gun?" Will laughed. "It's eighteen pounds heavier than a bolt-action M40 sniper rifle, but it's got twice the effective range, a bigger clip, and the .50-caliber rounds have more than twice the throw-weight of a .308 Winchester slug. Another reason that

I'm partial to this puppy is that they make 'em in Murfreesboro, Tennessee, which is about twelve miles from where I grew up."

"I suppose that this thing could do some damage," Anne said, looking at the fearsome-looking weapon that was nearly five feet long now that Casey had it fully assembled.

"Well ma'am, as I like to say, any of those jokers that I hit with this thing tend to stay dead for a very long time."

It had been an interesting ride getting to this bluff overlooking the Black Sea. The fat kid had never been on a horse before, but Dave Brannan was impressed by how willing he was to learn and the fact that he never complained. The professor on the other hand, rode as though she had been born on a horse. In fact, she was so good, even riding bareback, that Dave had put her in charge of one of the packhorses.

She not only kept pace, but she kept her horse moving as though she was trying to prove to him that a pair of unintended hangers-on would not slow down his operation. As they broke camp before dawn this morning, she had been the first one up and was making coffee before all the Raptors were awake. Even the fat guy was ready to go on time.

"That's it. That's the rat's nest," Jack Rodgers said as he walked noiselessly into their assembly area after climbing up the steep hillside. He had been gone for more than an hour, taking a closer look at Al-Zahir's compound.

"Are you sure?" Anne asked. "It looks more like a

movie star's house in Malibu. I thought all these people lived in caves somewhere."

"That's what they *want* you to think." Jason Houn laughed.

"There's a guard post at the turn of the road and another one at the side of the compound," Jack continued. "Perimeter security is minimal. They know that the Turkish authorities will leave them alone, and they know that without International Validation, the Americans can't touch them. There are a lot of rabbits and such critters in the woods leading up to it. I even saw a deer. That rules out motion sensors. The stone wall has barbed wire, but it's not electrified. I saw one guard with a night-vision goggles pack, but the others I saw didn't have them. They probably have more than one set, but there aren't enough to go around."

Dave Brannan unfolded the printout of an amazingly detailed high-angle view of the villa that had been taken by the Keyhole satellite, and the Raptors began dividing the site into sections and planning their assault. The place was surrounded by cliffs, so the obvious way in was by the main road. With this in mind, they planned only a diversionary attack here.

Greg Boyinson had been alerted and was planning to fly in just after dark. He would be overhead to provide air support for the ground attack, and would lighten his load of Hellfires when it came time to torch the place as a finale. Dave wanted the Raptors to take the house from the ground so that they could get a visual on Al-Zahir when they killed him.

They were going over the final details when they heard Anne say "*Oh* my God!"

She had borrowed Brannan's high-powered binoculars and had been looking at the villa.

"What is it?" Jack asked, looking at her staring down at the structure.

"The courtyard of this place is littered with Bronze Age Hittite sculpture. There are some like the ones from Sam'al that are in the Berlin Museum. I see a sphinx like the ones that were found at Gazientep. Whoever owns this place is a serious collector."

"More likely a pillager," Jason Houn interjected. "Antiquities are a big black market cash crop for organized crime and terrorists all over this part of the world. It's better than opium. You can dust it off, sell it to a rich European collector, and it looks legitimate sitting in his rec room."

November 19
8:09 A.M. Eastern Time

"**L**ET me do the talking," Rod Llewellan told his youthful partner. The talkative Erik Vasquez was the kind of energetic young man who one day would make a good agent, but he talked too much. Today called for listening more than talking. The two FBI men had taken the red-eye into Baton Rouge after wrapping up their day in the Chicago suburbs. According to his credit card records, Jack Rodgers's last known whereabouts was a motel on State Route 67, just north of Airline Highway and not far from the Baton Rouge Metro Airport.

Two men in suits strutting into his office at that hour of the morning made the proprietor a little nervous.

When Vasquez flashed his FBI identification, that made him a lot nervous.

"What can I do ya out of?" He grinned nervously.

"Ever see this man?" Llewellan asked, showing him a picture of Jack Rodgers.

"Seen a lotta white guys what look 'round about like that guy. Gotta name?"

"Rodgers. John Rodgers. Goes by Jack."

"When you reckon he stayed here?"

"Night of November 8? He was here on the next morning for sure."

"Oooh, lemme see," the proprietor said, slowly picking up his glasses and shuffling over to an adjacent table where he kept an accordion file full of receipts. The two G-men looked at one another. Was this old coot pulling their chains?

"That guy," he said at last. "Yeah, now I remember him. Yeah, he was drivin' one of Bobby Loreau's rent-a-wrecks."

"What's that?" Vasquez asked.

"Oh, y'know, old Bobby's got this place over on Choctaw Drive. Rents cars real cheap. Buncha old clunkers. Rents 'em cheap."

Armed with this information, Llewellan and Vasquez joined the morning commute into the downtown core of the Louisiana state capital. The fact the Bobby Loreau's "place" was downtown explained why the observant feds had not seen it when they picked up their own rental car at the airport.

Bobby had not yet opened for business, so they looked around and ascertained that Bobby did not take credit cards, which explained why the last two charges on Jack Rodgers's Visa had been for his ill-fated ride on Western Star Air and his motel room.

It was after nine when a man in a well-worn white suit and a Stetson pulled into the small parking lot in an aging Lincoln Town Car. It didn't take the well-honed intuitive powers of the FBI to know that this would be Bobby.

"Help you boys?"

"We're looking for a man," Erik told him.

"Can't help you there, son." Bobby chuckled. "I only deal in auto-MO-biles."

The playful smirk disappeared from his face when Rod showed him his federal identification.

As with the man at the motel, the picture of Jack Rodgers elicited no recognition, but an attentive search through Bobby Loreau's files resulted in a colorful series of expletives.

"Sumbitch clean drove outta here," Bobby explained. "Sumbitch took a Ford Taurus. Less'n 100,000 miles."

"He stole one of your cars?" Llewellan asked. He was incredulous that one of the men from the Raptor Team was a car thief, even if the Raptors were capable of slaughtering a room full of jihadis.

"He *did* send me four grand about a week later," Bobby admitted. "Probably more'n the old Ford was worth, but still, the sumbitch just drove off with her."

"Did you happen to remember what bank the check was drawn on?" Erik asked.

"Weren't a check. Cash. Sumbitch sent a big old wad o'cash."

"Did you happen to see where it was mailed from?" Erik asked.

"Think it was Seattle," Bobby said thoughtfully. "Yeah, pretty sure. Seattle."

November 19
9:26 P.M. Ankara Time

As night descended upon the Black Sea coast, the temperature was dropping and the Raptors were moving in for the showdown with Mujahidin Al-Akhbar. It was not as cold near the coast as it had been at higher elevations, so if a person kept moving, it was comfortable without a coat.

The main part of the two-story, U-shaped villa looked as though it had been built in the nineteenth century, but there was a wing that had been added around the 1950s or 1960s.

An old thirty-foot stone watchtower, measuring a bit less than a dozen feet on each side, extended above the building. It had probably been designed to give the original owner a good view of the Black Sea shoreline below, but tonight it was manned by two men with assault rifles and binoculars. In the hours that the Raptors had watched the villa, there had never been more than two. There wasn't enough room. But two were enough. Between them, the two guards in the tower had a clear view of the entire perimeter. This tower was the eyes of the villa's security apparatus. The Raptors thought it a safe assumption that at least two sets of night-vision goggles were up there.

On the ground, there was only one side that was sufficiently level to be approached by a vehicle, and hence there was just a single gate. It was guarded by a slightly elevated guardhouse that was not as high as the main tower. The two men manning it had a clear view of the road leading into the compound, and a heavy-caliber machine gun to cover the approaches. Barricades erected on this road would make it impossible for any kind of vehicle to approach the gate at high speed. Even the terrorists feared car bombs.

The biggest weapon visible at the compound was an old Russian-made Zhu-23 double-barrelled antiaircraft gun. Like the Kalashnikov rifles, Zhu-23s were of an old and simple design, but this made them easy to use, and they were very effective. The gun was located in an open area of the courtyard where it could track and kill helicopters approaching from any direction. On the ground, its 23-mm explosive rounds could make life difficult for most vehicles short of main battle tanks.

Inside the villa, things were peaceful. Logs had been added to the fires in both of the large hearths in the main part of the house. Most of the twenty-eight men at the compound were indoors. The four men who had gone to the remote site the day before were due back at any time. They were not yet overdue, so there was no alarm. They had not checked in because of Al-Zahir's strict orders to maintain cellular silence, and there were no landlines into the remote valley.

The compound was secure. There were two men in the tower with night-vision gear scanning the perimeter constantly. They were relieved every two hours to avoid fatigue.

The two men who had guard duty at the main gate were huddled into the guard shack with a portable electric heater. They kept watch over the road leading into the compound. With the concrete barricades to slow down any vehicle approaching the compound on the road, they could cut it to pieces with their heavy machine gun before it got anywhere near the gate. The gate itself was made of heavy-gauge steel armor plate and was impregnable anyway. The men who guarded the gate knew that it was impossible for anyone to get through the gate, and they knew that nobody had ever tried. For this reason, guard duty at the gate was considered to be the most boring assignment at the compound. More often than not, one of the two men usually slept while his colleague kept watch—not for potential gate crashers, but for senior Mujahidin Al-Akhbar leaders who might catch them trading naps while on duty.

Indeed, most of the men who guarded the compound found this duty tedious and almost pointless. They yearned for the fight. They had been swept up in the Mujahidin Al-Akhbar through the exhilaration of carrying the jihad to the infidel. They had watched the Great Satan as it had been attacked in its own heartland. They had wanted to be part of that, but knew that they would not see Americans nor smell their blood in this remote corner of Turkey. The men at the villa saw their brothers bathed in the blood of martyrdom, and longed to be there—anywhere but guarding a palatial Black Sea villa thousands of miles from the infidel heartland!

The men who had longed for action night after night in this distant place would not long remain disappointed. This night would be different, very different. They *would* see action—and martyrdom.

The first two men to be martyred were struck without

warning in the tower. The irregular terrain enhanced the villa's defenses, but also made it possible for Will Casey to get into position on high ground about 900 meters from the villa. He had a commanding view of the compound at half the effective range of his rifle. With his 100-power infrared telescopic sight, the jihadis looked to him as though they were standing in the next room.

Their Kevlar vests were no match for the .50-caliber rounds from Casey's elephant gun, but that didn't matter. The vests didn't cover their heads and necks.

A split second later, an M84 stun grenade exploded just inside the gate with a million-candlepower flash and a 180-decibel *ka-boom*. The stunned guards stood motionless. They were there to protect the gate against a vehicle that they would have seen coming, but out of nowhere there was a blinding—literally blinding—flash of light.

Standing motionless only made them better targets for the elephant gun, and they too joined the growing number of Mujahidin Al-Akhbar true believers who had been blessed with martyrdom by the Raptors.

Elsewhere in the compound, the jihadis reacted to the explosion at the front gate. They naturally assumed that the gate was under attack. Fourteen ran out of the building and across the courtyard, exposing themselves to the open field of fire from Casey's position.

When three jihadis, then eight, fell, the others wildly fired their automatic rifles into the darkness beyond the gate, supposing that the unseen attackers were there. In fact, nobody was there. Ray Couper, who had tossed the M84 grenade over the gate, was already more than ninety degrees around the circumference of the compound away from the gate.

The two jihadis who had the presence of mind to try to man the Zhu-23 died trying. The helicopter against which they might have reacted arrived moments later. It appeared without warning, although "appeared" is probably not the applicable word. Painted black, it could not be seen, except for a brief flash of reflection as it darted overhead. The sound of its engine was not even audible over the rattle of its pair of M134 six-barrel Gatling guns.

Greg Boyinson made a low-level pass, hosing the cluster of jihadis in the courtyard and blasting the wall of windows in the house that faced the courtyard. The latter was mainly for psychological effect. A couple of jihadis inside were hit, one fatally, but the attack was mainly to disorient the survivors.

The Little Bird's fly-past was the cue for the Raptors to come over the wall on the far side of the compound opposite the gate. They dashed toward the villa, which had been plunged into darkness the moment that the M84 had exploded at the front gate. During Jack Rodgers's reconnaissance that afternoon, he had noted the location of the main power supply.

They entered the U-shaped building at its base and moved calmly and systematically through the two wings, using their PVS-15 night-vision gear to peer into the shadows of the darkened building. The compound had now been under attack for less than fifty seconds.

Dave Brannan kicked open a set of double doors on the main floor, and found a huge room with a large table. The room comprised the main floor of that entire wing, dwarfing the huge table that would have seemed large anywhere else. He crouched down to see whether anyone was hiding beneath the table, saw one, and splintered the jihadi—as well as the table legs—with a burst from his MP5 submachine gun.

After a quick search of the room, Brannan and Brad Townsend ascended the stairs and cleared a series of upstairs rooms. At that same time, Jack Rodgers and Jason Houn were systematically doing the same on the opposite wing, while Ray Couper covered the base of the *U*.

Houn kicked in a door and found a jihadi in his underwear, squirming to open a window. It was almost comical. The man turned and stared at the Middle Eastern features and the beard of the Lebanese American Raptor. There was familiarity, and almost recognition, on his face.

"Brother," the man said to Houn in Arabic, "I can tell who you are. I see Lebanon in your face. Why are you siding with the infidel? His ways are not our ways. Join us in glory. God has spoken to the most holy Al-Zahir and he speaks to us through the most holy Al-Zahir. Join with those who share your blood. Join us to spill infidel blood—"

Jason had heard enough. He squeezed the trigger of his weapon. Just as Will preferred his elephant gun, Jason's weapon of choice was his "trench cleaner." The nickname was borrowed from the British Tommies of World War I, who sawed a foot off the barrels of their Browning shotguns and used them against the Boche trenches. Houn's trench cleaner was his Winchester model 1300 Black Shadow speed-pump shotgun. He had surgically removed about a foot of its twenty-six-inch barrel. A twenty-gauge round from this Winchester could clean a bedroom as easily as a trench.

"Man, you're talking to the wrong guy," Jason told the man whose body had now been hacked into two twitching, bleeding halves. "My family were Lebanese Christians. Your bunch were spilling *their* blood. Anyway, my brothers are all *American*, and you clowns have spilled way too much American blood."

It seemed strange to the Raptors that jihadis trained to be aggressively suicidal on the offensive had panicked when on the defensive. Five jihadis died while hiding under beds.

The wings took about two minutes to finish, and Raptors converged back at the base of the *U*. None of the jihadis in the house had night-vision equipment, and most had been unable to find their weapons in the darkness.

Here at the base of the *U* was the spiral staircase leading to the basement of the villa. Ray Couper dropped an M59 concussion grenade down the stairs, and there was a scream from the bottom as someone had his eardrums blown out.

Jack Rodgers carefully led the descent into the basement, stepping across two deafened jihadis who he shot as they writhed in pain from the concussion grenade. Jack was moving quickly, with the assumption that there was an escape tunnel somewhere and that a long chase through the surrounding woods lay ahead.

The appearance of the doors and woodwork upstairs had fit the period in which it had been installed—an uneasy juxtaposition of ornate Victorian and 1950s modern.

The basement was all business. The hallway had a cement floor and the doors that faced it were steel, with heavy industrial handles and locks. It reminded Jack of the bunkers in Iraq that Saddam Hussein had built for himself.

There were four doors in the hallway. Only one was open. Jack tossed an M59 through the door, and followed with a burst of 7.62-mm gunfire. There were no sounds of screams, so Jack and Jason entered cautiously.

"Holy shit, look at this," Jason said with disbelief. They were in a large improvised television studio. There was a camera on a tripod, studio lighting, racks of equipment, masses of cables, and a half dozen folding chairs. The grenade had pulverized a couple of the chairs and a large tripod, but most of the gear still stood as the technicians had left it.

Jack quickly searched the perimeter for any exit doors and kicked over a large rug on the floor looking for a trapdoor. Nothing. This room, with its concrete walls, was only and exactly as it appeared—a television studio.

"We'll have to give this a further look later," Jack said as they exited the room. Back in the hallway, Ray Couper had been keeping watch on the three remaining doors. He shook his head. He had heard nothing stirring behind any of them.

One by one, they blasted the three doors off their hinges. Upstairs, they had found messy workrooms and bedrooms that were far more comfortable than one would expect for terrorists that most people imagined living in caves.

Down here, each room was configured for a special-
ized purpose. Behind door number one was a large
room with chains hanging from the ceilings and walls,
clumps of clothing scattered about on the floor, and
large, dark stains that the Raptors could identify even in
the monochromatic world of their night-vision goggles.
There was no doubt about what happened in this room.

Door number two revealed a room that surprised the
Raptors even more than had the television studio. The
well-stocked wine cellar showed signs of having been
used recently. It was certainly not what one would expect from extremists whose religion considered the use
of alcoholic beverages to be a most grievous sin.

Behind door number three was the largest surprise of
all. A man was cowering in one corner with his palms
outstretched. He begged them in English not to shoot.
Jack was ready to ignore the plea, but he recognized this
man from somewhere.

November 19
9:36 P.M. Ankara Time

OVERHEAD, Greg Boyinson made his single pass
across the compound and began orbiting it at about
100 feet. He kept an eye on things, and communicated
with Brad Townsend through his AN/PRC-148 multiband
intrateam radio. As he stood guard at the intersection of
the two wings of the building, Brad gave both Greg and
Will the play-by-play of what was going on inside.

Out of the corner of his eye, Greg noticed something
moving on the road leading to the compound.

"There's an incoming truck about a quarter mile out," Greg reported. "I'm going to take a look."

The medium-sized Mercedes delivery truck had slowed down and cut off its headlights, but was continuing to approach the gate, where a small brush fire started by the M84 grenade still burned.

Greg sized up his target with his night-vision gear, put it in his sights, and cut loose with a Hellfire.

As the fireball engulfed the truck, he began surveying the road for other vehicles. After about two miles of seeing nothing, he banked hard and returned to his orbit above the compound. He noticed that the lights had been turned back on, and Brad told him that they'd be wrapping up pretty soon.

November 19
8:36 P.M. Central European Time

THE weather had grown cold and blustery in Paris. Rain was expected overnight, but it had yet to materialize. Muhammad Bin Qasim made his way along the Rue de Varenne, past the Rodin Museum and toward the Boulevard Raspail. It was a quiet street, but very upscale. The Italian Embassy was up ahead on the right, and the shops and galleries catered to those for whom price was no object. Bin Qasim wore a hat and had turned his collar up, as much to hide his face as to shelter himself from the cold. He fancied himself a recognizable public figure, but in reality, few people who had seen his face in televised news reports from the United Nations would remember the world body's Interna-

tional Validation Organization chief well enough to recognize him on this dark sidewalk.

He pressed the buzzer next to a heavy glass door and
waited patiently. Except for the absence of a sign or any
other sort of lettering, the entryway could have been
that of any number of the exclusive emporia that lined
Rue de Varenne.

At last, there was a short *ping*. The door hissed
slightly and popped ajar. Bin Qasim stepped inside. The
air was a perfect twenty degrees Celsius and smelled
vaguely of richly polished wood. The mauve carpet was
sumptuous and comfortable. A Chopin *Andante* could
be heard faintly in the background. A number of small
and precious impressionist watercolors hung on the
wall, each with its own small, low-wattage picture light.

"Bonsoir Monsieur Bin Qasim." A slender woman in
a Cardin suit emerged from a back room, graciously
greeting her customer as though he was a friend being
welcomed to her home. It was well past normal hours
for a gallery here on the Rive Gauche, but, as with a private salon, guests were friends and friends were always
welcome. The trade here at Gallerie l'Aiglon was by ap-
pointment only, and appointments could be arranged
whenever the exclusive clientele wished.

Adrienne Delacroix took Bin Qasim's coat and es-
corted him into a private viewing room, where he was
offered a cognac and told to make himself comfortable.

Tonight, he would be seeing several things from a
"private collection." There were two small Renoirs and
a Degas that had disappeared during the Nazi occupa-
tion of Paris. The Degas had hung on the wall of a
château overlooking Lake Geneva for decades, and now

it was being offered for sale by the estate of the man who had enjoyed its forbidden beauty for those many years.

This was the painting of which Bin Qasim had dreamed the night before. It had been described to him, but because of the seller's desire for privacy, it had not been possible for Gallerie l'Aiglon to e-mail a jpeg of it to him.

It was all that he had imagined. The hues were the colors of a sunset over the Gulf. He loved it. He had to have it.

Bin Qasim had also asked to be shown a selection of erotic etchings by an artist of the postwar Vienna School. He was buying a little gift for a friend in New York who collected erotica. Patronage had its price, but it also had its rewards.

November 19
9:39 P.M. Ankara Time

ANNE McCaine entered the foyer of the big villa shortly after the lights came on. Bodies and broken furniture were strewn in vast pools of blood. Even after what she had seen over the last few days, it was staggering to see so much carnage in the context of what had been a large and luxuriant living room. However, her first impression of the room was quickly pacified by the knowledge that these were the men who had planned, or at least celebrated, the murder of her husband. An eye had been exacted for an eye.

She walked slowly through the room, realizing that

she was looking at would-be martyrs who had hoped to bravely sacrifice their lives to destroy school buses and fourth graders on Indiana rural routes. They had never gotten that chance. Instead, they had died in the company of their comrades many thousands of miles from Hoosier cornfields.

Anne thought that it looked as though an angry monster had torn the place apart, but she knew that the angry monster was the man who had *lived* here.

Angry too was Dave Brannan as he came down the stairs from inspecting the two bodies that had met their martyrdom in the tower and in the sights of Will Casey's elephant gun.

"No sign of that bastard," he said. "I checked all the bodies on both sides and the two in the tower. I don't know which of the two heads up there in the tower goes with which body, but neither of 'em belong to Zahir."

"He's not out there either." Brad Townsend had returned from restoring the electrical power, and having taken digital photographs of each of the martyred jihadis in the courtyard.

"He's not downstairs, but look what we *did* find."

Jack Rodgers had emerged from the spiral staircase into the basement, pushing a dishevelled, shirtless man with his hands bound tightly behind his back.

Anne recognized the man from somewhere.

It dawned on her. The Olympic Airways airplane. She remembered the television pictures of this man. It was Muhammad Al-Abir. He had led that gang of hijackers who pushed all those women out the back door of the jetliner as it sat on the runway in Algiers—because they were Westerners not wearing veils. For not subscribing to his brand of religious law, they suffered a two-story fall to the concrete below. Anne had felt most sorry for the ones who *didn't* die in the fall, but who lay in pain for nine hours in the 100-degree heat, enduring a slow and excruciating death.

The Muhammad Al-Abir who stood on the thick, bloodstained Persian carpet in the Black Sea villa was a far cry from the defiant Muhammad Al-Abir of Algiers. The man in front of her had the expression of a trapped weasel. His watery eyes caught sight of Anne, with her tight fitting T-shirt, her unshrouded head, and her bare neck.

"I recall that you don't like looking at women's faces," she said, walking toward him. "I guess you've finally got yourself in a situation where you can't order us to put our heads in sacks."

Al-Abir tried to look away. He abhorred the sight of a woman's face, and Anne could see that. He had seen her face, her dark grey eyes, and her long slender *neck*. He had seen the contours of her breasts beneath her shirt and the hint of nipples beneath the fabric. He had seen her narrow waist and the curve of her hips. No man should have to look at such a thing. It was horrible.

"You are a blasphemer!" he snarled. "It is a sacrilege that you appear in the company of men without the hijab, without the burka!"

"Times have changed, asshole," Anne said calmly. "Welcome to the twenty-first century. Women don't have to take that sort of crap from homicidal maniacs like you anymore."

His head was spinning. No woman had ever dared to speak to Muhammad Al-Abir like that. She had to die.

He lunged at her. She slapped his face as Jack Rodgers jerked him back. Even Jack was startled by the force of the impact.

The sting of her slap caught Al-Abir off guard. The powerful bull of a man was no match for the Raptor who restrained him, but he suddenly realized that neither was he a match for the strength of will that was so tightly coiled within this small woman who had just struck him.

His mind could not grasp such a thing. No woman had ever struck him. None had dared. He saw her face staring at him with disgust, the way one would stare at a maggot, the way that Muhammad Al-Abir would stare at a woman. He felt his body in convulsion. He felt his bladder explode, and he felt the warm and humiliating wetness streaming down his pant leg.

November 19
9:11 P.M. Central European Time

MUHAMMAD Bin Qasim reverently placed the bottle of Moët & Chandon in his refrigerator. Tomorrow it would be there for him as he welcomed the Degas into his life. He smiled, poured a splash of Cartais-Lamaure cognac to warm him against the coolness of the evening, and stepped outside to the balcony overlooking Quai Louis Blériot and the Seine. From here, he could see the lights of the Eiffel Tower, which was just across the river and a bit to the north. There were a few raindrops in the air, and a storm was blowing in, but Bin Qasim felt so cozy here in his comfortable

Sixteenth Arrondisement apartment. He and Baudouin Abuja Mboma shared a fondness for the finer things in life. They both loved the excitement of New York City, even though they hated the culture that had created it. But for both, the City of Lights was without equal. This was the true crossroads of world culture.

Bin Qasim removed two of his extensive collection of Persian miniatures from above his silk brocade sofa and smiled at the empty space. Tomorrow at this time, his Degas would occupy this honored place. The Moët & Chandon would be opened. As he stepped backward to marvel at it, he spilled a bit of cognac on his eighteenth-century Persian prayer rug. He dabbed at it with his monogrammed silk handkerchief and decided to check his e-mails before it got too late. His office in New York City might have something for him. He could take care of this, slip into his bath, and go to bed early.

The messages were mostly either routine or junk, but the last one to load made him hold his breath. It was from the man whose screen name was "chevelnoir." He had not had a message from chevelnoir for nearly a year. He was coming to Paris and needed Bin Qasim's help. How could chevelnoir know that he was in Paris?

This was unexpected. This was distressing. The timing could not be worse. Or could it?

November 19
10:11 P.M. Ankara Time

"**A** little light reading?" Dave Brannan said, noticing that Anne McCaine was thumbing through a leather-bound volume with glossy photographs of what appeared to be small sculptures.

The Little Bird was on the ground, and the Raptors were preparing for exfil. Had it not been for Robert Pauwel, who recalled seeing a large tank of commercial-grade kerosene at the safe house in the canyon where they had been yesterday, Boyinson would have had to make two round trips to Dodge City in order to get enough fuel to lift everyone out. This would have taken all night, and it would have more than doubled the danger to the team. Thankfully, the Allison 250 engine that powered the Little Bird was a very robust piece of equipment.

"See this," Anne said, pointing to one of the photographs. "It's a Hittite bronze sculpture of a Zebu Bull. Something like that would date from between 2000 B.C. and 1000 B.C. See the background in the picture."

"Uh-huh." Dave nodded impatiently.

"See that wall over there," Anne said, pointing across the room. There was no doubt that the small bronze statue had been photographed against the wall to which Anne pointed.

"It's not there now," Dave said impatiently. "Probably got moved. It could've gotten knocked over when we busted in here. We weren't exactly watching out for the knickknack shelves."

"It's not a knickknack," Anne corrected him.

"I'm sorry," Dave said, feigning contrition.

"It's actually quite a valuable piece of art. So are all of the other pieces in this book," she said, flipping through the pages. "What they all have in common is that they were photographed here in these rooms, and they aren't here now."

"So, somebody stole them?"

"I don't think so," Anne said thoughtfully. "Remember when I said that a serious collector lived here? I think that he's on a selling trip. I think . . . I'm sure . . . that when you find the objects in this book, you'll find Fahrid Al-Zahir. And *I* can help you find the objects in this book!"

FOURTEEN

"**H**E'S *back!*" Steve Faralaco, the president's chief of staff said as he burst into Thomas Livingstone's office.

The president was trying to work his way through some briefing materials that were related to the Forest Service appropriations. The speaker of the House had suggested a compromise that would get it through, and Livingstone had said that he wanted to take another look before it went to the floor. In the scheme of things, it was inconsequential, but it kept his mind off the terrible external dangers faced by the nation.

"Who's back?" Livingstone was startled by the sudden interruption. He had thought that Faralaco was better trained than to just burst in.

"Mr. President. It's Badr. He's on television right now."

Livingstone hurried into the room where the staff was clustered around a large-screen television. Seeing him enter the room, one of the secretaries picked up the TiVo remote and rewound to the place where a commentator in an Atlanta control room introduced the dreadful quality recording as having just been picked up from an Arab news channel in the Middle East.

"To our deepest regret, Mujahidin Al-Akhbar has refused to listen to the people calling upon them to reject the ridiculous and dim-witted Fahrid Al-Zahir."

The English text crawled rapidly across the bottom of the screen as the man with the long beard with the distinctive grey patch, dressed in a black kaftan with embroidery near the collar and a grey skullcap, spoke.

"The matter of Fahrid Al-Zahir worsens as previous wrongdoings were followed by mischiefs of greater magnitudes. It is no longer possible to be quiet. It is essential to hit Mujahidin Al-Akhbar, which has become corrupted as the enemy of the righteous people. I cannot give a blind eye to this affair."

As he droned on and on, without saying much of anything substantive, Livingstone and the others in the room found themselves watching the images on the tape, rather than reading the words of translation. It was fascinating. In the past, terrorist leaders sat in front of banners or other drapery, or they used a fixed background. Badr moved about in a recognizable room, with recognizable furniture. Now he was pointing angrily to objects on the floor of the room.

"Look at that!" Steve Faralaco gasped.

"It's a body!" shrieked one of the secretaries.

"It's two, no three, bodies," the president corrected grimly.

The camera moved through the room, zeroing in on body after body, showing close-ups of faces, most with bullet holes in them. There were nearly a dozen bodies. When the camera returned to Badr, he was explaining that these were Mujahidin Al-Akhbar jihadis who had died a coward's death in a luxurious palace dripping with Western pleasures.

Everyone watching in the White House could see that the rooms through which Badr walked were indeed more than comfortable, or had been before the blood-bath took place within them. There was even a fifty-inch plasma screen television on one wall.

The picture changed, and they saw Badr seated on a sofa with another man, a balding man in a black cloak, a huge man with an aquiline nose, black beard, and fierce, piercing eyes. Badr pledged solidarity with the man, shaking his fist and angrily denouncing Mujahidin Al-Akhbar and Fahrid Al-Zahir. The other man just sat and stared angrily at the camera.

"Who did he say that was?" Faralaco asked.

"It's Muhammad Al-Abir," the president said through clenched teeth.

"*The* Muhammad Al-Abir?" If Faralaco seemed horrified, it was for good cause. "The one who killed all those women in Algiers?"

Thomas Livingstone just nodded. He felt like he was going to be sick.

November 20
7:36 P.M. Ankara Time

FAHRID Al-Zahir was speechless. He had watched the latest Badr tape on Al-Jazeera while cooling his heels in a modest Istanbul apartment. It was the most horrible nightmare he could imagine. He was filled with boundless fury.

The evil bastard was in Al-Zahir's own home. He flaunted the fact by strutting through his rooms. There could be no doubt. Badr had defiled his safest of safe houses. It was guarded by his bravest and most loyal, and he had slaughtered them. Now he was rubbing his camera in their faces. Badr must have two hundred men, possibly more. And Al-Abir. That devious sodomite Al-Abir had betrayed him. *Both of them must die!*

Al-Zahir raged, his mind flooded with outrage. He felt like he was going to be sick. He trained his 9-mm automatic on the small television sitting on the low cedar table and emptied the clip.

November 20
9:36 A.M. Pacific Time

ROD Llewellan was going through the motions. It would not have been necessary for he and Erik Vasquez to travel all the way to Seattle to search for Bobby Loreau's Ford Taurus. They could have just e-mailed the license and registration to the Washington State Patrol. He knew that it was pointless, but he was killing time, keeping the FBI, his own agency, as far from Jack Rodgers's trail as possible.

"Where do you suppose he is?" Vasquez asked rhetorically as they drove north on Interstate 5 from their meeting at patrol headquarters in Olympia. "Do you suppose they'll find the car?"

"Rodgers would have put it in a place where the sun doesn't shine, and probably in a place far from Seattle," Llewellan replied. This was true. Rodgers would not have left the car in plain sight anywhere.

"A place where the sun doesn't shine? That would *include* Seattle." Vasquez laughed, nodding to the windshield wipers sloshing their way through the Pacific Northwest rainstorm that was turning the interstate into a river.

Llewellan's cell phone rang. To his surprise, their inquiry at the Washington State Patrol had already turned up a hit. Someone at the Seattle Division of the King County Jail had a picture from a surveillance tape of a man matching Jack Rodgers's photo.

November 20
9:12 P.M. Central European Time

BIN Qasim strolled along the Quai Saint-Bernard, with the Seine on his left and the facade of the Gare d'Austerlitz visible ahead. He wore his hat, and his collar was turned against the storm. The rain had let up for the moment, but the wind was brutal. Certainly few people would have recognized him here this evening—even if he had been the recognizable public figure that he imagined himself. On the other hand, no one would recognize the man whom Bin Qasim was meeting tonight, the man whose e-mail address was "chevelnoir."

Just as Bin Qasim cut a dashing figure on the world stage—or imagined himself this way—the man called chevelnoir inhabited the shadows. He was an Egyptian educator—or was he a Lebanese doctor? Whatever he was professionally, chevelnoir had been a useful connection for Bin Qasim and vice versa. Based in Dubai— or was it Bahrain?—chevelnoir was well connected in the world of Middle Eastern and Southwest Asian art and antiquities.

He had brokered a sizable proportion of the blasphemous art that the Taliban had claimed to have destroyed in Afghanistan. One year, he proudly boasted that he made more money for the Taliban than they had netted in the opium trade.

"Bonsoir mon ami." The voice materialized out of nowhere, startling Muhammad Bin Qasim.

"Good evening my old friend," Bin Qasim replied in Arabic, kissing chevelnoir on both cheeks. "How did you know I was in France?"

"A public figure such as yourself has a high profile. When I heard you were coming, it was most auspicious timing. I have a matter with which you might be able to help me."

"What is it?" Bin Qasim asked. "How can I be of assistance?"

"I have a client. An old friend known to us both. He has a substantial collection that he wishes to move at top price. I was hoping that you might ask l'Aiglon to arrange a private showing for their select clients. I know that their mailing list is extensive."

"What sorts of things is your, our, old friend making available?"

"Hittite pieces. Mainly small sculptures, works in terra-cotta, bronze and so forth. Some very nice pieces, dating mainly between 2500 and 1500 B.C. There are nearly a hundred."

Often, chevelnoir had deals that were simply too good to be true.

Bin Qasim liked dealing with Gallerie l'Aiglon. He enjoyed the security of knowing that everything was fully documented, regardless of the cost of the documentation. He also, frankly, liked being pampered. Tonight he had been given an opportunity to return the favor.

November 20
11:12 A.M. Pacific Time

"**N**O, he was not an inmate," said the heavyset woman in the crisply starched uniform shirt at the Seattle Division of the King County Jail. "No, he was here to bail out an inmate. Saw that picture on that alert this morning and the old alarm bells went off. Old Marilu has got a mind for faces, and that picture set the alarm bells to ringin'. I matched it to the surveillance tapes from that day."

"Which day?" Rod Llewellan asked.

"November 10 at 9:14 in the morning," Marilu said proudly, handing a printout to the two FBI agents.

"Do you have his name?"

"Sure do," Marilu said with a smile. "Right here in the book. His name was Charles W. Fairbanks. Showed an Indiana driver's license. He was with another fella, a Hiram Johnson from California."

"Great, let's run these guys through the FBI database," Erik Vasquez said eagerly.

"Don't bother," Llewellan said, shaking his head. "Charles Fairbanks and Hiram Johnson are the two guys who ran for vice president with Teddy Roosevelt. I can pretty much guarantee that they weren't in the King County jailhouse on November 10."

Marilu had an uncanny knack for remembering faces. The images on the surveillance tape printouts were virtually indecipherable. However, she had *no* knack for intuiting aliases.

"Do you have a copy of the check they used when they bailed their guy out?"

"Paid cash."

"Cash?"

"Listen, we got more that 1,500 inmates in this house. On a good day nearly half are comin' and goin'. Cash is almost the same as money down here."

"Who was the guy they bailed out?" Llewellan asked. "Don't tell me it was William Jennings Bryan with a Nebraska ID."

"Lessee here," Marilu said, not recognizing the illustrious statesman who headed the opposition ticket the year that Roosevelt himself became vice president. "Bryan, Bryan, Bryan. Nope, but close. It's a *B* all right. Boyinson. Gregory Boyinson. Mr. Boyinson was in for assault. He beat up a guy in a bar. Said he insulted the flag. Beat him half to death. In the end, the other gentleman chose not to press charges."

"Good choice," Vasquez said as an aside.

Llewellan could see now how Colonel Brannan had assembled the Raptor team. It was like a buccaneer crewing a pirate ship—he had emptied the jails of criminals and sociopaths.

FIFTEEN

November 21
11:33 A.M. Eastern Time

"**B**UCK, do *you* know what they're doing out there?" President Tom Livingstone was meeting his confidant on the fly again. This time in an underground passageway at the Pentagon. Peighton maintained a "Secret" clearance. Unlike "Top Secret" or higher classifications, it didn't give him access to every nook and cranny in the five-sided symbol of American military might, but it got him into places where prying eyes were few.

"You know I can't tell you the details," General Buckley Peighton reminded his old friend. "Your own ground rules."

"Okay, Buck. I didn't ask you *what* is going on with my American Volunteer Group, I just asked whether *you* know."

There was a long pause, and finally the chagrinned former general admitted, "Not exactly. It's also on a need-to-know basis."

"I think I really need to know," Livingstone said, almost pleading. "I don't know what the hell your guys are doing, but meanwhile this terrorist thing is mushrooming all over the place. First, this guy Badr suddenly showed up. He materialized out of nowhere. Nobody had heard more than a word or two about him, and suddenly he's competing with Fahrid Al-Zahir for terrorist of the year."

"Maybe things are not what they seem?" Peighton suggested.

"Muhammad Al-Abir sure as hell seems to be what he seems," Livingstone said angrily. "The whole world freaked out when they aired this tape from inside a big house somewhere and he's sitting on the sofa with Muhammad Al-Abir! This is horrifying."

"I couldn't agree more about the seriousness of Al-Abir being mixed up in this," Peighton admitted.

"As far as I can see, your guys have just vanished. What are they doing?"

"They stopped the Downers Grove attack," Peighton reminded Livingstone. "That would've been terrible. That would've been the third major assault on this country in just ten days. There have been none since. That has to mean something."

"I don't know *what* it means," the president said sadly. "Does it mean that they're doing their job, or is this just the calm before a really terrible storm?"

"I'm sure that they're doing their job."

At least Peighton hoped they were. He had not seen

Brannan since November 12. That was the night before the raid at Rancho de los Bichos, the one for which Badr had taken credit. He had been assuming that the Raptors had something to do with Badr, but even he was deeply troubled about Al-Abir's involvement.

"I really put my neck out on this thing," Livingstone said. "I may end up having to resign if this American Volunteer Group idea backfires. Whose idea was this, anyway?"

"Yours."

"That's a rhetorical question," the president said. "How much money have we given them?"

"You authorized fifty million through the bank in the Caymans," Peighton reminded the president.

"I'll leave this in your hands, but if you're not satisfied with what they're doing in forty-eight hours, freeze the account."

November 21
5:33 P.M. Central European Time

MUHAMMAD Bin Qasim left the Gallerie l'Aiglon and walked east toward that little brasserie on Rue Sainte-Guillaume. His friends at the gallery had been very interested in the little works in terra-cotta and bronze that were offered by Bin Qasim's unnamed client.

A public show would take time. A date would have to be selected, invitations engraved, and a commemorative poster commissioned. Then, perhaps there would be the necessity of a color catalogue. When Bin Qasim replied by explaining that the client needed to move quickly, his friends at Gallerie l'Aiglon got the idea. They nodded and winked. A private showing would be much more easily arranged. Adrienne would take the small photographs that chevelnoir had left with Bin Qasim. She would scan these and e-mail a few to special private clients. They would RSVP via e-mail and that would be that. It would be like guests in the home. Very intimate.

Bin Qasim took a table near the bar and ordered a glass of Gevrey-Chambertin. The slender man with the unusually thick glasses at the next table was drinking coffee and reading a fresh copy of *France Soir*.

"Have the games begun?" Bin Qasim asked in French as he sipped his wine.

"*Mais oui.* They are en route to Canada as I speak."

"Canada? What is in Canada?"

"I cannot say." The man shrugged, folding his paper and standing up to leave. "I've said too much already."

Muhammad Bin Qasim breathed easily and savored the musky aroma of his deep red beverage. It didn't matter what was in Canada or where it was in Canada. His plan was in motion. The French would deal with Khaleq Badr quickly and efficiently. And *quietly* too, he hoped.

November 21
11:33 A.M. Eastern Time

"**THIS** gang war has taken a most ominous turn." The somber-faced Director of National Intelligence led the briefing for the special joint task force. He didn't have to tell them how serious it was that Badr had been joined by the frightening Muhammad Al-Abir, but he did. He spoke on the subject for several minutes. Maybe it was cathartic.

For Rod Llewellan, it was both horrifying and confusing. Jack Rodgers had smiled at him, and had as much as said that Badr was no threat. Perhaps this was the case. Badr was an unknown. He had appeared out of nowhere. Nobody had much information on him. Al-Abir was another matter entirely. His angry face was one of the most recognized and most feared in the world. How could Badr *not* be a threat if he had joined forces with Al-Abir? What in the world were the Raptors doing?

"Do we have any idea where the thing was filmed?" someone asked.

"We are analyzing the architectural detail," one of the analysts spoke up. "It's hard, because the picture quality is terrible. It's almost certainly nineteenth century, and it's almost certainly in Europe or the Middle East. The detail on the door casings might be late-nineteenth-century Ottoman."

"That could mean a lot of things," another agent said, exasperation showing in her voice. "Egypt. Syria. Lebanon. Iraq. Even Turkey."

"Do we know who any of these people are?"

Llewellan sat numbly, listening to bits and pieces of the exchange. He did not want to entertain thoughts that the whole Raptor affair had devolved into a walk on the dark side. What if Peighton and the Raptors were part of some complicated and evil double cross? Llewellan

did not want to think that he had been duped—at least
not yet.

November 21
6:33 P.M. Ankara Time

"**S**EE this? Just click here and type in those fourteen
letters that we got on that other site." The overweight graduate student was explaining the nuances of
his handheld satellite download device to the veteran
Special Forces operative.

As Robert Pauwel instructed, Jack Rodgers carefully
typed the numbers, and suddenly the screen blossomed.
Jack was feeling his age. This fat kid who inhabited the
imaginary world of video games had just helped him
hack into a direct download of KH-12 satellite imagery,
bypassing the National Reconnaissance Office center. Of
course, without a great deal of proprietary information
known only to the Raptors, Robert could not have gotten
close, but with that, the big guy easily navigated the cor-
ridors of cyberspace to put a series of images on Jack's
laptop that should have never been viewed on a hill overlooking an apricot warehouse in the middle of Turkey.

It was cold, but clear, and it was quiet up here away
from the hive of activity at Dodge City. Fahrid Al-Zahir
had slipped the noose at the Black Sea villa, but he was
on the run. Western governments still dreaded this man
in the way that they had once dreaded Osama Bin
Laden, but the back-channel chatter painted a picture of
a man on the edge. It was Khaleq Badr who had made
him that way.

Badr had succeeded beyond what anyone had imagined. A spur-of-the-moment idea by Dave Brannan at Rancho de los Bichos had given Jason "Call Me Badr" Houn the theatrical role of a lifetime.

Frankly, Jack had thought Jason was a bit over the top when they were taping at the Black Sea villa. He was an irrepressible ham in real life, and he had played his role to the hilt back there before they torched the place. At one point, Jack thought he could hear himself snicker off camera as Jason strutted through the big house ranting and raving. The point was to show off the place for Al-Zahir's benefit, and that had been accomplished. Al-Zahir had now seen *two* of his safe houses penetrated, not by the United States armed forces, but by the renegade Badr.

Now Al-Zahir was on the run, and the Raptors were trying to figure out where he would go to rest and regroup for his next round of mass homicides of soccer moms and Little League players.

The information that the Raptors had received from Rod Llewellan had gotten them to Turkey, and they'd found out a great deal at the two Turkish safe houses. Now they needed the equivalent of a Refresh button.

They could send somebody back to the United States to contact Llewellan again, but that would break Dave Brannan's "moving parts" rule. The more moving parts, he believed, the exponentially greater chance of something going wrong. Thanks to Robert, they didn't have to make a transatlantic round-trip.

Jack instinctively looked up at the stars that were starting to appear in the gathering dusk. Somewhere up there, a satellite the size of a Greyhound bus was looking back and watching the highways and byways of the Middle East. The big Keyholes were keeping tabs on terrorists that the United States could see, but could not touch. The United States lay imprisoned by the need for an International Validation to strike them, while they operated with impunity. Meanwhile, there was no need for Mujahidin Al-Akhbar or Al-Qaeda to procure an International Validation in order to cross borders to do their mischief.

Jack smiled. The Raptors didn't need an International Validation either.

SIXTEEN

November 22
9:29 A.M. Eastern Time

"**R**OD, I took the liberty of pulling the file on this Boyinson character that Rodgers is mixed up with." Erik Vasquez handed the bulging folder across the steel government-issue desk at FBI headquarters. Between the flight back from the Northwest and the round of briefings with the director of National Intelligence, Rod Llewellan had forgotten about Erik's introduction to Greg Boyinson's reputation as a marauding miscreant.

"No wonder this man was in the King County lockup. His military service record runs the gamut from drunk and disorderly to incredible heroism. He's a *schitzo!*"

Llewellan leafed through the file. A page documenting a horrific barroom brawl was filed next to his two

Silver Star citations, and he had even been written up
for a Medal of Honor that was never awarded. His skill
as a pilot seemed uncanny. Apparently one of his most
memorable street fights occurred in Bosnia. He saved a
platoon of British SAS commandos by flying back and
forth through city streets just a few feet off the ground.
With his rotor tips nicking the bricks of buildings adjacent to the streets, he shot up an entire Serbian battalion
and destroyed seven T-55 tanks.

Rod hadn't spoken to Peighton since he briefed Jack
Rodgers in Winchester on November 15. He had met
Boyinson only one time, and hadn't really gotten to
know him. Llewellan was indeed the man who knew too
much who was coming to realize that he knew so little.
He was starting to think again about being tried for trea-
son.

He had assumed that the Raptors were headed over-
seas, proabably to Turkey, but he wasn't completely
sure. The bloodbath on Badr's tape might have been the
work of the Raptors, but how did Al-Abir figure into
this?

Llewellan stared at the photograph of the wild-eyed
Greg Boyinson in the personnel file. What if Vasquez
was right? Never mind, he *was* right. Boyinson really
was a *schitzo*! He was certainly capable of wildly erratic
behavior. Rod Llewellan had lived and worked in a disciplined environment all his life. He couldn't fathom
what it was about brain chemistry that created a man
like Boyinson.

Rod stood up. He had to get out and make a call.
Halfway to the elevator, he caught himself and went
back to put the Boyinson file in a locked drawer. There

was no way that he wanted to have that file floating around.

Outside, he strolled up Tenth Street for a couple of blocks, bought a Diet Pepsi, and stepped into a phone booth in the lobby of the IRS Building.

"It's Rod," he said when the man answered the phone.

"Glad you called," the voice replied. "I'm in town. Meet me."

November 22
3:29 P.M. Central European Time

"**I** certainly believe that this showing will be of interest to Herr Stabl." Adrienne Delacroix typed the e-mail message quickly and efficiently. She had more than three dozen e-mails to get out today, but she was personalizing a few for potential clients who she thought would be *especially* anxious to know about the Gallerie l'Aiglon show that was now scheduled for November 25.

Hermann Stabl was a wealthy German industrialist with a weakness for Near Eastern antiquities. His home near Freising was said to contain an extensive collection of museum-quality Hittite sculptures.

Adrienne had just met Fiona Richardson, Stabl's Cambridge-educated personal curator. They had crossed paths online during another auction for a small number of pieces being sold in Milan. Adrienne had been doing some online research on Hittite bronzes, and Fiona had proven to be very helpful. She was extremely knowledgeable on the subject, and Adrienne told Fiona that she looked forward to meeting her and Herr Stabl should they choose to attend the showing at Gallerie l'Aiglon on November 25.

November 22
5:47 P.M. Eastern Time

BERT'S Crab House was a noisy no-nonsense place just off the Old Richmond Highway south of Alexandria. Those not interested in digging through a plastic bucket and eating soft-shelled crab with their bare hands had plenty of other choices of a place to dine out. It was still early, but the spot was starting to fill up with its usual boisterous clientele.

General Buckley Peighton was sitting by himself and enjoying a glass of beer when Rod Llewellan came in. Soon they had spilled the contents of their first bucket across the kraft-paper tablecloth and were tearing the succulent crustaceans limb from limb.

They had quickly established that they both shared a feeling of being out of the loop with what was going on with the Raptors.

"The tape had to be them," Peighton said. "The timing was right. It would've been Turkey. That's where they went."

"What about you-know-who being on that tape?" Llewellan said, making reference to Muhammad Al-Abir.

"That's sure bothering the hell out of Tom!" Peighton said, making reference to Thomas Livingstone.

"It's sure bothering the hell out of *everybody* down where I work," Llewellan said, making reference to the National Intelligence establishment. "Not to mention the media. You can't pick up a paper without seeing it."

"Frankly, it bothered me too," Peighton said, taking another sip of Foggy Bottom lager. "Then I got to thinking."

"Thinking about what?"

"Ask yourself. Your bosses and the big boss and everybody is all freaked out about these guys. Okay, so ask yourself, who in the world is probably the *most* freaked out of anybody?"

Llewellan thought for a moment, but before he could answer, Peighton mouthed the word "Fahrid."

"As I told Tom, I don't know what they're doing," Peighton continued. "And I guess I really don't *want* to know. I have never been a micro-manager. Delegate to somebody you trust who knows what the hell they're doing and let them do their job. That's always worked for me. Figure it still does."

"So you think this is all for *his* benefit?" Llewellan said, making reference to Fahrid Al-Zahir.

"Step away past arm's length and look at it. What would upset him worse?" Peighton smiled. "I'll bet you dollars to doughnuts that the house in those pictures was *his* house."

"Still lots of unanswered questions," Llewellan said cautiously. "You know that my office has been investigating Rodgers."

"I did not know that. What for?"

"To track him down. He was on the flight. Somebody connected him to the Chicago thing. Thought it was him who killed that guy in the hospital. Traced a rental car to Seattle. Did you know that him and somebody else . . . probably Brannan . . . bailed Boyinson out of *jail* up there?"

"Greg's a real sunuvabitch." Peighton smiled, shaking his head.

"Sunuvabitch on an *assault* charge up there," Llewellan added. "You know what this looks like? It's looking like a real bunch of wild men on the loose somewhere, and terrorists sprouting up like mushrooms."

"Who would you rather have doing this?" Peighton asked. "You need somebody arrested, you send a trained law enforcement professional . . . such as yourself. You want somebody killed, you send a *killer*."

"Well, killers were certainly doing their thing at that place on the tape," Rod said, shaking his head. "It was a bloody mess."

"We're up against bastards that are fighting dirty, really dirty." Peighton shrugged. "Dontcha think it's time for the 'wild bunch' to be fighting dirty *back*?"

Suddenly the general's cell phone rang.

"Hey Buddy, what's up?" Peighton asked. "Oh yeah. Um-hmm. Nope. Yep. See ya."

"Good news?" Llewellan asked, seeing that the older man had a pleasant look on his face.

"Possibly. That was the airline."

"When are you flying back?"

"Oh no. Not *my* airline. No, that was another airline. They'll be on the move soon. Not sure where."

"Who's on the move?" Llewellan asked.

"It's your 'wild bunch.' " Peighton grinned. "Your bunch of wild men is on the loose."

November 23
12:47 A.M. Ankara Time

FIONA Richardson logged on to check her e-mails. There were nearly a dozen from galleries and collectors as far afield as Japan. Several had sent beautiful thumbnails of pieces that would make wonderful additions to Herr Stabl's collection.

She clicked on the one originating at Gallerie l'Aiglon in Paris. There was a nice note from Adrienne Delacroix mentioning an upcoming private showing. Would Herr Stabl like to attend?

There was an attachment. Fiona opened it, and a short series of jpegs spilled across her screen. It sent chills down Fiona's spine. It had happened the way that she had hoped, but it had happened so much faster than she had expected. Every one of the images was familiar. Indeed, they were copies of the same pictures that Fiona had in the binder that lay on her desk. She picked up the binder and simply shook her head.

The desk at which Fiona Richardson worked was not in the comfortable Bavarian *schloss* that Adrienne had imagined when she sent the e-mail. Such is the deceptive world of Internet communications. Things are not as they seem. Fiona's desk was actually an apricot crate in a barn, not in Bavaria, but at a place called Dodge City in the Anatolian backwoods of Turkey. Fiona, of course, was not Fiona.

She stood up and walked across the dirt floor to where Dave Brannan was cleaning his Heckler & Koch.

"Sprechen sie Deutsche?"

"Ja," he answered, trying to figure out why Anne

McCaine would ask him whether he spoke German. *"Einige worter, aber warum?"*

"Wir gehen zu einer partei." Anne smiled, proud of the fact that her hours at the laptop under the assumed identity of a rich guy's personal assistant had finally hit pay dirt. They were going to a party.

SEVENTEEN

November 23
3:16 P.M. Central European Time

FAHRID Al-Zahir was exhausted. He had been on the road for three days, travelling across Europe in a series of vehicles owned by friends and followers. Getting into Bulgaria from Turkey had caused him some anxious moments, but after he had reached Hungary, he never saw another border guard. Bless the Europeans and their trusting openness. Last night, in a small room at a safe house in Bobigny, a working-class suburb of Paris, he had gotten his first good night's sleep since he left his Black Sea villa on the morning of November 19.

This morning, as he drank coffee with the men at this house, he found himself wondering who he could trust. Who remained loyal to Mujahidin Al-Akhbar, and who now held in his heart an allegiance to Khaleq Badr and Ikhwan Al-Jihad?

As the fully draped women came and went, refilling coffee cups and offering breads and sweets, Al-Zahir studied the faces of the men. Each was an unquestionably zealous jihadi with the fire of hatred for America and all things Western in his eyes.

Each and every one of them expressed the will and the desire to kill Americans whenever and wherever they could. They swore an allegiance to Mujahidin Al-Akhbar, but they could just as easily have sworn an allegiance to Al-Qaeda or Ikhwan Al-Jihad. They were all part of that ambiguous generation whose only true allegiance was to killing, and to thoughts of the swarms of virgins that awaited them in heaven. Gang leaders came and went, but only the "true ideals" of unlimited virgin flesh were truly immortal.

Al-Zahir had spent the morning taping a speech, a fatwa that would be released later in the day when he was sure that all of America would be awake to hear it broadcast by Al-Jazeera.

When he was finished, he exchanged his robes for the nondescript clothes of a nondescript French laborer and took the RER commuter train into Paris. He got off at the Gare de L'Est and hurried up Rue de Paradis to a nondescript building just a few doors from the posh Baccarat glassware showroom.

The kindly old Egyptian doctor whose e-mail address identified him as chevelnoir greeted Al-Zahir warmly.

"Would you care for a drink?" the older man asked.

"Thank you," Al-Zahir replied in Arabic. "I've been drinking nothing but tea and coffee for a week."

A group of packing crates lay on the floor in the small but comfortable apartment. All had been opened, and most had been resealed. The man called chevelnoir had displayed several of the small bronzes and terracotta sculptures on the table.

"You have some beautiful things here, my friend," he told Al-Zahir. "I especially like this little bronze Zebu Bull."

"It's Hittite. Bronze Age. Probably between three and four thousand years old," Al-Zahir replied. "I expect that it might net me 7,000 Euros."

"At least. I would think eight or nine would not be unreasonable."

"I hope so," Al-Zahir explained, "I have a great deal of work to do in America, and money is the key to getting my activities back on track. There has been a small setback."

"So I've heard." Chevelnoir nodded sympathetically.

November 23
9:16 A.M. Eastern Time

EILEEN Koznowski was heading home from the supermarket on North Laurel Park Drive when she noticed something suspicious. Three SUVs that seemed to be tailgating one another passed her. They moved as though they were attached. It was a good thing that it was not still snowing. They all made a quick right turn onto a residential street without signalling. That made her curious. She had an hour to kill, so she decided to follow them. It wasn't that there wasn't enough excitement for a

mother of two in Livonia, Michigan, it was just that there
was still a streak of that old Nancy Drew curiosity in
Eileen.

By the time that she made the turn, the three SUVs
were up around the next corner, and they had stopped.
Eileen drove past, looped through the cul-de-sac, and
parked where she could watch. Eight or ten men had
gotten out of the vehicles and were surrounding a small,
older ranch-style home.

It's a drug bust!

Eileen had never seen a drug bust go down before. It
was a little bit scary, but very exciting.

Oh my goodness, one of the men had a gun! Another
man was banging on the door.

Suddenly, Eileen heard police sirens. The men appeared startled. Two of them started to run. Why were
they running if they were the police? Eileen was confused.

Two police cars squealed to a stop in front of the
house. Another man started to run. A policeman ordered
him to stop, and he did. The man who had the gun had
dropped it and put up his hands. There was a great deal
of shouting, but Eileen couldn't tell exactly what they
were saying.

More police cars had arrived now, along with a
SWAT vehicle. A half dozen men dressed as what
looked like soldiers got out, and now they started banging on the door. A man with a beard who was wearing
pajamas answered the door.

By now, a crowd of onlookers had started to gather,
and the police were telling them to go away. Eileen decided that she had seen enough. She started her car and

took the long way home. There would be a lot to talk about at dinner tonight!

November 23
12:45 P.M. Eastern Time

"**F**ROM this, we can conclude that Khaleq Badr is definitely in the United States," the Director of National Intelligence announced proudly. He was trying to put a positive spin on the unfolding news from Livonia, Michigan.

Much to his chagrin, nobody in the American national security apparatus had any idea that a twelve-man strike team from the Groupement d'Intervention de la Gendarmerie Nationale (GIGN), the French National Gendarmes Intervention Group, had entered the United States. Nor did anyone under the control of the Director of National Intelligence have any idea that there was a Mujahidin Al-Akhbar sleeper cell snoozing in this Detroit suburb.

Somebody made a snide comment that the same army that surrendered to the Germans in five weeks during World War II had now surrendered to the Livonia, Michigan, Police Department in less than five *minutes*. Nevertheless, the director was angry that the whole thing had come as a surprise to his department:

"Do the local police have any idea of the source of the anonymous tip?" someone asked.

"It was male, it sounded American and the reception was very bad," replied an analyst sitting next to the Director of National Intelligence at the big table in the front of the briefing room. "It was an untraceable cell phone. We'll be analyzing the tape in detail."

"What are we getting from the French agents?" Rod Llewellan asked.

"Nothing at first," the Director of National Intelligence explained. "They claimed Diplomatic immunity. The local police were ready to go to the media with it, so they made a call to the French Embassy. The embassy called us, and we cut a deal to keep the French part quiet from the media if they told us what they know. They did. They were acting on a tip that Badr was connected to that house. I guess they were right. The house was strewn with anti-American literature and bomb-making stuff. There were three very surprised jihadis in the place. One of them tried to detonate something, but it didn't go off."

November 23
12:45 P.M. Eastern Time

"**WHAT** in the world were the GIGN doing operating in *our* country?" The president of the United States was furious. He had the French ambassador and the American secretary of state in the Oval Office. The GIGN had been created as an antiterrorist organization in the early 1970s after the incidents at the Munich Olympics and at the Saudi Arabian Embassy in Paris. It operated wherever and whenever the French government sent it.

"We had reliable information that Khaleq Badr was at that house," the ambassador replied.

"Isn't it customary for governments of civilized nations to *cooperate* in antiterrorist operations?" Livingstone scolded. "Why were we not informed that you were planning this operation?"

"I was not informed myself of this," the ambassador admitted. "It was being kept very clandestine."

"What were they thinking?"

"They hoped to execute Badr and leave quickly and quietly."

"Why is the French government suddenly so interested in Badr?" the president demanded. "You showed no interest in going after Fahrid Al-Zahir, even after Mujahidin Al-Akhbar attacked the United States on two separate occasions, killing all those innocent people."

"It has been our policy not to provoke the terrorist groups," the ambassador explained. "If they are angered, they will attack. We did not want to anger Al-Zahir. With Badr, we had information that he might attack in France, that he may wish to destroy targets in Europe. It was the reasoning of our government that he should be eliminated quickly and quietly."

"And is it the reasoning of your government that so long as you move quickly and quietly and don't make Al-Zahir mad, you will be safe from terrorist attack?" Secretary of State Edredin interjected.

"Of course."

"You are not a student of history, Monsieur Ambassador," Livingstone said angrily. "If you believe that appeasement buys you protection from the likes of Fahrid Al-Zahir, then you don't remember that Daladier and Chamberlain thought that they had pacified Adolf Hitler

when they handed him Czechoslovakia at Munich back
in 1938. That didn't work out so well . . . certainly not for
your country about two years later."

The French ambassador merely turned pink and
squirmed slightly in his chair. He was a diplomat, and
the diplomatic thing to do was to say nothing. Indeed,
what could he say about one of the more embarrassing
moments in his country's recent history?

**November 23
1:24 P.M. Eastern Time**

"I call upon all true believers to join me, and join with
me now, to become soldiers in the holy jihad of Mujahidin Al-Akhbar," Fahrid Al-Zahir growled angrily. "I
call upon all true believers to fight not only the Zionist
Crusader, but also the false prophet Badr whose lies are
like locusts consuming the truth. He has come to humil-
iate the people. I call upon all true believers to fight and
slay the pagans and the blasphemers wherever you find
them. Lie in wait for them. Seize them and beleaguer
them. All these crimes and sins are a clear declaration
of war on Al-Zahir, God's messenger who hears God's
voice and who speaks to God."

The face and embodiment of Mujahidin Al-Akhbar
terror had lost none of his fire. To a world that was unaware that Badr's second taped message had originated
from Al-Zahir's violated inner sanctum, he was as fear-
some and as frightening as ever.

The French ambassador heard the diatribe on the car
radio as his limousine passed Georgetown University

and headed up Reservoir Road toward his embassy. He realized that what the president had said was true, and it worried him. His government had pretended in 1938 that appeasement bought protection, and his government believed that now. Indeed, all of Europe felt that as long as they distanced themselves from the Americans, all would be well. They were kidding themselves, and the ambassador knew it. He didn't have to read between Al-Zahir's lines to know that.

Thomas Livingstone watched the televised iteration of Fahrid Al-Zahir's fiery fatwa at the White House. The speech was long on rhetoric and short on specifics, but the rhetoric was frightening. It was a call to arms, a call to jihadis everywhere to murder Americans everywhere. Nearly three weeks had gone by since he had met with Buck Peighton in that hangar in Denver, and Al-Zahir was still burning up the airwaves.

Al-Zahir was still out there. So too were Khaleq Badr and Muhammad Al-Abir. Where, oh where, was his American Volunteer Group? Were, *they* still out there at all?

November 23
7:31 P.M. Central European Time

"**Y**OU won't hear this on the news," Muhammad Bin Qasim told chevelnoir. "But you should tell our friend that Khaleq Badr is in the United States. He will pose no threat in Europe."

The two men had met at their usual place of rendezvous along the Quai Saint-Bernard near the Gare d'Austerlitz to discuss the transfer of the objects to Gallerie l'Aiglon, and they had joined a cluster of Parisians to watch the Fahrid Al-Zahir speech on a television set mounted on the wall inside a sidewalk cafe.

Bin Qasim didn't mention that he had heard on the whispered back channels of diplomatic chatter that the GIGN had failed in their attempt to kill the rival warlord. This was not good news, but at least Badr was confirmed to be in the United States. It was certainly better to have him, and the terrorist civil war between him and Al-Zahir, confined to the United States.

It would have been good if the GIGN had gotten Badr, but as he watched Al-Zahir, Bin Qasim was confident that the Mujahidin Al-Akhbar would not fail to finish the job, and the finishing would take place in America.

But the man believed to be Khaleq Badr was *not* in the United States, he was minutes away from setting foot on French soil, barely more than twenty kilometers from where the two men were sitting.

November 23
7:31 P.M. Central European Time

THE big 747-200F freighter touched down at Aeroport Charles de Gaulle, which was more or less an hour—depending on traffic—northeast of Paris. Thanks to FedEx and the support of the French government, it had become the largest air freight airport in Europe. With the hundreds of passenger jets and the mushrooming number of freighters, one more 747 garnered little notice, especially when an Apex Air flight came into this busy hub from points east five evenings each week.

The Ford Broncos with the Turkish plates had remained behind. A pair of mismatched Renault delivery vans with French plates would take their place. The Little Bird had come to Paris, but she was scheduled for a very serious repainting.

EIGHTEEN

November 24
8:17 A.M. Eastern Time

"**T**HEY came up with a positive ID for the voice on the Livonia 911 tape," Erik Vasquez said proudly, as though it had been his own detective work that had developed this nugget of information. "It's our guy. It's that John Rodgers whose handiwork is all over this case. The Army Special Forces had records of his voice profile. I guessed as much, so I had them run his voice first."

Rod Llewellan might have guessed as much as well, but he feigned surprise. Of course it was Rodgers. It had to be him, or Boyinson, or one of the other mercenaries that Buck Peighton had sent running around the world. He had been thinking about what Peighton had said at Bert's Crab House the other night. Just because what he was seeing from afar didn't make sense, didn't mean that the total picture was wrong. Of course Jack Rodgers had made the 911 call. Of course Jack Rodgers had been at the hospital. He was operating beyond the horizon. Llewellan was seeing things that could not be seen by the national intelligence apparatus. Each time that he had appeared, it had seemed to be erratic, but it was precise. Rodgers was there to save lives. He had personally saved more than a hundred that Llewellan knew about. Boyinson may have been a criminal, but he was also a hero.

Buck Peighton had asked Rod whether a law enforcement professional or a trained killer was right for the job. Buck Peighton had been right when he had picked the Raptors. The president had been right to pick Buck Peighton.

After all his soul-searching, Rod Llewellan knew that he had a role to play in all of this. He had been trained to follow orders, even if they didn't seem to make sense at the time. Now, even though the situation was utterly and completely beyond his understanding, he would play his part and do his job.

"Rod, hey, you daydreamin' or what?" Erik Vasquez was speaking. He had said something, and Rod had been, indeed, daydreaming.

"Rod, the Director of National Intelligence wants to see you. He wants us to find those guys. Bring 'em both in. They're now officially 'persons of interest.'"

"Well, we're the guys for the job." Llewellan smiled. He was glad to be on the trail of Rodgers and Boyinson again. That way he could continue to make sure that they would *not* be found.

November 24
2:17 P.M. Central European Time

"**THE** explosives are in a warehouse near here," Ghassan Aswad told his most holy boss. "The detonators I can have in one hour. Two at the most."

"Good," Fahrid Al-Zahir said thoughtfully. "We must strike tomorrow night."

Al-Zahir was desperate to regain the initiative from Badr. He was sure that the renegade was planning something big in the United States, and he had to beat him to the punch. Al-Zahir decided to make his move soon, and to supervise the details himself. This meant making his move here in Paris before Badr did something.

"May I be permitted to know where?" Aswad asked.

"All in due course, my little brother." Al-Zahir smiled patronizingly. "Just get me the detonators and await my call."

Al-Zahir knew that Aswad could be relied upon. There were a few others. He wasn't sure how many. When he had looked around the table at the safe house again this morning, he could see it in their faces. Their loyalty fluctuated. Each and every man would gladly trade his own life for a busload of infidels, but a narrowly disciplined commitment to Mujahidin Al-Akhbar was necessary to bring down the Great Satan.

Narrow discipline required leadership. Al-Zahir had thought he had found this in Khaleq Badr when he made the man one of his lieutenants. He had been wrong about Badr. He had been deceived. Tommorrow, he would plan and lead this operation himself. He would control every step.

The explosives needed detonators. The detonators were worthless without the cyclonite or the cyclotrimethylene trinitramine. A bomb was impotent as long as the two ingredients remained apart. As long as they were kept separate, Al-Zahir would remain in control.

November 24
2:17 P.M. Central European Time

"**T**HE guy in the white cap just came back."

The fat guy with the iPod playing video games in the arcade was the last person that anyone would expect to be conducting surveillance of the Mujahidin Al-Akhbar safe house in Bobigny. He was too young, too overweight, and he looked too much like the kind of underemployed kid that one would expect to find killing time at a working-class video arcade.

"Thanks Robert, I've got him on the mike now." Based on the paperwork found at the safe houses in Turkey, and on Jack Rodgers's downloads from the KH-12 spy satellite, the Raptors had located the Bobigny house and had managed to place five microphones on it. Arabic-speaking Jason Houn could listen from the van around the corner, but Robert was literally across the street and could provide the visual element. His iPod was actually a short-range, two-way transmitter.

Dave Brannan was not pleased that they had missed Fahrid Al-Zahir again here in Bobigny. After placing the bugs the night before, they had ascertained that Al-Zahir *had* been there in the morning, but that he had moved on. At least they were getting close.

As Robert had seen and reported, Ghassan Aswad had just come back from meeting with Al-Zahir. The Raptors were just a few hours behind him.

Aswad began barking commands. The hair on the back of Jason's neck stood up. There was talk of explosives. Aswad insisted that someone named Sedik go somewhere and pick up some explosives. First, Aswad wanted him to drive past an address and to plan to martyr himself there tomorrow.

Ray Couper, who was in the van with Jason, casually got out and strolled to a phone booth that was well out of sight from the safe house. Here, he phoned Brannan on a landline. A car bomb was a serious turn of events, but why here? A car bomb in Paris didn't fit Al-Zahir's pattern.

Brannan's last words to Couper were to order him to follow this guy named Sedik. By doing this, they'd know *what* was going to be hit, and they'd have a day to figure out what to do about it.

Meanwhile, Anne McCaine had come up with an alternate plan to snare Al-Zahir that was certainly crazy enough to try, and perhaps crazy enough to work. Dave Brannan was betting on it.

November 24
8:17 A.M. Eastern Time

"**TELL** me again about this Gregory Boyinson," the president demanded.

Livingstone had the Director of National Intelligence in his office for a briefing on the growing number of links between two former Army Special Forces men and the situations involving the terrorists.

"He's a real loose cannon," the Director of National Intelligence told the president, happy to be pointing the finger at the idiosyncracies of someone from a department other than his own. "His service file is full of appalling incidents of drunken violence and broken regulations."

"I understand that there were some decorations and commendations."

"Yes, Mr. President, Boyinson could be, and frequently was, a genuine hero. He saved countless lives of other service personnel, including a British SAS detachment in the Balkans."

"Why was he not dishonorably discharged?"

"His time was up." The Director of National Intelligence shrugged. "Better to just let him go."

"How is he involved with this man Rodgers?" Livingstone asked. "He's the same Rodgers that was the hero on the Western Star flight, correct?"

"Yes, that's correct. They're linked because they served together in the army, and because Rodgers bailed Boyinson out of jail in Seattle. By the way, Rodgers's service record is very much like the one side of Boyinson's. Commendations a mile long, plus a Silver Star and a DSC."

"So you'd say that they are both loose cannons?" Livingstone asked.

"There is no 'drunk and disorderly' in Rodgers's record, but several instances of him going a bit far to get the job done. Essentially, they are both heroes with a record of breaking the rules to accomplish their missions.

That's probably why they both got out of the service. They had both made captain, and neither had a future in the army without punching his ticket with a staff job somewhere."

"And you think that they may now be involved in the terrorist attacks?" Livingstone asked. "It would seem unlikely, given that Rodgers was the one who thwarted a terrible tragedy."

"No sir, we do not suspect them of being *involved*. Rodgers certainly stopped that hijacking, but it is terribly peculiar that he may have been at the Downers Grove hospital, and then he made the 911 call that brought police to the Livonia house. It has to be more than a coincidence."

"I agree, but what *is* it, if not a coincidence?" Livingstone asked nervously.

"We have two Special Forces men, and two separate situations where at least one was in the same place as an incident involving the terrorists. We have developed a theory over at National Intel."

"And that is?"

"We think that they've decided on their own that they're going to go after Al-Zahir and Mujahidin Al-Akhbar. We think that Rodgers and Boyinson have decided to turn *vigilante*. I've issued orders to have them picked up as 'persons of interest.' "

"Who do you think may be behind their having turned vigilante?" Livingstone asked. His nervousness now bordered on panic, and he hoped that it would not show. "Do you know who might be financing their operation? Are others involved?"

"At the moment, it looks like just the two of them

and maybe one other guy. We haven't gotten close
enough to find any trail of financial transactions to follow."

The president had started to exhale a sigh of relief
when the Director of National Intelligence added, "But
if it's there, we *will* find it."

November 24
3:28 P.M. Central European Time

SEDIK took the N3 Autoroute into Paris, his old Citroën delivery truck swirling in a cloud of black
smoke whenever he slowed, which was often. At one
point, Ray Couper referred to the vehicle as an "old
bomb," not realizing the double entendre until he'd said
it out loud. Jason Houn just nodded.

The Raptors tried not to lose him in the heavy city
traffic along Avenue Lafayette. The black smoke that
the "old bomb" belched was useful in this regard, even
in a city that takes emissions standards with a grain of
salt. More important, they tried to figure out where he
slowed to study a location. The sinister fact that he was
scouting the intended location of a car bomb attack
added urgency to their mission.

At Boulevard Haussmann, Sedik made a left and
headed past the Paris Opera. Houn and Couper looked
at one another. Bounded by busy streets on five sides,
and with the Place de l'Opera on the sixth side, this
Paris monument was easy pickings for a potential car
bomb. However, Sedik hardly slowed, except when a
large Mercedes nearly cut him off. He shot past the

Opera and picked up Boulevard des Capucines. He was continuing in generally the same south-by-southwest direction that he had followed since Bobigny.

Moments later, he led them past the great neoclassical Church of the Madeleine, another monument encircled by busy streets. Again, there was no sense that Sedik was pausing to look something over.

It was eerie to be following someone who knew that the next time he drove this route it would be the last time that he drove anywhere. The promise of unlimited virgins in heaven will do that to a man.

Sedik made such a sharp right off Rue Royale that Couper almost lost him. They now found themselves on Avenue Gabriel, with the Hôtel de Crillon just ahead and the Place de la Concorde on the left. Just as Couper accelerated to catch him before the next intersection, Sedik's brake lights came on for no obvious reason.

This was it. Sedik had slowed to take a close look at Number Two Avenue Gabriel, the four-story, neoclassic United States Embassy!

November 24
3:28 P.M. Central European Time

ADRIENNE Delacroix smiled as she offered coffee to her guests. She always served coffee to guests of Middle Eastern origin whom she did not know. It was never good to make a faux pas, and always better to be safe than sorry. She knew that Monsieur Bin Qasim would probably enjoy a cognac, but his colleague might be more orthodox and might take offense. So coffee it was. The little man known to the world as chevelnoir identified himself today as Monsieur Haroum. He smiled politely, warmly thanking her in French for the coffee.

"Monsieur Stabl will be attending the showing tomorrow evening, but he has a particular interest in several of the pieces," Adrienne Delacroix explained, having filled them in on the enigmatic Bavarian industrialist. "He asked me to convey a special request on his behalf. He would like to arrange a private meeting with the seller to discuss these certain pieces. Pending a personal inspection by his curator, who will be traveling with him, he would be willing to pay 15 percent over the asking price, plus the gallery commission."

"This is quite irregular," Muhammad Bin Qasim said nervously.

"Which pieces are of particular interest?" Monsieur Haroum asked calmly.

"Four of the bronzes," Adrienne replied pointing to a color printout of the jpegs that she had e-mailed to her special list. "The Hittite Zebu Bull, the one of the goddess Astarte, and these two others."

"I assume that his banker's draft is in order?" Haroum asked.

"Monsieur Stabl asks whether you would be able to accept cash?" Adrienne queried. "He would be prepared to pay in American dollars."

The man called chevelnoir did the math in his head. A single sale of pieces of this value at 15 percent over, *and* in cash, was extraordinary. It was chevelnoir's role to make money for his client, and this was real money. On top of what could be picked up from the sale of

about a hundred other pieces, tomorrow would be a
very good night. For someone who wanted to pay in
cash, 15 percent over was great. Usually, these people
wanted discounts for cash.

"We could arrange the meeting at *your* apartment?"
Haroum asked, looking at Bin Qasim.

As they left Gallerie l'Aiglon and walked down Rue
de Varenne toward the Invalides, Bin Qasim was appre-
hensive.

"You know better than I the identity of this man for
whom we are setting up this meeting," Bin Qasim said.
"He is a wanted man. Perhaps the most sought fugitive
in the world. Is he going to want to be seen in public?"

"Don't worry, my friend," Monsieur Haroum said
calmly. "First of all, it is not in public. It is in a situation
of which we have complete control. As for his being a
fugitive, this is France. They would never arrest him if
they could avoid it. And finally, if this man is paying
cash for such a purchase, and he is doing so in private, it
is more than obvious that he has some very large skele-
tons in *his* closet."

NINETEEN

"**W**HEN I so capriciously undertook this misadventure, I had thought it would *help* me sleep at night. I thought I'd rest easier knowing that *something* was being done," President Thomas Livingstone said. He was dashing to his car after having given a speech in Raleigh, and General Buckley Peighton had "coincidently" appeared.

"You are now characterizing your American Volunteer Group as a 'misadventure?' What other way do you have of getting at Mujahidin Al-Akhbar?"

"It's a misadventure because Fahrid Al-Zahir is still out there, and so are Khaleq Badr and now Muhammad Al-Abir. When we started, we had one terrorist chieftan. Now there are *three!* It's a misadventure because my own Director of National Intelligence has the FBI trailing two former Special Forces people who he thinks are involved in some vigilante hunt for terrorists."

"And who are these two people?" Peighton asked.

"I know that you won't tell me whether these individuals are involved in the American Volunteer Group, but their names are John Rodgers and Gregory Boyinson."

"I see," Peighton said thoughtfully, trying not to let on that the president had just identified two members of the Raptor Team.

"If these guys are involved, and the FBI gets hold of them *and* they start talking, I'm finished. Remember Watergate? A president of the United States isn't supposed to have freelance agents with a shadowy past running around doing his dirty work."

"Richard Nixon was involved in Watergate to get himself reelected," Peighton reminded Livingstone. "He had CIA guys doing dirty tricks that were designed just to keep him in office. They were aimed at Nixon's personal and political enemies, not enemies of the American people who want to slaughter us by the thousands."

"I'm not sure that the loyal opposition in Congress would find my operating outside the law so benign. I also think that it would also be a hard pill for the director of National Intelligence to swallow, knowing that I didn't bring him into the loop."

"Isn't the defeat of Mujahidin Al-Akhbar worth getting some feathers ruffled?"

"It's not just feathers, it's my political future, maybe even my *future*," the president said, his voice straining. "And I don't see Mujahidin Al-Akhbar being defeated.

I see only that we have triple the number of terrorist bosses that we had a couple of weeks ago. I want you to pull the plug on this thing. I want you to freeze their bank account."

November 25
3:31 P.M. Central European Time

"**T**HERE'S a 'Bay'n'Pay' around the next corner," Dave Brannan told Anne McCaine as they strolled down the posh and busy Rue de Rivoli, directly across the street from the Louvre.

"What in the world kind of bank is a 'bay and pay?' It sounds like a seedy check cashing parlor. I can't imagine one of those chucked in here next to Hermes and Gucci."

"It's the Banque Nationale de Paris." Brannan laughed. "The initials sound roughly like 'Bay'n'Pay' if you say them in French. I've used this 'Bay'n'Pay' branch before. They always have plenty of cash on hand for the high rollers that pass through this neighborhood."

If Hermann Stabl was going to pay cash, he'd need some cash. He had Hiram Johnson's American Express platinum card, but nothing said "cash" like real American dollars.

"What if they record us on their surveillance cameras, Colonel?"

"That's why we're wearing shades, Professor."

Anne thought they were wearing sunglasses because the weather was bright and sunny again after several days of rain, but she was a bit impressed with Brannan's

fast comeback. In fact, the sunglasses were to disguise
them, and he had brought Anne because a middle-aged
couple would arouse much less suspicion than a lone
man of any age.

The platinum card, a passport, and a few words to
the assistant manager got the casually dressed Americans into a private office, where a slender young man
with a powder blue ascot typed a specified number
given to him by Mr. Hiram Johnson into a computer.

He wrinkled his nose, typed some more, paused, and
wrinkled his nose again.

"Un moment," he said, standing up and leaving the
room.

"What's wrong?" Anne asked. The cloak-and-dagger
stuff was actually a bit of fun when played online at a
laptop, but the field operations aspect was different.
Withdrawing over two hundred grand in American dollars from a bank in a foreign country while using forged
identity papers was enough to make anyone nervous.

"Nothing," Brannan said calmly, casually flipping
through the copy of *Paris Match* that had been beneath
the ashtray on the coffee table.

Through the open door, Anne could see the slender
young man speaking to an older man. The colonel
seemed not the least bit concerned as five minutes
ticked by. To Anne, it seemed like thirty.

"Pardon, monsieur et madame," the young man
said, returning to the room and reseating himself at the
computer. He wrinkled his nose, typed some more,
paused, and wrinkled his nose again. Finally, he looked
at Brannan and asked in what denominations he would
like to have his currency.

November 25
3:31 P.M. Central European Time

THE bearded man carrying the large case and the music stand was hardly noticed as he squeezed through the throng at Espace Pierre Cardin. The haughtily chic department store was known as much for musical events and fashion shows as for the couture of which it was one of the signature purveyors in Paris. Therefore, musicians in tuxedos were nearly as common a sight here as supermodels or the emaciated young aspirants to the runway.

Espace Pierre Cardin was located overlooking the Jardin des Champs-Elysées, just a short distance from the tony boulevard of the same name—and just across Avenue Gabriel from the four-story, neoclassic United States Embassy.

When Jason Houn had overheard on the Bobigny bugs that Sedik was going to deliver the explosives, but *not* the detonators for the car bomb, it had seemed odd. Why would the jihadis bring the two necessary components together at the target site rather than put the whole thing together at a safer location?

It took Robert to suggest the only plausible suggestion. "Maybe Al-Zahir doesn't *trust* his flunkies to do the right thing."

Robert was right. It was like the key safety feature of an ICBM silo. It took *two* people acting simultaneously to launch a nuclear-armed missile. One person acting alone couldn't go off his rocker and launch. Al-Zahir had built in a safety link to be sure that his jihadis did as they were told.

Colonel Brannan decided that they should take out the vehicle with the detonators in a very public place, preferably near the embassy. That way, when the police cordoned off the street, which they were likely to do immediately, Sedik's smoky van and its load of C4 would be found. Will Casey suggested that he could throw a round into the driver of each vehicle. A .50-caliber slug taking off a person's head through a windshield on a busy street would make a pretty obvious splash with minimal collateral damage.

Casey was on Avenue Gabriel within an hour of Sedik's drive-by. He did a walk around of the embassy and headed into Espace Pierre Cardin. He couldn't tell the fashion models from the wannabes as they passed through the large portico with their perfect bodies, pouty lips, and massive shopping bags, but it was an interesting exercise to try guessing. He gave up on this distraction and refocussed his attention on the job at hand.

The big store was such an obvious place for a sniper, he imagined that the Marine guards at the embassy kept a pretty good eye on it. Of course, every window in the embassy had glass thick enough to bulletproof it from a 7.62-mm round, and probably a .50-caliber slug. That would keep them pretty relaxed. Men who lived in impregnable fortresses had time to relax.

On the third floor, there was a large section that was roped off for a change of display. A few Gallic workmen in blue coveralls were pretending to work at hanging a large partition. Casey decided when he made his first walk-through that they would be gone by the time that the musician returned with his music stand and his instrument.

He had been right, and now he was back. The view was perfect. The embassy was visible without being directly in view. This meant that he could see the street at a good angle to watch approaching vehicles.

As he carefully unpacked his Barrett M107 elephant gun, he saw a man on the roof of the embassy with binoculars. He routinely scanned the perimeter, seeming more interested in the numerous paths and thick woods of the Jardin des Champs-Elysées. It was certainly a probable route for an attack. Lots of cover. Lots of options for exfil.

The boy from Tennessee set his 9-mm with the silencer where he could get at it easily in case he had any visitors, plugged in the AN/PRC-148 earpiece, and sat back to wait.

November 25
11:47 A.M. Eastern Time

G **ENERAL** Buckley Peighton pulled his big car into the rest stop off Interstate 95, and unpacked his new cell phone. When he declined the nights-and-weekends plan offered by the teenager behind the counter at the phone store, she had looked at him like he was nuts. Maybe he was, but he didn't need the nights-and-weekends plan for a phone that he would only use once. Modern warfare was sure as hell a lot different than what they had predicted when he was back at the Army War College.

He quickly dialed the number with the 345 area code. The man whose car was buffeted by the cold wind of a

Virginia winter was instantly connected with a woman in a bank in the Cayman Islands who could look out her open window at gently swaying palms.

"I'd like to freeze an account."

"Close an account?" the woman with the British accent asked.

"No, just freeze it against being accessed remotely."

"I understand."

She asked for the password, and she opened the account on the computer.

"Could you tell me when my account was last accessed?" he asked.

"Yes, sir. The last transaction was at 1447 Greenwich Mean Time today. There was $215,000 withdrawn at the Banque Nationale de Paris office on Rue Rivoli in Paris. Is there anything else, sir?"

"No. Thanks. That's all."

Buck Peighton punched the Off button. It was a pity. It was a cute little phone.

A semitruck thundered past, sending a surge of slush into the rest stop. Buck could imagine Dave Brannan in the City of Lights. He grinned and shook his head. *You beat me to the punch, you old devil. Go for it buddy, I wish you luck and good hunting.*

November 25
5:47 P.M. Central European Time

FAHRID Al-Zahir paced the floor nervously. Outside the apartment, and five stories below, the traffic was dashing past quickly on the Quai Louis Blériot.

Muhammad Bin Qasim's newly acquired Degas hung on the wall. *What rubbish. What Zionist rubbish.* Such affectations as impressionist art were the embodiment of Western decadence. Bin Qasim wallowed in such crap, but he was not an infidel. He despised the Americans as much as anyone, and his place of power made him a very useful ally of the jihadi.

Al-Zahir picked up the bronze Zebu Bull and kissed it good-bye. *Go little bull. Go with the German stranger whose past is filled with darkness.* Al-Zahir loved the art of the Hittites, and so too did this German. The art of the Hittites was so real, so pure, so deeply rooted, and so unlike decadent Western impressionism! *Go little bull, let my sacrificing you bring me the treasure that will make the world tremble.*

Tonight was going to be a great and glorious night for Fahrid Al-Zahir. As he made his quiet transaction, the operation that he had so meticulously planned would be making the world tremble. It would establish Mujahidin Al-Akhbar as the preeminent society of martyrs in the holy jihad against the infidel, against the Zionist, against the Great Satan! Tonight would make Khaleq Badr tremble. Tonight would make that sick sodomite Muhammad Al-Abir tremble!

Fahrid Al-Zahir did not know that he was running from ghosts. Khaleq Badr, or at least most of his bones that had not yet been gnawed by coyotes, still lay in a shallow, rocky grave in Luna County, New Mexico. He had died a martyr's death to serve a cause that he could never have imagined in life. Muhammad Al-Abir too, had achieved martyrdom, although it was not quite the magnificent martyrdom that he had imagined. In fact, it had been the most humiliating martyrdom imaginable. The last thing that the great and glorious jihadi had done in his life was to wet his pants. And this is the way the Turkish police would find him when they came to investigate two days later.

Even worse, the last thing he had *seen* in his life was the face of an unshrouded woman.

Fahrid Al-Zahir was running from ghosts, but he was running hard and planning not to finish second.

November 25
5:47 P.M. Central European Time

GHASSAN Aswad left Bobigny in an aging green Fiat and headed south on the A86, the freeway that rings Paris on the east and south about ten or so miles outside the city limits. A Renault delivery van was in the next lane and about five to seven car lengths behind. There was plenty of traffic, and much of it consisted of anonymous light-commercial vehicles.

The fat guy with the iPod who had been playing video games in the arcade across the street had limped past the green car about a half hour before. Aswad had not noticed when he stopped next to his Fiat to tie his shoe.

Jason Houn was now monitoring the car in case Aswad made any cell phone calls as Jack Rodgers maintained a comfortable distance from the Fiat. Robert lounged in the back of the van, resting the ankle that he'd sprained in Turkey. He was taken with the excitement of the caper. Who would have thought when he signed up for this semester abroad that it would turn out like this?

Shortly after Aswad got on the freeway, he had made one call to someone to say that he was on his way. This was probably the guy who was supplying the blasting caps. Since then, Aswad had been quiet, and Houn was treated to the sound of the Arabic-language music station that he was listening to on the radio. Jason would have rather that Aswad tuned to a station with some Johnny Cash, but at least it wasn't hip-hop.

Immediately after crossing the Seine due south of Paris, Aswad signalled for the *sortie* at Choisy-le-Roi and took the road south to an industrial building directly across the river from the big plant where Renault reconditioned powertrain components for the European market. Jack Rodgers turned into a Total gas station nearly across the street and went through the motions of filling the tank of his truck.

Jason wished that he had been able to figure out a way for Robert to bug Aswad himself, and not just his car, but he was thankful for what he *had* been able to do. The cup was definitely half full.

Aswad could be seen talking to someone inside the car repair shop. They disappeared for a moment, and Aswad returned carrying a gym bag emblazoned with the logo of a regional French soccer team. He looked up and down the street and climbed back into his Fiat. He hadn't looked across the street at the gas station.

Jack Rodgers finished his transaction at the gas pump and made a note of the coordinates of the shop on his GPS tracker. This would soon be added to Greg Boyinson's to-do list for the evening.

November 25
5:47 P.M. Central European Time

"**G**REG Boyinson was pacing the smooth concrete floor of the hangar at Charles de Gaulle that was leased by Apex Air. He was anxious for action. All of the other Raptors were on the move and he was standing by his AN/PRC-148 multiband intrateam radio waiting for his cue. Being in the hangar with the smell of JP-4 and big jets reminded him of being in that bar back on November 4 when this nightmare had begun with the demise of another big jet. Boyinson had wanted to strangle the bastards with his bare hands. A couple days later, he had tuned up a clown who thought it was all America's fault, but today wasn't the same. The jerk in Seattle just needed an attitude adjustment. The Mujahidin Al-Akhbar bastards needed the full treatment.

Over the past several weeks, as the Raptors had begun to systematically dismember Mujahidin Al-Akhbar, all of the others had taken on the jihadis face-to-face. Even Will Casey, with his elephant gun, had seen faces. Greg had been compelled to content himself with hitting his targets at a distance. Not that he minded starting fires with Hellfires. He had cooked plenty of martyrs and made things difficult for Mujahidin Al-Akhbar, but still, he wished he could look one in the eye as he went to jihadi heaven.

Now, Greg was pacing the floor, waiting for the go-code. There would be a couple of fires in Bobigny, and now another would be added in Choisy-le-Roi. After that, some extractions and whatever Jack Rodgers called for. Jack was running the show tonight as Dave

Brannan went undercover to nail the big SOB. If anybody deserved the pleasure of taking out Fahrid Al-Zahir, it was Dave Brannan. After that deadly and disappointing night at Shakaraband back in 1997, Dave deserved to be the man.

November 25
11:47 A.M. Central Time

"**H**E said he had a friend that needed his help."

Rod Llewellan and Erik Vasquez were back in the South, in the city of Port Allen, Louisiana, across the Mississippi from Baton Rouge. This time they had tracked Jack Rodgers back to his missed interview with the head of the huge midsouth retail chain.

"I appreciate loyalty in a man," the company president told the two FBI agents. "Sure, I was pissed off that he didn't come to work here. To get a former Special Forces guy, especially a *decorated* former Special Forces guy, would've been a great coup. But, y'know, to pass up a job to go off and help out a friend kinda shows character, doncha think?"

"Do you have any idea *where* this friend was?" Vasquez asked.

"Didn't say. Not that I'd remember anyway. Seem to recall he said he was going to drive, so it couldn't have been all that far. Of course, that was the week the airlines weren't flying."

As the two agents got up to leave, the retail executive leaned back in his big chair and changed the subject.

"You guys on the Feds' antiterrorist squad?"

"The Bureau is involved in such things, but as you probably know, we couldn't talk about our specific lines of inquiry," Llewellan replied.

"Yeah, I know all of that, but I was just thinkin'. Since old Jack kinda skipped town on me, I still am in need of some good men to help me out with security. I've got a lot of trucks, a lot of warehouses, and a lot of stores to worry about. I sure could make it worth the while of a man or two who knows his stuff."

"Thank you, that's very generous," Llewellan told him, watching the flicker of thought processing in Erik's expression. "But we're both gainfully employed."

"Well, y'all think about it. You know where to find me."

The trail was going backward and getting colder every day. Llewellan remembered his trepidation back on the day that he drove all of that pirated national security data out to Winchester. That was the last time that he had seen Rodgers. When the director sent them out on this wild-goose chase, Rod could have just come out and told what he had seen on November 15. That was a much fresher sighting than anything that he had come up with as he went through the motions with Vasquez.

Of course, he'd also have to tell a great deal more, including the admission of actions that were—without an improbable presidential pardon—serious felonies. Llewellan would keep quiet and carry on, but he was becoming more comfortable with the idea that he was doing the right thing.

"You know," Vasquez said as they climbed back into their rental car that was not, of course, one of Bobby

Loreau's rent-a-wrecks, "the more I hear about this Jack
Rodgers, the more I'm getting to like him."

Rod Llewellan just smiled.

November 25
7:50 P.M. Central European Time

DAVE Brannan fastened his cuff links and looked
out the hotel window. Rue Vaneau was quiet. Brad
Townsend and Ray Couper were in place.

Brannan's first purchase after completing the transition at the Bay'n'Pay on Rue Rivoli had been a briefcase. He went for utilitarian and wanted to get the first
inexpensive black leather one that he saw when they
walked into Dunhill. Anne suggested the understated el-
egance of a deep maroon calfskin case with brass fittings that might pass for gold in subdued light. She had
also picked out the cuff links. He took her suggestions.

They hailed a cab and headed for the Left Bank.
Townsend and Couper followed at a discrete distance to
make sure that they weren't being followed, and to be in
place to act as backup later in the evening as Brannan
closed in on Al-Zahir.

Brannan and his companion had checked into the
Hotel Maurice Char as Hermann Stabl and Fiona
Richardson. The location met the Dave Brannan "moving parts rule"—it was a ten-minute walk from Gallerie
l'Aiglon. They were given two rooms on the third floor
at opposite ends of the hall. When Fiona had reminded
Herr Stabl that they were dressed a bit too casually to
attend the showing at Gallerie l'Aiglon, he had said that

they had better go shopping. He handed her a wad of hundred dollar bills and suggested they meet back at the hotel a half hour before the soiree.

Dave Brannan was the only Raptor old enough to reasonably impersonate the imaginary Hermann Stabl. Fortunately, he spoke enough German to avoid getting into trouble. In any case, his curator, Fiona Richardson, would do all the talking. After all, Anne McCaine had forgotten more about Hittite sculpture than Dave Brannan would ever know.

He straightened his tie, picked up Herr Stabl's brief-case, checked the time on Herr Stabl's new Rolex, and headed down the hall to Miss Richardson's room.

For a split second it didn't register to Brannan that the beautiful woman who answered the door was the same person as the dust-covered Anne McCaine whom he'd first met in a box canyon in Turkey with a knife strapped to her leg. The exquisite creature was wearing a V-necked satin dress the color of sapphires, with a full skirt that fell to the knees of her perfectly proportioned legs. It shimmered as she moved, like a sapphire.

The three-inch heels of her slingbacks made her appear taller and more graceful as she walked across the room. Except for the barely discernable lines around the corners of the large, dark eyes, he could have easily taken her for being ten or fifteen years younger than the woman who had led the packhorse for a day and a half across impossibly rugged terrain. He noticed that her nails were no longer chipped and rough. Her manicure had given her the hands of a sophisticated woman who earned her living by touching nothing rougher than a keyboard.

"You look good," he said, as though acknowledging that this understatement was self-evident. In fact, he thought she was gorgeous. Brannan was given to verbal understatement, but Anne caught enough of what he was really thinking by the look in his eyes. She was pleased to know that her companion found her attractive, even if tonight would be all business.

"You send a girl shopping in Paris, and a girl can get what she needs to look good." Anne smiled. "You seem to have made the transition pretty well yourself, Herr Stabl."

Brannan had bought himself a good suit, not a *very* good suit, but good. He couldn't really push himself to get a ridiculously expensive suit, but he bought a really good silk shirt and the most expensive necktie that he could find. It was one that not only was expensive, but which looked expensive enough to confirm Herr Stabl's status as a high roller.

"I like your earrings," he said, noting the vague resemblance to a Hittite motif in the golden baubles dangling from Anne's ears.

"I found these at a little place on the next street over," she said. "I thought that they might get noticed."

"I don't think you'll need those for *you* to get noticed."

November 25
7:50 P.M. Central European Time

ACROSS town, Will Casey watched Avenue Gabriel through his sniperscope. He had seen Sedik's pale blue Citroën delivery truck cruise past, return, and park near the Jardin des Champs-Elysées. He was getting updates from Jack Rodgers through his AN/PRC-148 earpiece and was patently waiting for a green Fiat.

If all went according to Fahrid Al-Zahir's plan, Ghassan Aswad would arrive and arm the car bomb. Sedik would then floor his accelerator and hit a predetermined place as close to the United States Embassy as the concrete traffic barriers would allow.

There were probably enough high explosives in the blue Citroën to do considerable damage to the facade of the Chancery building, and even more damage to the prestige and confidence of the United States. Al-Zahir would show Khaleq Badr that he wasn't afraid to hit the United States anywhere.

November 25
8:08 P.M. Central European Time

I T was a beautiful evening in Paris. It was very cold, but the air was crystal clear. The City of Lights shimmered like a box of jewels as well-dressed people scurried from place to place in taxis and limousines bound for the gastronomical adventures or the entertainment venues for which Paris is legendary.

In few places was the jewel box appearance more obvious than from the glittering crown jewel of the City of Lights, the 986-foot Eiffel Tower. Diners were already studying wine lists and enjoying their escargot appetizers at the Jules Verne, the restaurant on the tower's second platform. With a private elevator, Jules Verne was as exclusive a restaurant as could be found in a national monument anywhere.

Security for the patrons of Jules Verne was strict, but not intrusive, as the staff hurried about with the delicacies and service that guaranteed the restaurant its coveted star in the Michelin Red Guide.

November 25
8:08 P.M. Central European Time

HERMANN Stabl and Fiona Richardson arrived at Gallerie l'Aiglon fashionably late. The security guard confirmed their identities, and the porter took their coats. He offered to take Herr Stabl's briefcase, but the German industrialist politely declined. The porter nodded. He understood.

There were about two dozen well-dressed people already there. They were milling about and looking at the art from the private collection that was being offered for sale. Only a handful of Hittite sculptures existed in European museums, and far fewer in private collections. Tonight's show afforded a unique opportunity for private collectors like Herr Stabl and the others who were gathered here.

It was dazzling. Fiona had never seen anything quite like it. The objects in the room were exquisite. Indeed, no museum had such a collection.

"These are cute little guys," Stabl whispered to his curator, pointing to a row of small gold figures presented on a blue black velvet backdrop. "They remind me of your earrings."

"They're Hittite deities from the thirteenth century B.C.," she replied. "They remind me of some similar ones from Carchemish in Turkey that are in the British Museum. They're inlaid with lapis lazuli. I *wish* I had earrings like those."

"I guess if they're thirteenth century, the lapis would've come out of Afghanistan," he said, looking at the tiny figurines.

"Herr Stabl, you surprise me," she said. "You certainly are a wealth of knowledge."

"I only *ride* like a cowboy," he said.

"Welcome to Gallerie l'Aiglon," a well-dressed woman with a narrow chin interrupted them. "I'm Adrienne Delacroix."

"Bonsoir mademoiselle." Fiona smiled. "I'm Fiona Richardson. "We've spoken online."

"Of course, I am so pleased to put a face to the name, and so pleased to welcome you this evening."

"And this is my employer, Herr Hermann Stabl."

"Guten Abend," Stabl said, stiffening in formal Prussian manner and extending his hand.

"I have been looking forward to meeting you, Herr Stabl." Mademoiselle Delacroix smiled warmly and shook the German's hand. "Did you know that these figurines are based on carvings from an open-air shrine at Yazilikaya near the Hittite capital of Hattusa in central Anatolia?"

"Ah yes," Stabl said, feigning interest. "Near Bogazkoy."

"That's right," Mademoiselle Delacroix said, pleased to see that the German knew the modern Turkish name for Hattusa off the top of his head. "They were found in a grave from the seventh century B.C."

As she watched Adrienne touching Herr Stabl's arm much more than necessary, Fiona felt a tinge of jealousy, but quickly tried to put it out of her mind. She could easily see why Mademoiselle Delacroix might be attracted to the tall and powerfully built German. There was what she probably knew was in the briefcase, but there was more to it than that. Adrienne recognized what Fiona already knew. This big guy was attractive, espcially in a suit and tie.

Fiona carefully took the little caviar hors d'oeuvre that was offered and moved to another perfectly lit glass case. It contained a circular Hittite stamp seal that had been found near Yozgay. She knew some of the people who had worked on the excavations there. How did that monster Al-Zahir get hold of *this* piece?

"It's from the fourteenth century B.C.," he said softly. Fiona had hardly noticed the little man. "That was the period when the Hittites expanded their empire from Syria to the Aegean shore. It's made from hematite."

"Because that's a very hard stone." Fiona smiled. "And it will make a very good impression."

"It is difficult to cut." The little man smiled. "But hematite is very durable and very reliable."

"What is this in the center?" another man asked, barging in on the conversation.

"This is the name and title of the owner," Fiona explained. "It's in Hittite hieroglyphics. Around it is a seated god holding a bird. See the stag's head and the spears and tree?"

"There is much to see," the little man added. "See the bull-headed men kneeling beside an altar, and a bird-headed figure pouring wine? There are similar scenes on many Hittite seals, beginning around 1500 B.C."

"Beer," Fiona said succinctly. Both men looked at her. "In central Turkey by this time, as well as throughout Mesopotamia, it was more likely that they would've used beer rather than wine. Professor Solomon Katz at the University of Chicago has found Sumerian recipes for beer that date back nearly four millennia."

"And coincidentally, seals of this type have been found at places that served as storehouses for agricultural commodities," the older man added. "And one of the most important was *barley*, the essential ingredient in beer."

"That would make this an important artifact of ancient commerce." The younger man smiled. "Are you planning to make an offer on this piece?"

"Be my guest." The older man smiled.

She was good. Brannan could tell that Anne had worked far more cocktail parties than he had. It was second nature. She also seemed to know what there was to know about Hittite sculpture. People were asking her opinion. She knew the subject, but Brannan was amazed at how well she stayed true to the mission at hand, the way that she avoided putting fingerprints on anything. She had her hands everywhere. She touched wrists and shoulders, and little toasts with Caspian fish eggs, but never a glass, a fork, or anything that would confirm her presence in this room when she had gone.

She looked good. She was so animated, so graceful, and so beautiful in that iridescent blue satin dress that shimmered as she moved. Brannan hadn't fallen for a woman for so long that he had forgotten what it felt like. People came and went in his life, often without a second thought. The professor, though, Dave felt certain that he was going to miss her when this mission was over.

The other man took a flute of champagne and moved on, but the soft-spoken little man remained.

"*Je m'appelle Monsieur Haroum.*"

"Fiona Richardson, I'm the curator for Herr Stabl, the Bavarian collector."

"More Hittite objects for Germany?"

"The Berlin Museum has the Sam'al sculptures," Fiona stated. "Bavaria has a growing *private* collection."

"I see," the man said, nodding to Adrienne Delacroix, who excused herself from two Japanese men with whom she was talking.

"If you and Herr Stabl would like to come with me, there is someone that I would like you to meet," Mademoiselle Delacroix whispered softly to Fiona.

November 25
8:08 P.M. Central European Time

GHASSAN Aswad had backtracked on the A86 and picked up the A4, the Autoroute de l'Est, for the final few miles to the gates of Paris at Porte de Bercy. Here, he picked up the Périphérique, the aptly named multilane freeway that forms a continuous ring around the periphery of Paris along its city limits boundary. The jihadi with the gym bag full of detonators headed north, travelling counterclockwise around the city.

Jack Rodgers followed as Aswad's Fiat darted in and out of traffic toward his rendezvous with death. Rodgers wondered whether the deaths that Aswad would abet to-night were intended to include his own. Was he planning to martyr himself at the United States Embassy tonight, or just deliver his deadly cargo and live to die another day?

About halfway around the circle of the Périphérique, Aswad exited at Porte Maillot to enter the city. This put him in a direct line with Sedik and his old Citroën delivery truck near the United States Embassy. Just as Aswad passed the Concorde Lafayette high-rise luxury hotel on Avenue de la Grande-Armée, his cell phone rang. Jason Houn instinctively pressed the earpiece into his ear.

"What? Where? But?" Aswad said in Arabic, obviously disturbed. Jason wished that he'd been able to bug his cell phone. At least he was hearing half the conversation. The cup was half full.

"No, I'm not there yet. Of course, master. As you wish, my lord. Of course. I will do so now."

"What the hell?" Jack asked.

"Sounds like a change of plans."

"To what?"

"I can't tell."

The two vehicles were now in heavy traffic at the Place Charles de Gaulle, the circular multispoked plaza surrounding the gaudily illuminated Arc de Triomphe. Drivers entering this crowded, dozen-lane traffic circle had a dozen streets on which to spin off, including the Avenue des Champs-Elysées—at the opposite end of which lay the United States Embassy.

Rodgers turned his Renault into the circle, straining to follow the Fiat in a sea of cars, most of which seemed to be changing lanes.

"Where the hell is he?" Jack said. "I think I lost him."

"There he is," Robert said after what seemed like an eternity of the three pairs of eyes looking every which way. "He took that street there by the billboard with the snake on it."

"That's Avenue Kléber." Jack had missed the turn, so he accelerated to get around the circle and make the exit on his next pass. "That's the wrong way to get to the embassy."

"He's not going to the embassy anymore," Jason said.

November 25
8:19 P.M. Central European Time

THE moment that the door closed, the loud murmur of voices in the Gallerie l'Aiglon disappeared. Adrienne Delacroix had brought Fiona Richardson and her boss into the soundproofed inner sanctum. The carpets were lush, the lighting soft, and the faint sound of a Chopin *Nocturne* set the mood.

"Monsieur Stabl and Mademoiselle Richardson, may I present Monsieur Bin Qasim," Adrienne said. "Monsieur Bin Qasim has generously offered to make the arrangements for the private showing that you requested."

Both of the disguised Americans successfully hid

their surprise as they greeted the chief of the United Nations International Validation Organization.

"Monsieur Stabl, I understand that you are prepared to make an offer on several pieces," Muhammad Bin Qasim said.

"I'm sure that Mademoiselle Delacroix has explained which pieces, and the terms that we offer," Fiona Richardson replied.

"They are very munificent terms indeed," Bin Qasim admitted. "Why are you being so generous? Why didn't you simply purchase them here at the gallery?"

"Provenance. I am anxious to know the provenance of the pieces and to speak directly to the seller on this matter," Stabl said in perfectly German-accented French. "I am an old-fashioned collector who prefers dealing face-to-face. I want to look the man in the eye."

"He is definitely very old-fashioned," Fiona Richardson added.

"Mademoiselle Richardson, I understand that you are quite knowledgeable on the subject of Hittite sculpture," Muhammad Bin Qasim said, looking directly at her with cold, penetrating eyes.

"I've made it a substantial part of my professional career," she replied.

"Where did you study?"

"Cambridge. As an undergraduate, I was involved in geoarchaeological projects with the McBurney Laboratory on the neolithic sites discovered at Avebury. In graduate school I worked on the nomadic pastoralist settlements in Israel and Jordan."

"Did you know Ian Buehler?" Mademoiselle Delacroix asked.

"Yes. I took a class on the alluvial systems in New Mexico and Montana from him."

Muhammad Bin Qasim found himself distracted as the attractive Mademoiselle Richardson crossed her legs.

"And Perry Cross?"

"No, I knew who he was, but I didn't know him. He was at the McDonald Institute for Archaeological Research. He died last winter . . ."

"I'm sure that the young ladies would enjoy discussing mutual friends all evening, but I am here to acquire some objets d'art and I wish to get on with it," Hermann Stabl said impatiently. He knew that the Delacroix woman was grilling Fiona Richardson to determine her true credentials, and he wanted to seize the momentum of the conversation and put a stop to this line of inquiry.

"I suggest that you arrange a luncheon with Mademoiselle Delacroix. We *will* be in Paris for two more days."

"Are your financial arrangements in order, Monsieur Stabl?" Bin Qasim asked.

"Of course," Stabl said, placing the deep maroon calfskin briefcase on the table. The brass fittings that passed for gold in the subdued light made almost no sound as he opened them. She was good, that woman who suggested—who insisted—that he buy this briefcase. "I assume that these financial arrangements will meet with your approval."

The International Validation Organization chief picked up two of the bundles from opposite corners of the case and thumbed through them. The bills did not have sequential serial numbers, and they showed varying age and wear. This was the real thing. He felt like a character in a gangster movie, and he realized that he perhaps *was* a character in the real-life equivalent. He replaced the bills in the case and nodded.

"Now I have a question for Monsieur Bin Qasim," Stabl said as he closed his case. "Why are *you* involved in this transaction? Aren't you a bit outside your element?"

"I'm just an art lover who was asked by the parties to help arrange a transaction," Muhammad Bin Qasim replied.

"In that case, let us conclude this transaction," Stabl said, standing up. "I'm an art lover who wants to meet the seller, now."

November 25
8:19 P.M. Central European Time

"**T**HERE he is!" Robert shouted. "He just made the light."

Jack Rodgers maneuvered through the traffic on Avenue Kléber, trying to catch up with the old Fiat without running any of the crazy Parisian cabdrivers onto the sidewalk, and without Ghassan Aswad seeing him and getting spooked. By the time that Jack had gotten off Place Charles de Gaulle, Aswad was a block ahead and gaining.

"Ghassan is headed away from the target," Jack announced over his AN/PRC-148 link to the other Raptors deployed across the French capital.

Fortunately, the red lens of the Fiat's left brake light was broken so they were able to see Aswad far ahead as he maneuvered through Place du Trocadero and made a left turn toward the Pont de Bir-Hakeim. They followed him across the Seine, with the Metro tracks thundering overhead.

"He just turned again," Robert reported, even though the hard left onto Rue Desaix was evident.

Jack floored the accelerator just as a truck made a sharp turn in front of him. There were the screeching of brakes, Jack's leaning on the horn, and a rude gesture from the truck driver, but the two vehicles were miraculously spared a fender bender. Precious time, however, was lost. By the time that the Renault made the left onto Rue Desaix, Aswad was nowhere to be seen.

November 25
8:19 P.M. Central European Time

"**S**EDIK'S on the move, now," Will Casey announced. "Get me outta here."

"I'm already on the way!" Boyinson replied. As soon as he had heard that Aswad had diverted away from the United States Embassy, Boyinson had been airborne. "I figured you'd decide you needed me someday!"

As Sedik drove away in the old truck, the Little Bird dashed across the Paris sky, garishly painted with the logo of the independent rock music station Radio Métal Dur. The lettering was red, and the background was dark blue with a flat finish. In daylight, it looked like any typical commercially marked helicopter. At night, it was evident to the trained observer that the colors chosen were extremely low-visibility. For night operations, military aircraft are often painted flat black and given red markings.

Boyinson flew at rooftop level without lights, guaranteeing that he was hardly noticed. The Little Bird was so quiet that it was audible only for the couple of seconds that it was flying overhead, and most people were sufficiently used to hearing helicopters that those few seconds were hardly worth looking up. At this altitude, he was also lost in ground clutter and essentially invisible to radar.

"Meet me on the roof," Greg told Will. "I'll be coming in from the south. The next helicopter you'll see at zero-zero will be your ride."

"I'm headed for the stairs now," Will told him. "Sure you wanna do the south? The south side is the Champs-Elysées. It's wall-to-wall bright lights."

"If I come from the north, that's the embassy side. I'm not the least bit worried about the fuckin' French cops. I just don't want the U.S. Marines at the embassy to decide I'm a threat and start shootin' at me."

"Pardonnez-moi monsieur."

Casey stopped in his tracks. There was a security man shining his flashlight at him standing on the staircase leading to the roof of Espace Pierre Cardin.

November 25
8:27 P.M. Central European Time

"**S**HALL I call for a taxi?" Adrienne Delacroix offered as they left the Gallerie l'Aiglon and stepped out into the cold night air.

"No, we'll take my car," Muhammad Bin Qasim asserted. He raised his hand and a jet black luxury car with diplomatic plates glided across the street. Bin Qasim's driver scampered around to open the door for Mademoiselle Richardson as Adrienne bid them *bonsoir* and went back into the gallery.

As Hermann Stabl climbed into the plush backseat of Bin Qasim's Mercedes S500, he was reminded that no matter how much trouble the United Nations always had making ends meet, they certainly managed to find a way to take care of their senior personnel.

"I believe that you'll be quite pleased with the pieces that you've selected," Muhammad Bin Qasim promised, making small talk as the car floated smoothly through the Paris streets.

"We certainly hope so," Fiona Richardson assured him. She wondered how well she was playing her role, but she sensed from the completely relaxed expression on her companion's face that it was so far, so good.

November 25
8:27 P.M. Central European Time

"**I'VE** lost him!" Jason Houn said as he listened to the bugged Fiat, and as they searched frantically for a visual sighting of the car on which he had been eavesdropping. They couldn't *see* Ghassan Aswad, but at least Houn could *hear* him. The cup was half full.

"Either that or he's turned off his radio. *Wait!* I just heard a car door slam. Aswad's out of the car."

"He can't be too far ahead," Jack said hopefully, and

the three pairs of eyes scanned the numerous side streets that crisscrossed the park that lay ahead of them.

"There it is!" Again, Robert had been first to spot the elusive vehicle.

Jack wheeled the Renault to within twenty feet of the car. It was parked on a small lane that ran through the park.

The two Raptors approached the car cautiously, their weapons ready. It was empty, and the gym bag was not to be seen.

"Oh shit!" Robert cried as they returned toward their own vehicle. He was looking up through the trees.

"Oh shit, indeed!"

They were parked in the Champ de Mars, looking up at the Eiffel Tower.

"Do you suppose . . . ?" Jason asked, already knowing the answer.

"That sunuvabitch Al-Zahir is going to show the Frogs that he isn't playing favorites with the Americans," Jack said, summarizing the situation. "Let's spread out and find Aswad."

November 25
8:27 P.M. Central European Time

THINKING quickly, Will Casey explained to the security guard that he was one of the musicians performing at the fête down on the second floor. He was on break and going up for some fresh air and a cigarette.

As the guard studied him carefully, Will listened on his earpiece, waiting for Greg to arrive and ask where the hell he was. Will knew that he could drop the guard with his silenced 9-mm before the poor guy knew what hit him, so he slowly started to reach for his sidearm. Just as his hand closed on the pistol, the guard abruptly told him to have a good night and walked away.

The guy had no idea how lucky he was!

The door to the roof was locked, but Casey forced it and stepped out into the cold night air. The view was spectacular. The lights of Paris were like jewels on velvet. As he looked at the Eiffel Tower, it was suddenly blacked out by a shadow—like an eclipse of the moon. Only then did he hear the Little Bird.

Greg Boyinson barely touched the surface of the roof, and was airborne again before Will managed to get both feet into the helicopter. He banked hard to the left, rolled off the building, and descended to treetop level. Suddenly, they were directly over a street that was so brightly illuminated that it was like a river of light.

"I always wanted to see the Champs-Elysées," Boyinson said calmly as the Little Bird raced westward, so low that they could see people on the broad sidewalks ducking.

Casey looked up and saw the brilliantly lit Arc de Triomphe racing toward them at the speed of a Formula One race car.

"Oh, what the fuck?" Greg asked himself as he jinked the helicopter to a slight angle. The brief reverberation of the engine noise as the helicopter slashed beneath the arch was the only clue Casey had that he had survived the maneuver. Normally, he had no fear of flying, but this time, he had closed his eyes.

November 25
8:32 P.M. Central European Time

THE driver wheeled the Mercedes S500 into a re-
served parking space on Quai Louis Blériot and
opened the doors for Muhammad Bin Qasim's guests.
They were directly in front of Bin Qasim's building.
Diplomatic license plates carried certain privileges.

"I'm afraid that I must insist on one more formality,"
Bin Qasim said as they passed through the lobby of the
grand apartment building. "Our friend upstairs is a bit
sensitive."

Hermann Stabl stiffened slightly as the driver gently
patted his jacket and pant legs for the telltale lump of a
weapon. He knew the drill. He raised his arms slightly
to facilitate the search. Herr Stabl had already ascertained where the driver was carrying his own weapon.

"Merci, monsieur," the driver said, almost apologetically, turning to Mademoiselle Richardson.

For an awkward moment, all eyes were on the beautiful woman in the V-necked satin dress the color of sapphires, with a full skirt that fell to the knees of her
perfectly proportioned legs. Finally, she disdainfully
handed him the black Yves Saint Laurent overcoat that
she was carrying over her arm. He patted it down as she
showed the contents of her black leather Prada handbag
to Bin Qasim.

The driver knelt and put his hand on her thigh and
was moving it upward when Bin Qasim nervously told
him, "That will be fine."

For an instant, as the driver reluctantly removed his
hand from her leg, she saw Herr Stabl's eyes brimming

over with anger. She imagined him about to attack the driver, and she knew who would win.

The moment that the driver stood, Stabl's calm and businesslike expression returned. He was certainly playing his role well tonight.

November 25
8:32 P.M. Central European Time

JACK Rodgers and Jason Houn spread out and walked toward the Eiffel Tower. It was very cold, and no one was walking in the Parc du Champ de Mars. Nobody that is, except the two blackclad Raptors and the big guy in the University of Colorado Windbreaker with the iPod and the limp.

"I see him," Robert announced. "He's almost there. See the guy with the bag?"

"You have awfully good eyes, man," Jason told him. Robert Pauwel was not used to getting compliments, and he was proud to be useful. It chipped away at the inferiority complex that he had carried with him all his life, like he carried his many extra pounds. The men with whom he had travelled for the past week were powerfully athletic, and in such contrast to someone whose own body was a cumbersome impediment to his own mobility, yet they treated him with growing respect. If he got through this mad adventure—*when* he got through it—he promised himself that he would do anything it took to get his embarrassing carcass into shape.

"He's already to the base of the tower," Jack said with angry disappointment as he studied the brightly lit area beneath the tower through his binoculars. "It looks like he's getting into the elevator. Yes, he did. He had a pass."

"It's probably an employee pass," Jason observed. "That's the tradesman's elevator for the Jules Verne restaurant."

"Where the hell is Sedik?" Jack asked. "They can't blow this thing without the C4."

"It's already up there," Robert suggested meekly.

"What?"

"It's probably already up there. What I think I've learned from you guys is that the explosives are the heaviest and the hardest to move. I'm personally very aware of being too heavy and hard to move. I understand that. I figure they already have the explosives up there."

"There's no way in hell that we can get up there before he does!" Jason despaired. "And we can't hit him from here with an M4A1, even with an AN/PEQ-2."

"We need a sniper," Jack said.

November 25
8:41 P.M. Central European Time

THE driver stood aside observantly as Muhammad Bin Qasim graciously welcomed his guests to his apartment. He was proud of this apartment, his home. He was proud of his collection of precious little Persian miniatures, and he was especially proud of his new and prominently displayed Degas. The large living room was tastefully decorated with the classical beauty of nineteenth-century France. It seemed an incongruous place to be meeting a man who had dedicated himself to the destruction of Western civilization.

Three men sitting in various parts of the room stood and stared as they entered the room. Each had a black beard and wore a light-colored skullcap. Each was heavily armed, but none of them was Fahrid Al-Zahir.

Dave Brannan grimaced slightly. Could it be that the evil bastard had eluded him again?

Seconds later, his eyes fell on the partially opened French door that led to the balcony overlooking Quai Louis Blériot and the Seine, the balcony from which the lights of the Eiffel Tower were visible. A shadow on the balcony moved, and a man entered the room. At last he was staring face-to-face with the mastermind of the Mujahidin Al-Akhbar, the global arch-villain whose pathological hatred for America found its manifestation in mass murder.

It was an unlikely meeting. Al-Zahir was in the role of a gentleman art collector. Dave Brannan was in the clothes of Hermann Stabl, gentleman art collector.

As Muhammad Bin Qasim introduced them, Al-Zahir displayed the suspicion of a terrorist meeting strangers from beyond his insular world. Hermann Stabl conveyed only the calm and businesslike demeanor of a German industrialist about to negotiate a deal. For Stabl, meetings with strangers were second nature.

Anne McCaine took her cues from her companion. Her first sight of Al-Zahir as he entered the room was one of sickening, almost paralyzing horror. But the way that Dave Brannan conducted himself in his role gave her the sense of security that would allow her to play her own role as Fiona Richardson with relative composure. As long as she had her protector near her, she felt at ease. Standing in the same room with the man responsible for the murder of her husband seemed an odd time to start falling for a guy, but then she realized that she had been smitten by this large and powerful man since that day—that seemed so long ago—when he saved her life in Turkey.

"Please sit down," Bin Qasim invited as the two men stared at one another. He spoke in English, evidently because Al-Zahir spoke neither French nor German. Herr Stabl demonstrated an equal facility for German-accented English as for German-accented French.

They sat on the three sofas that were arranged around a large, low, coffee table. The four Hittite bronzes that Hermann Stabl had wished to purchase were arranged in a row near one edge of the table. Fiona Richardson seated herself there, and Herr Stabl sat on the adjacent sofa next to Muhammad Bin Qasim, placing his briefcase on the table.

"I have brought the precise amount of the asking prices, plus the promised 15 percent surcharge and the gallery commission," Stabl explained, opening the briefcase and turning it so that Al-Zahir could see the contents across the table. "Monsieur Bin Qasim has examined the currency and has pronounced it as genuine, which it most certainly is. When Miss Richardson has examined the pieces and pronounced *them* as genuine, and when I am content with the provenance, you will be welcome to count the cash yourself. That will conclude our transaction. Miss Richardson, please take your time."

She took that as an indication that he wanted her to make more than a cursory examination of the items. She calmly opened her handbag, took out the large magnifying glass that she had purchased earlier in the day at Dunhill, and picked up the first piece.

"As Mademoiselle Delacroix described it, this piece represents the goddess Astarte," she said, looking at Hermann Stabl.

"The Hittite fertility goddess," he said in a perfunctory way. She had briefed him well.

"Yes, but more than that, she was also seen as a goddess of wisdom or of love, or even of war. She was a very powerful woman."

She couldn't resist adding that last comment, nor could she stifle the urge to glance at Fahrid Al-Zahir. He had been uncomfortable shaking the hand of a woman, and he was obviously ill at ease. As Anne examined the small votive sculpture, she wondered about the mothers of such men, and how they could grow to adulthood with such disdain for women. She wondered how the status of women in that part of the world could have sunk so far since the era when Astarte had been revered, but she did not wonder out loud.

"It was listed as dating from between 2100 B.C. and 1600 B.C. By the detailing and the rendering of the eyes, I'd say that it is comfortably a second millennium piece. Very nice."

"And the provenance?" Stabl asked, looking directly at Al-Zahir.

"Northern Syria," he said. "I obtained it from a man who was close to a British excavation in the 1950s. I have had it for eighteen years. It has had two owners since it came out of the ground, and I am the current one."

"I'm familiar with the British work in that time frame," Fiona said. "But I was unaware that any of the pieces were sold."

"It was a gift," he said indignantly. "It was baksheesh, a gratuity given to someone who made things happen a certain way."

November 25
8:41 P.M. Central European Time

"**W**HERE are you, Will?" Jack Rodgers called on the AN/PRC-148.

"Directly above the Eiffel Tower. What a pretty sight. Where are you?"

"Just below. Do you have your elephant gun?"

"Yep."

"I need you to take out a target who's here to make it *not* a pretty sight. Now!"

"Who and where?"

"Guy in a blue coat. Carrying a gym bag. He just got into the elevator."

Will Casey was already reassembling his Barrett M107.

Greg Boyinson descended to 300 feet and hovered over the Champ de Mars about 900 feet south of the resplendently lit tower. For all practical purposes, the Little Bird was now invisible. At that distance, the helicopter would not be visible from the tower because of the glare, and anyone standing in the open air anywhere on the observation decks would have a hard time hearing it.

"I can see him," Will said, training his scope on the windows of the rising elevator.

"Can you get a shot?" Greg asked.

"Not until he gets out of the elevator. It's too crowded."

"Shall I get closer?"

"Can you?"

"Is the Pope Italian?" Greg asked, implying that his ability to get closer should be self-evident.

"Actually, he's not."

"I know that." Greg chuckled as he moved the Little Bird closer. "That was a joke."

He moved the helicopter as smoothly as a nurse rolling a hospital bed.

"Okay, you can stop. I got him, he's getting out."

Will Casey studied the scene. A man in a white waiter's jacket was in the way. He could see Aswad's black beard and glistening teeth. He was smiling at the guy in the coat. They were pointing and nodding.

Just outside the kitchen of the Jules Verne, Ghassan Aswad had been greeted by young Abbas, his cousin who had been a waiter at the restaurant for more than a year. Just inside the door was a cart draped with a white linen tablecloth. Beneath the cloth was nearly seventy-five kilos of cyclotrimethylene trinitramine mixed with a few grams of plasticizer and other chemicals. It was neatly packed in a box identifying it as pastry dough, which it vaguely resembled.

In the gym bag that Aswad carried were some used

work-out clothes, sufficiently foul-smelling to deter any but the most thorough inspection. Beneath the sweaty sweats was a cheap disposable camera, and within the camera were three short-period delay detonators.

The next move for the cousins had been practiced until it could be accomplished in twenty-five seconds or less. The camera's wrapper would be torn back. The exposed metal fittings would be removed and inserted in the "pastry dough." After that, the "short-period delay" of the detonators was measured in milliseconds.

The explosion would destroy one of the four corners of the tower. With the center of gravity thus altered, all of the structure above would collapse toward the corner with no support. The weight of eight million pounds of iron suddenly falling on the remaining structure would crumble the Eiffel Tower.

Abbas was prepared for the explosion that would encompass his own martyrdom, but he was not prepared for the sight of his cousin's head exploding in a cloud of blood and bone. He tasted fragments of raw human flesh that were accelerated into his mouth and he felt the prickle of wet bone fragments sandblasting his face. Abbas would not have long to ponder this situation.

"Two for the price of one," Will Casey said calmly as he lowered his rifle.

November 25
8:41 P.M. Central European Time

SLOWLY and methodically, Fiona Richardson examined the Hittite bronzes displayed on the large coffee table at the apartment on Quai Louis Blériot. She had looked at the Zebu Bull and the goddess Astarte. She had moved on to a sculpture of two figures that had looked almost like a Picasso when she had first seen it in a book on another coffee table in a villa overlooking the Black Sea.

Fahrid Al-Zahir was explaining to Hermann Stabl about the origin of the piece near Houran in Syria. The three armed men in skullcaps, who had scrutinized the outsiders so closely when they had first entered, were now lounging about, bored to tears by all this chatter about bronze detail and this excavation or that. Two of the men were sitting in chairs against the far wall. The third was looking out the window, his back to the room, his hands in his pockets. Sitting in a comfortable chair near the door, Muhammad Bin Qasim's driver had actually dozed off. This is what Herr Stabl had in mind when he asked Fiona to take her time.

Nobody took particular notice as Herr Stabl removed his suit jacket. None of the guards had time to take notice when he reached to the small of his back and brought out a Heckler & Koch Mk.23 pistol with a lightweight silencer.

Whap! Whap! Whap!

The sounds of their bodies hitting the floor were louder than the sound of the shots.

A fourth round impacted the upper edge of the driver's cheekbone just as he opened his eyes to the sound of the three bodies dropping on the oak parquet.

The man who masqueraded as Hermann Stabl stood up, now pointing the gun at Fahrid Al-Zahir.

"Game, set, match, Zahir," Dave Brannan said. "I'm

operating under the direct orders of the president of the
United States, and your little crime spree has been officially terminated."

The terrorist boss quickly regained his composure
and rose to face the American who had duped him.

"The whining jackal Thomas Livingstone," Al-Zahir
said angrily. "He has no idea with whom he is dealing.
He threatens *me* . . . Fahrid Al-Zahir who speaks with
God? He threatens that he will stop *me* from imposing
the glorious justice of the law of Mujahidin Al-Akhbar
upon the world? He cannot do this. He can only sit and
whine in his White House."

"Apparently you're wrong about that." Dave Brannan
smiled, nodding to the four dead men. He thought of
how those people on that Western Star flight must have
reacted to the idea of the "glorious justice of the law of
Mujahidin Al-Akhbar." He thought about Anne Mc-
Caine's husband. Dave had never met him, but Anne
idolized him, and she deserved a little justice.

"When your little drones brought the glory of your
Mujahidin Al-Akhbar justice to those people at the
NothalCorp Tower in Denver, this young lady's husband
was among those who didn't get out," Brannan ex-
plained as he carefully reached over and pressed the
Heckler & Koch into Anne's hand.

"The infidels in that tower deserved to die. If I do not
slaughter them and spill their blood, then my mother
must be insane!" Al-Zahir said, wrathfully paraphrasing
one of Osama Bin Laden's more infamous and peculiar
analogies. "They deserved to die because they refused
to obey the law as instructed by Osama Bin Laden, as

instructed by *me*! I speak to God and God speaks to *me*! Infidels must die."

"I'd say that you're already a walking, talking embodiment of that diagnosis about your poor mother," Anne replied. "It probably drove the poor woman *crazy* to realize that she had raised a psychopath like you."

As she squeezed the trigger, Anne thought about her husband and about the insanity of the madman who had engineered his death. She could not fathom what madness must have led this man to believe that the world should obey his twisted worldview under pain of violent death.

The .45-caliber hollow-point ripped through Al-Zahir's abdomen, shattering his seventh thoracic vertebrae. In turn, his spinal column was severed by shards of splintered bone. Below that point, his body went numb, but the horrible torment above his belt was so distracting that he didn't notice.

Long ago, in the misty distant past, three or four millennia ago, when the women of the Middle East had not yet become property to be hidden in sacks, Astarte and her sisters of the ancient pantheons had held great power over the fate of human civilization. In the twenty-first century, Astarte's sisters still held power—despite those men who preached otherwise. A small woman from Colorado had just proven that, more by her skill in tracking this monster, than by the almost anticlimactic act of granting him martyrdom.

The man who took almost orgasmic pleasure in the pain of people he hated but never met, now felt throbbing agony. His useless legs had collapsed beneath his torso as he crumpled clumsily to the floor.

"You never get an instantaneous kill with a shot to the midsection," Dave Brannan said mildly, looking down at the writhing terrorist. He was calmly critiquing her work, even though he could imagine that she had probably placed her shot exactly where she intended.

"I hunted deer when I was a girl," Anne explained. "My father always cautioned me against a gut shot. He told me that it was painful and inhumane for the animal. It's always fatal, but it takes a very, very long time for them to bleed out. I always remembered that, but in this case, I guess fairness sort of demands a shot that's painful for the animal."

November 25
8:41 P.M. Central European Time

JACK Rodgers watched the gym bag plummet to the ground together with a few random fragments of what had been the bodies of Ghassan Aswad and his cousin.

Because it had occurred around a corner and beyond soundproof glass, nobody inside Restaurant Jules Verne had yet noticed that two men had just died their martyr's deaths. Jack thought about those fancy folks picking at their steak tartare, and wondered how long it would take before someone noticed the small fragments that had splattered on the outside of the window near the kitchen.

Two cars raced past on the Allée Thomy-Thierry, one of the streets that knifes through the Champ de Mars near the Eiffel Tower. Each one throbbed with the sound of classic Led Zeppelin. Both radios were tuned

to Radio Métal Dur. The news of the rock station's helicopter darting beneath the Arc de Triomphe had spread
rapidly, and people had tuned to Radio Métal Dur to be
part of whatever promotion they had going. The switch-
boards lit up. The disc jockey on duty knew nothing of
a helicopter, but he decided to milk it for what it was
worth. *Of course it was our helicopter!*

One of the few car radios in Paris not tuned to Radio
Métal Dur tonight was in the old Citroën delivery truck
that Sedik had driven across town from the Avenue
Gabriel. Aswad had phoned. There was a change of
plans. He was to park as close as possible to the Eiffel
Tower. Aswad told him that fire trucks and emergency
vehicles would be arriving. He didn't ask why, he just
promised Aswad that as soon as they did, he could detonate his explosives using his jumper cables.

"It looks like we have company," Jason Houn said,
nodding across to the far side of the Champ de Mars.
The pale blue truck was ambling slowly toward the Eiffel Tower. "That looks like our friend Sedik."

"Can you cut him off?" Jack Rodgers asked, having
alerted Greg Boyinson to the slowly moving Citroën.
He knew the answer.

Sedik couldn't believe his eyes. A shadow had blot-
ted out his view of the shimmering Eiffel Tower. Inside
the shadow were two men bathed in faint red light. Was
this a vision, or merely a hallucination?

He slammed on the brakes. The helicopter was about
twenty meters distant, and moving slowly toward him.
One of the men gestured with his middle finger.

Sedik slammed the transmission into reverse and
glanced in his mirror. Directly behind him was a Renault

van with its lights dimmed. It was a vision. He had to act immediately. He jumped from the car and began digging under his seat for his jumper cables.

Greg Boyinson gently set the Little Bird down and unsnapped his harness.

"I'll take him," Will Casey said, stepping out onto the ground with his elephant gun.

"No, Will," Greg said. "This bastard's *mine*."

Sedik saw the man coming toward him. He was short and stocky, with angry eyes. On his flight suit was a small embroidered patch. It was the *American flag*. The Great Satan!

Calling upon his polished skill in the martial arts, Sedik would make quick work of this man. With blinding speed, his leg arched toward the infidel's face. Abruptly, his leg stopped. It was in the man's grip, and Sedik felt the excruciating pain of his femur being dislocated.

As he collapsed to the ground, Sedik saw his old Egyptian-made Helwan automatic pistol beneath the driver's seat and reached up for it.

Greg Boyinson saw the punk grab the Beretta knock-off, and he saw him swing it up to aim it. With one kick, he smashed the gun into the joker's face. With a second kick, another brave jihadi was aided into martyrdom by the Raptor Team.

November 25
8:56 P.M. Central European Time

"**I** think that your carpet already had a few bloodstains on it," Anne McCaine said, noticing that Muhammad

Bin Qasim was staring transfixed as the dreaded Fahrid Al-Zahir slowly bled to death on his eighteenth-century Persian prayer rug.

"I'm not part of this," Bin Qasim insisted. He had watched in stunned surprise as Dave Brannan had popped the four armed men in his luxurious apartment on Quai Louis Blériot. He was dazed by the sight of a beautiful woman dispatching Al-Zahir toward martyr-dom five feet from where he now stood.

"You certainly seem to have gotten yourself in with some bad company," Brannan said in an almost sympa-thetic tone. "I'd say finding Fahrid Al-Zahir and his gangsters hanging out in the apartment of the head of the United Nations International Validation Organiza-tion could be pretty awkward to explain."

"I was *not* involved in any terrorist act," Bin Qasim assured them. "I certainly would have alerted the proper authorities if you hadn't resorted to violence."

"Oh, I'm sorry," Brannan said sarcastically. "We really *meant* to apply for our International Validation before we took out the most dangerous man in the world. You know, all this paperwork, it just backs up and the next thing you know, your papers aren't in order."

"That's quite all right," Bin Qasim said nervously, looking at Al-Zahir lying on the floor. He was still alive, but his breathing was shallow, and a pink foam was ooz-ing from his mouth as he moved closer toward the cli-max of his martyrdom.

"Thank you, Mr. Bin Qasim," Dave told the man. "But it's you who's got himself into a really bad situa-tion here. Tomorrow, somebody is going to find Fahrid

Al-Zahir in your apartment. That is not going to look very good. In fact, it's going to look very bad."

"Al-Zahir broke in here?" Bin Qasim said, suggesting a possible alibi. "I could do nothing? I shot him myself?"

"No, I think that even the French cops are not going to believe that story," Dave said, shaking his head in mock sympathy.

"Any way it goes, it goes badly for you," Anne told the nervous United Nations bureaucrat. "Any way it goes, there will be an investigation. I'm not a clairvoyant, but even I can predict that the investigation will find this isn't the first bit of mischief that you've been involved in. And I'll bet there are other people in your food chain who will not want to be troubled by what an investigation will inevitably uncover."

Muhammad Bin Qasim started to respond, but he couldn't. What could he say?

"The young lady is right," Brannan said. "I think that the noble thing for you to do would be to spare other gentlemen the embarrassment of an investigation."

November 25
9:02 P.M. Central European Time

IT was a beautiful evening in Paris. It was very cold, but the air was crystal clear. As Dave helped her on with her coat he found himself captivated by her fragrance.

"*Soir de Paris* by Bourjois," Anne smiled. "Thank you for noticing, Colonel."

"I was a bit preoccupied for the last couple of hours, but I've cleared my schedule. Could the gentleman buy the lady a drink?"

"The lady would like that, Colonel." She smiled, taking his arm as he offered it.

A small crowd was gathering on the sidewalk adjacent to Quai Louis Blériot. The well-dressed man had fallen for several stories, and people were speculating from which floor. One woman said she thought she recognized him. She was sure that she had seen him coming and going in the building, but it was hard to tell. His face was badly damaged when he was killed in the fall.

The sound of the approaching ambulance could be heard in the distance. The haunting voice of James Douglas Morrison echoed from a car racing past with its radio tuned to Radio Métal Dur. "No one here gets out alive," said the Lizard King before his voice was swallowed by the roar of fast-moving traffic.

Nobody noticed the well-dressed, middle-aged couple who left the building just before the ambulance arrived. They walked arm in arm into the night and faded into the darkness.

EPILOGUE

November 26
8:11 A.M. Eastern Time

"**W**HO owned that helicopter?" Rod Llewellan asked, nodding to the newspaper that his part-ner was reading at the Tennessee truck stop diner.

The media was saturated this morning with news reports out of Paris. The biggest news was the violent death of the hated and feared Fahrid Al-Zahir in the Paris apartment of Muhammad Bin Qasim, the head of the United Nations International Validation Organiza-tion. The world was stunned with the good news, but saddened to learn that Bin Qasim was also dead, having jumped or been pushed from the apartment's balcony.

In Paris, the gendarmes were baffled. They couldn't speculate. That was up to the rumormongers, and there were plenty of them this morning. Buried on the back pages was news that four buildings in the industrial suburbs of Paris had blown up and burned to the ground overnight. The police were sure that these incidents were unrelated to the death of Al-Zahir. Just a coincidence.

Especially intriguing was the story about the helicopter pilot who had killed the driver of a van carrying nearly 400 kilos of C4 high explosives less than 100 meters from the base of the Eiffel Tower.

"It says here that the chopper had the logo of a rock radio station in Paris," Erik Vasquez answered as he scanned the article.

"So a rock station is responsible for saving the Eiffel Tower?" Llewellan said, shaking his head. "That's incredible."

"That's the way the media is playing it, but there's one problem that makes the story *literally* incredible," Vasquez said thoughtfully.

"What's that?"

"The station says that they don't *have* a helicopter."

November 26
2:33 P.M. Eastern Time

BUCK Peighton handed his old friend a pair of photographs. The first one showed Fahrid Al-Zahir in death. His eyes were still open and a pool of blood could be seen on the floor beneath him. On his chest, just below his bearded chin was a small embroidered patch. It was a United States flag, such as is worn on the uniforms of American soldiers.

The message in the first photograph was plain as day. The second photograph was confusing. It was of a familiar man with a long beard with a distinctive grey patch, dressed in a black kaftan with embroidery near the collar and a grey skullcap. It was the clearest picture that Livingstone had ever seen of Khaleq Badr. What confused the president was that Badr, who always sneered and scowled, was grinning and winking. The two fingers of one hand were raised in a peace sign. The other hand held a small, embroidered American flag.

The president handed the pictures back to Peighton. He knew that they were his to see, but not his to keep.

"Your American Volunteer Group is out there working for you, Tom," the old general said. "They were, and they still are. Even when you doubted it the most, they were in the mud and muck, working to carry out their mission. They have done it. They have done their duty."

"How could I have doubted it?" Livingstone asked, sadly shaking his head. "How could I have sat here and worried what the media was going to say and do if all this came to light? I had wanted to rise above all of that. I should have realized that you, and those guys, whoever they are, wouldn't let me down . . . or more important, that they wouldn't let down our country."

"Well, there was a great man who once said that it is not the critic who counts; not the man who points out how the strong man stumbles, or where the doer of deeds could have done them better," Buck Peighton said, looking at his old friend. "He said that the credit belongs to the man who is actually in the arena, whose face is marred by dust and sweat and blood; who strives valiantly; who errs, who comes short again and again, because there is no effort without error and shortcoming; but who does actually strive to *do the deeds*; who knows great enthusiasms, the great devotions; who spends himself in a worthy cause; who at the best knows in the end the triumph of high achievement, and who at the worst, if he fails, at least fails while daring greatly, so that his place shall never be with those cold and timid souls who neither know victory nor defeat."

"That truly sums up what has happened over the past month," President Thomas J. Livingstone said grimly. "Who said this? Who is this quote from, this quote that you seem to have committed to memory?"

"It's from a speech that was originally delivered in Paris of all places, the same town where this adventure of ours finally came to a head. It was back in 1910. The guy who said it used to work in the same office as you. His name was Theodore Roosevelt."

Also from

Bill Yenne

Secret Weapons
of the Cold War

The highly classified Doomsday weapons that agents on
both sides of the Iron Curtain once
risked their lives to protect.

Military expert Bill Yenne reveals the sophisticated
weaponry that would have launched Armageddon if the
Cold War had turned hot—weapons so closely guarded
that people would kill to learn their secrets.

0-425-20149-X

Penguin Group (USA) Online

What will you be reading tomorrow?

Tom Clancy, Patricia Cornwell, W.E.B. Griffin,
Nora Roberts, William Gibson, Robin Cook,
Brian Jacques, Catherine Coulter, Stephen King,
Dean Koontz, Ken Follett, Clive Cussler,
Eric Jerome Dickey, John Sandford,
Terry McMillan, Sue Monk Kidd, Amy Tan,
John Berendt…

You'll find them all at
penguin.com

*Read excerpts and newsletters,
find tour schedules and reading group guides,
and enter contests.*

Subscribe to Penguin Group (USA) newsletters
and get an exclusive inside look
at exciting new titles and the authors you love
long before everyone else does.

PENGUIN GROUP (USA)
us.penguingroup.com